Kirk Munroe

Through Swamp and Glade

A Tale of the Seminole War

Kirk Munroe

Through Swamp and Glade
A Tale of the Seminole War

ISBN/EAN: 9783744753579

Printed in Europe, USA, Canada, Australia, Japan

Cover: Foto ©Andreas Hilbeck / pixelio.de

More available books at **www.hansebooks.com**

THROUGH
SWAMP AND GLADE

A TALE OF
THE SEMINOLE WAR

BY

KIRK MUNROE
AUTHOR OF "THE WHITE CONQUERORS," "AT WAR WITH
PONTIAC," ETC., ETC.

ILLUSTRATED BY VICTOR PERARD

NEW YORK
CHARLES SCRIBNER'S SONS
1896

Norwood Press
J. S. Cushing & Co. — Berwick & Smith.
Norwood Mass. U.S.A.

TO MY READERS

THE principal incidents in the story of Coacoochee, as related in the following pages, are histori-
cally true. The Seminole War, the most protracted
struggle with Indians in which the United States
ever engaged, lasted from 1835 to 1842. At its
conclusion, though most of the tribe had been removed to the Indian Territory in the far west, there
still remained three hundred and one souls uncap-
tured and unsubdued. This remnant had fled to
the almost inaccessible islands of the Big Cypress
Swamp, in the extreme southern part of Florida.
Rather than undertake the task of hunting them
out, General Worth made a *verbal* treaty with them,
by which it was agreed that they should retain that
section of country unmolested, so long as they committed no aggressions. From that time they have
kept their part of that agreement to the letter,
living industrious, peaceful lives, and avoiding all
unnecessary contact with the whites. They now
number something over five hundred souls, but the

tide of white immigration is already lapping over the ill-defined boundaries of their reservation, while white land-grabbers, penetrating the swamps, are seizing their fertile islands and bidding them begone. They stand aghast at this brutal order. Where can they go? What is to become of them? Is there nothing left but to fight and die? It would seem not.

KIRK MUNROE.

BISCAYNE BAY, FLORIDA, 1896.

TABLE OF CONTENTS

viii TABLE OF CONTENTS

LIST OF ILLUSTRATIONS

THROUGH SWAMP AND GLADE

CHAPTER I

A BIT OF THE FLORIDA WILDERNESS

THE scene is laid in Florida, that beautiful land of the far south, in which Ponce de Leon located the fabled Spring of Eternal Youth. It is a land of song and story, of poetry and romance; but one also of bitter memories and shameful deeds. Its very attractiveness has proved its greatest curse, and for weary years its native dwellers, who loved its soil as dearly as they loved their own lives, fought desperately to repel the invaders who sought to drive them from its sunny shores.

Although winter is hardly known in Florida, still there, as elsewhere, spring is the fairest and most joyous season of the year, and it is with the evening of a perfect April day that this story opens.

The warm air was pleasantly stirred by a breeze that whispered of the boundless sea, and the glowing

B   1

sun would shortly sink to rest in the placid bosom
of the Mexican Gulf. From the forest came sweet
scents of yellow jasmine, wild grape, and flowering
plumes of the palmetto mingled with richer perfumes
from orange blossoms, magnolias, and sweet bays.
Gorgeous butterflies hovered on the edge of the
hammock and sought resting-places for the night
amid the orange leaves. Humming-birds, like living
jewels, darted from flower to flower; bees golden
with pollen and freighted with honey winged their
flight to distant combs. From a ti-ti thicket came
the joyous notes of a mocking-bird, who thus unwittingly disclosed the secret of his hidden nest. A
bevy of parakeets in green and gold flashed from
branch to branch and chattered of their own affairs;
while far overhead, flocks of snowy ibis and white
curlew streamed along like fleecy clouds from feed-
ing-grounds on the salt marshes of the distant coast
to rookeries in the cypress swamps of the crooked
Ocklawaha. Some of these drifting bird-clouds
were tinted or edged with an exquisite pink, denot-
ing the presence of roseate spoonbills, and the effect
of their rapid movement against the deep blue of
the heavens, in the flash of the setting sun was inde-
scribably beautiful.

Amid this lavish display of nature's daintiest
handiwork and in all the widespread landscape of
hammock and savanna, trackless pine forest that had
never known the woodman's axe, and dimpled lakes

of which a score might be counted from a slight elevation, but one human being was visible. A youth just emerged from boyhood stood alone on the edge of a forest where the ground sloped abruptly down to a lakelet of crystal water. He was clad in a loose-fitting tunic or hunting-frock of doeskin girded about the waist by a sash of crimson silk. In this was thrust a knife with a silver-mounted buckhorn handle and encased in a sheath of snakeskin. His hair, black and glossy as the wing of a raven, was bound by a silken kerchief of the same rich color as his sash. The snow-white plume of an egret twined in his hair denoted him to be of rank among his own people. He wore fringed leggings of smoke-tanned deerskin, and moccasins of the same material. The lad's features were handsome and clear cut, but his expression was gentle and thoughtful as might become a student rather than a mere forest rover. And so the lad was a student, though of nature, and a dreamer not yet awakened to the stern realities of life; but that the mysteries of books were unknown to him might be inferred from a glance at his skin. It was of a clear copper color, resembling new bronze; for Coacoochee (little wild cat) belonged to the most southern tribe of North American Indians, the Seminoles of Florida. Indian though he was, he was of noble birth and descended from a long line of chieftains; for he was the eldest son of Philip Emathla (Philip the leader), or "King

Philip," as the whites termed him, and would some day be a leader of his tribe.

Now, as the lad stood leaning on a light rifle and gazing abstractedly at the glistening clouds of home-returning birds that flecked the glowing sky, his face bore a far-away look as though his thoughts had outstripped his vision. This was not surprising ; for to all men Coacoochee was known as a dreamer who beguiled the hours of many an evening by the camp-fire with the telling of his dreams or of the folk-lore tales of his people. Not only was he a dreamer of dreams and a narrator of strange tales ; but he was a seer of visions, as had been proved very recently when death robbed him of his dearly loved twin sister Allala.

At the time Coacoochee was many miles away from his father's village, on a hunting-trip with his younger brother Otulke. One night as they slept the elder brother started from his bed of palmetto leaves with the voice of Allala ringing in his ears. All was silent about him, and Otulke lay undisturbed by his side. As the lad wondered and was about to again lie down, his own name was uttered softly but plainly, and in the voice of Allala, while at the same moment her actual presence seemed to be beside him.

It was a summons that he dared not disobey; so, without rousing Otulke, the young hunter sprang on the back of his pony and sped away through the moonlight. At sunrise he stood beside the dead form of the dear sister whose fleeting spirit had called him.

Since then he had often heard Allala's voice in the winds whispering through tall grasses of the glades, or among nodding flags on the river banks; in waters that sang and rippled on the lake shore; from shadowy depths of the hammocks, and amid the soft sighings of cypress swamps. Fus-chatte the red-bird sang of her, and pet-che the wood dove mourned that she was gone. To Coacoochee, she seemed ever near him, and he longed for the time when he might join her. But he knew that he must be patient and await the presence of the Great Spirit, for he believed that the hour of his own death had been named at that of his birth. He also knew that until the appointed time he would escape all dangers unharmed. He felt certain that Allala watched over him and would warn him of either death or great danger. Being thus convinced, the lad was absolutely without fear of dangers visible or unseen; and, dreamer that he was, often amazed his companions by deeds of what seemed to them the most reckless daring.

At the moment of his introduction to the reader Coacoochee, bathed in the full glory of the setting sun, wondered if the place to which Allala had gone could be fairer or more beautiful than that in which he lingered.

Although he was without human companionship he was not alone; for beside him lay Ul-we (the tall one), a great shaggy staghound that the young Indian had rescued three years before from the wreck of an English ship that was cast away on the lonely coast more than one hundred miles from the nearest settlement. Coacoochee with several companions was searching for turtle-eggs on the beach, and when they boarded the stranded vessel, a wretched puppy very nearly dead from starvation was the only living creature they found. The Indian boy took the little animal for his own, restored it to life through persistent effort, nursed it through the ills of puppyhood, and was finally rewarded by having the waif thus rescued develop into the superb hound that now lay beside him, and whose equal for strength and intelligence had never been known in Florida. The love of the great dog for his young master was touching to behold, while the affection of Coacoochee for him was only excelled by that felt for his dearest human friend.

This friend was a lad of his own age named Louis Pacheco, who was neither an Indian nor wholly a paleface. He was the son of a Spanish indigo planter and a beautiful octoroon who had been given her freedom before the birth of her boy. The Señor Pacheco, whose plantation lay near the village of King Philip, had always maintained the most friendly relations with his Indian neighbors; and, Louis having one sister, as had Coacoochee, these four were united in closest intimacy from their childhood.

At the death of the indigo planter his family removed to a small estate owned by the mother, on the Tomoka River, some fifty miles from their old home; but this removal in nowise weakened their friendship with the red-skinned dwellers by the lake. Frequent visits were exchanged between the younger members of the two families, and when Allala was taken to the spirit land, none mourned her loss longer or more sincerely than Louis and Nita Pacheco.

Louis, being well educated by his father, taught Coacoochee to speak fluently both English and Spanish in exchange for lessons in forest lore and woodcraft. The young creole was as proud of his lineage as was the son of Philip Emathla, and bore himself as became one born to a position of freedom and independence.

It was some months since he and Coacoochee had last met, and at the moment of his introduction to us the latter was thinking of his friend and meditating a visit to him. It would seem as though these thoughts must have been induced by some subtle indication of a near-by presence; for the youth was hardly conscious of them ere Ul-we sprang to his feet with an ominous growl and dashed into the thicket behind them. At the same moment the young Indian heard his own name pronounced in a faint voice, and wheeling quickly, caught sight of a white, wild-eyed face that he instantly recognized. Ul-we had but time to utter one joyful bark before his young master stood beside him and was supporting the fainting form of Nita Pacheco in his arms.

CHAPTER II

MR. TROUP JEFFERS PLOTS MISCHIEF

For a full understanding of this startling interruption of the young Indian's meditations it is necessary to make a brief excursion among the dark shadows of a history which, though now ancient and well-nigh forgotten, was then fresh and of vital interest to those whose fortunes we are about to follow.

Florida had only recently been purchased by the United States from Spain for five millions of dollars, and its vast territory thrown open to settlement. Being the most nearly tropical of our possessions, it offered possibilities found in no other part of the country, and settlers flocked to it from all directions. As the Spaniards had only occupied a few places near the coast, the interior had been left to the undisturbed possession of the Seminoles and their negro allies. The ancestors of these negroes escaping from slavery had sought and found a safe refuge in this beautiful wilderness. By Spanish law they became free at the moment of crossing the frontier boundary line, and here their descendants dwelt for generations in peace and happiness.

With the change of owners came a sad change of fortunes to the native inhabitants of this sunny land. The swarming settlers cast envious glances at the fertile fields of the Seminoles, and determined to possess them. They longed also to enslave the negro friends and allies of the Indians, whom they discovered to be enjoying a degree of freedom and prosperity entirely contrary to their notions of what was right and fitting. Slavery was a legally recognized institution of the country. The incoming settlers had been taught and believed that men of black skins were created to be slaves and laborers for the benefit of the whites. Therefore to see these little communities of black men dwelling in a state of freedom and working only for themselves, their wives, and children was intolerable. Slaves were wanted to clear forests and cultivate fields, and here were hundreds, possibly thousands, of them to be had for the taking. The villages of these negroes and those of their Indian allies were also affording places of refuge for other blacks who were constantly escaping from the plantations of neighboring states, and seeking that liberty guaranteed by the Constitution of the United States to all men. This condition of affairs could not be borne. Both the Indians and the free negroes of Florida must be taught a lesson.

General Andrew Jackson was the man chosen to teach this lesson, and he entered upon the congenial task with a hearty relish. Marching an army into

Florida, he killed all the Indians whom he encountered, killed or captured all the negroes whom he could find, burned villages, destroyed crops, and finally retired from the devastated country with a vast quantity of plunder, consisting principally of slaves and cattle.

To impress this lesson more fully upon the Indians, General Jackson compelled an American vessel lying in Appalachicola Bay to hoist British colors in the hope of enticing some of them on board. Two Seminole chiefs, deceived by this cowardly ruse, did venture to visit the supposed British ship. When they were safely on board, his Majesty's ensign was hauled down, that of the United States was run up, and beneath its folds the too confiding visitors were hanged to the yard-arms without trial or delay.

After this General Jackson summoned the Indians to come in and make a treaty; but they were fearful of further treachery, and hesitated. Finally some thirty warriors out of the entire tribe were bribed to lay aside their fears and meet the Commissioners. These signed a treaty by which the Seminoles were required to abandon their homes, villages, fields, and hunting-grounds, in the northern part of the territory, and retire to the distant southern wilderness, where they would be at liberty to clear new lands and make new homes. The tribe was also bound by the treaty to prevent the passage, through their country, of any fugitive slave, and to deliver all such seeking refuge among them to any persons claiming to be their owners.

The United States on its part promised to compensate the Indians for such improvements as they were compelled to abandon, to allow them five thousand dollars annually in goods and money for twenty years, to feed them for one year, and to furnish them with schools.

With the signing of this alleged treaty the trials and sufferings of the Seminoles began in earnest. They were literally driven from their old homes, so eager were the whites to possess their fertile lands. Most of their promised rations of food was withheld, that they might be induced by starvation the more speedily to clear and cultivate new fields in the south. The goods issued to them were of such wretched quality that they were contemptuously rejected or thrown away ; and on one pretext or another nearly the whole of their cash annuity was declared forfeited. The most common excuse for thus defrauding the Indians was that they did not display sufficient activity in capturing the negroes who had sought refuge in their country.

Any white man desirous of procuring a slave had but to describe some negro whom he knew to be living among the Seminoles and file a claim to him with the Indian agent. The latter then notified the Indians that they were expected to capture and deliver up the person thus described, or else forfeit his value from their annuity. Thus these liberty-loving savages soon discovered that, under the white man's interpretation of their treaty, they had bound themselves to deliver into slavery every man, woman, and child found within their territory, in whose veins flowed one drop of negro blood, including in some cases their own wives and children, which crime they very naturally refused to commit.

Although Philip Emathla had thus far avoided an open rupture with the whites, an event of recent occurrence caused him grave anxiety. On the occasion of his last expedition to St. Augustine to receive that portion of the annuity due his band he had been persuaded by Coacoochee and Louis Pacheco, who happened to be visiting his friend at that time, to allow them to accompany him. The Indians camped at some distance from the town, but were permitted to wander freely about its streets during the daytime — a permission of which the two lads took fullest advantage. Thus on the very day of their arrival they set forth on their exploration of the ancient city, and Louis, who had been there before with his father, kindly explained its many wonders to his less travelled companion.

The massive gray walls of Fort San Marco, with their lofty watch towers, and black cannon grinning from the deep embrasures, possessed a peculiar fascination for Coacoochee, and it seemed as though he would never tire of gazing on them. From the gloomy interior, however, he shrank with horror, refusing even to glance into the cells and dungeons, to which Louis desired to direct his attention.

"No," he cried. "In these I could not breathe. They hold the air of a prison, and to a son of the forest that is the air of death. Let us then hasten from this place of ill omen, lest they close the gates, and we be forced to leap from the walls for our freedom."

So the Wildcat hastily dragged his friend from that grim place, nor did he draw a full breath until they were once more in the sunny fields outside. He was infinitely more pleased with the interior of the equally ancient cathedral, and lingered long before the mystic paintings of its decoration. Its music and the glowing candles of its richly decked altar affected him so strangely, that even after they had emerged from the building and stood in the open plaza, listening to its chiming bells, he was for a long time silent.

Louis, too, was occupied with his own thoughts; and as the lads stood thus, they failed to notice the curiosity with which they were regarded by two men who passed and repassed them several times. One of these men, Troup Jeffers by name, was a slave-trader, who was keenly alive to the possibility of making a good thing out of the present embarrassment of the Seminoles. The other man, who was known as Ross Ruffin, though that was not supposed

to be his real name, was one of those depraved char-
acters found on every frontier, who are always ready
to perform a dirty job for pay, and who so closely
resembled the filthiest beasts of prey that they are
generally spoken of as "human jackals." With
this particular jackal Mr. Troup Jeffers had already
dealt on more than one occasion, and found him
peculiarly well adapted to the requirements of his
despicable trade.

"Likely looking youngsters," remarked the slave-
dealer, nodding towards the two lads upon first
noticing them. "Pity they're Injuns. More pity
that Injuns don't come under the head of property.
Can't see any difference myself between them and
niggers. Now them two in the right market ought
to fetch — "

Here the trader paused to inspect the lads more
closely that he might make a careful estimate of
their probable money value.

"By Gad!" he exclaimed under his breath, "I'm
dashed if I believe one of 'em is an Injun!"

"No," replied his companion; "one of 'em is a
nigger. Leastways, his mother is."

"You don't say so?" remarked Mr. Troup Jeffers, his eye lighting with the gleam of a man-
hunter on catching sight of his prey. "Who owns
him?"

"No one just now. Leastways, he claims to be
free. He lives with his mother and sister in the

Injun country. I've been calculating chances on 'em myself for some time."

"Tell me all you know about 'em," commanded the trader, in a voice husky with excitement, while the evil gleam in his eyes grew more pronounced.

When Ross Ruffin had related the history and present circumstances of the Pachecos to the best of his knowledge, the other exclaimed:

"I'll go yer! and we couldn't want a better thing. Agent's in town now. I'll make out a description and file a claim this very evening. We'll claim all three. Jump this young buck before he has a chance to get away. It'll make the other job more simple too. Get all three up the coast, easy as rolling off a log. 'Quick sales and big profits' — that's my motto. I'll divvy with you. On the square. Is it a go? Shake."

Thus within five minutes, and while the unsuspecting lads still listened in silence to the tinkling chimes of the old cathedral bells, there was hatched against them a plot more villanous than either of them had ever conceived possible. Not only that, but the first link was forged of a chain of circumstances that was to alter the whole course of their lives and entwine them in its cruel coils for many bitter years to come.

CHAPTER III

THE SLAVE-CATCHERS AT WORK

The following day was also passed by Coacoochee and Louis in pleasant wanderings about the quaint little city whose every sight and sound was to them so full of novel interest. At length in the early dusk of evening they set forth on their return to Philip Emathla's camp, conversing eagerly as they walked concerning what they had seen. So occupied were they that they paid little heed to their immediate surroundings, and as they gained the outskirts of the town were startled at being commanded to halt by a man who had approached them unobserved. It was Troup Jeffers, the slave-catcher, who had been watching the lads for some time and awaiting just such an opportunity as the present for carrying out his evil designs.

"What's your name?" he demanded, placing himself squarely in front of the young creole.

"Louis Pacheco."

"Just so. Son of old Pacheco and a nigger woman. Nigger yourself. My nigger, sold to me by your dad just afore he died. Hain't wanted you up to this time. Now want you to come along with me."

"I'll do nothing of the kind!" cried the lad, hotly. "When you say that I am your slave, or the slave of any one else, *you lie*. My mother was a free woman, and I was born free. To that I can take my oath, and so can my friend here. So stand aside, sir, and let me pass."

"Ho, ho! my black fighting cock," answered the trader, savagely; "you'll pay sweetly for those words afore I'm through with ye. And you'll set up a nigger's oath and an Injun's oath agin that of a white man, will ye? Why, you crumbly piece of yellar gingerbread, don't you know that when a white man swears to a thing, his word will be taken agin that of all the niggers and Injuns in the country? Cattle of that kind can't testify in United States courts, as you'll find out in a hurry if you ever try it on. Now you're my property, and the sooner you realize it, the better it will be for you. I've filed my sworn claim with the agent, and it's been allowed. Here's his order for the Injuns to deliver you up. So I'd advise you to go along peaceably with me if you don't want to get yourself into a heap of trouble. Grab him, Ross!"

Mr. Troup Jeffers had only talked to detain the lads until the arrival of his burly confederate, who was following at a short distance behind him. As the moment for action arrived, he seized Louis by one arm, while Ross Ruffin grasped the other.

Coacoochee, knowing little of the ways of the

whites, had not realized what was taking place until this moment; but with the seizure of his friend the horrid truth was made clear to him. He was called a dreamer, but no one witnessing the promptness of his action at this crisis would have supposed him to be such. Ross Ruffin was nearest him, and at the very moment of his laying hands on Louis there came a flash of steel. The next instant Coacoochee's keen-bladed hunting-knife was sunk deep into the man's arm just below the shoulder.

With a yell of pain and terror, the "jackal" let go his hold. Louis tore himself free from the grasp of his other assailant, and in a twinkling the two lads were running with the speed of startled deer in the direction of their own camp, while an ineffective pistol shot rang out spitefully behind them.

A few minutes later they had gained the camp, secured their rifles, told King Philip of what had just taken place, crossed the San Sebastian, and were lost to sight in the dark shadows of the forest on its further side.

They had hardly disappeared before St. Augustine was in an uproar. An Indian had dared draw his knife on a white man who was only exercising his legal rights and claiming his lawful property. An Indian had actually aided in the escape of a slave, when by solemn treaty he was bound to use every effort to deliver such persons to their masters. The act was an intolerable outrage and must be promptly punished.

Within an hour, therefore, an angry mob of armed citizens headed by Troup Jeffers had surrounded Philip Emathla's encampment. They were confronted by his handful of sturdy warriors, ready to fight with the fury of tigers brought to bay, and but for the determined interference of the Indian agent, who had hastened to the scene of disturbance, a bloody battle would have ensued then and there. This officer begged the whites to leave the affair with him, assuring them that the Indians should be made to afford ample satisfaction for the outrage, and taught a lesson that would prevent its repetition. At first the citizens would not listen to him; but the cupidity of the slave-catcher being aroused by the promise of a handsome pecuniary compensation for his loss, he joined his voice to that of the agent, and finally succeeded in persuading the mob to retire.

Two thousand dollars of government money due King Philip's band was in that agent's hands and should have been paid over on the following day. Now that official gave the aged chieftain his choice of delivering Coacoochee up for punishment, and Louis Pacheco to the man who claimed him as his property, or of relinquishing this money and signing for it a receipt in full.

The alternative thus presented was a bitter one.

The loss of their money would involve Philip Emathla and his band in new difficulties with the whites, to whom they were in debt for goods that were to be paid for on the receipt of their annuity. The old man knew that his creditors would have no mercy upon him, but would seize whatever of his possessions they could attach. Nor could mercy be expected for his son and Louis Pacheco should they be delivered into the hands of their enemies.

Long did the perplexed chieftain sit silent and with bowed head, considering the situation. His warriors, grouped at a short distance, watched him with respectful curiosity. At length he submitted the case to them and asked their advice.

With one accord, and without hesitation, they answered: " Let the Iste-hatke (white man) keep his money. We can live without it ; but if one hair of Coacoochee's head should be harmed, our hearts would be heavy with a sadness that could never be lifted."

So Philip Emathla affixed his mark to the paper that the agent had prepared for him, and was allowed to depart in peace the next day. Of the money thus obtained from the Indians two hundred dollars served to salve the wound in Ross Ruffin's arm, and eight hundred satisfied for the time being the claim of Mr. Troup Jeffers, the slave-trader. What became of the balance is unknown, for the agent's books contain no record of the transaction.

Coacoochee and Louis had halted within friendly shadows on the edge of the forest, and there held themselves in readiness to fly to the assistance of their friends, should sounds of strife proclaim an attack upon the encampment. Here they remained during the night, and only rejoined Philip Emathla on his homeward march the following day. When they learned from him the particulars of the transaction by which their liberty had been assured, both of them were bitterly indignant at the injustice thus perpetrated.

The indignation of the young creole was supplemented by a profound gratitude, and he swore that if the time ever came when it should lie in his power to repay the debt thus incurred, he would do so with interest many times compounded. Now, feeling secure in the freedom for which so great a price had been paid, he returned to his home on the Tomoka, where for several months he devoted himself assiduously to labor on the little plantation that afforded the sole support of his mother, his sister, and himself. During this time of diligent toil, though he found no opportunity for communicating with his Indian friends of the lake region, they were often in his thoughts, and his heart warmed toward them with an ever-increasing gratitude as he reflected upon the awful fate from which they had saved him.

While the busy home life of the family on the Tomoka flowed on thus peacefully and happily, there came one evening a timid knock at the closed door of their house, and a weak voice, speaking in negro dialect, begged for admittance.

Louis, holding a candle, opened the door, and as he did so, was struck a blow on the head that stretched him senseless across the threshold. As Nita, who was the only other occupant of the house at that moment, witnessed this dastardly act, she uttered a piercing scream and was about to fling herself on her brother's body, but was roughly pushed back by two white men, who entered the room, and dragging Louis back from the door, closed it behind them.

One of the men, who were those precious villains Troup Jeffers and Ross Ruffin, bound the wrists of the unconscious youth behind him, while the other ordered Nita to bring them food, threatening to kill her brother before her eyes in case she refused. The terrified girl hastened to obey; but, as with trembling hands she prepared the table with all that the house afforded in the way of provisions, her mind was filled with wild schemes of escape and rescue. Her mother was absent, having gone to sit with the dying child of their only near neighbors, a negro family living a short distance down the river.

While the girl thus planned, and strove to conceal her agony of thought beneath an appearance of bustling activity, the slave-catchers dashed water in her brother's face and used other means to restore him to consciousness. In this they were finally successful.

The moment that he was sufficiently recovered to realize his situation and recognize the men who had treated him so shamefully, he demanded to be set at liberty, claiming that he was free by birth, and that even if he were not, the price of his freedom had been paid several times over by the annuity that Philip Emathla had relinquished on his account.

"Oh no, you're not free, my lad, as you'll soon discover," replied Mr. Troup Jeffers, with a grin. " You're property, you are. You was born property, and you'll always be property. Just now you're my property, and will be till I can get you to a market where your value will be appreciated. As for the cash handed over by that old fool of an Injun, it warn't more than enough to pay for the cut that young catamount give my friend here, and for my injured feelings. It warn't never intended to pay for you. So shut your mouth and come along quietly with us, or we'll make it mighty oncomfortable for ye. D'ye hear ? "

" But my father was a white man, my mother was a free woman, and I was born — "

"Shut up ! I tell ye !" shouted the trader, angrily.

Determined to be heard, the youth again opened his mouth to speak, when, with a snarl of rage, the brute sprang forward and dealt him several savage

kicks with a heavy cowhide boot that proved effective in procuring the required silence.

While the attention of both men was thus engaged,
Nita managed to slip unobserved from a back door
of the house.   With the swiftness of despair she fled
along the shadowy forest trail that led to the neigh-
bor's cabin, a quarter of a mile away.   There she
hoped to obtain help for her brother's rescue.   When
she reached it, she found to her dismay that it was
dark and empty.   Its door stood wide open, and the
poor girl received no answer to her terrified callings.

CHAPTER IV

CAPTURE AND ESCAPE OF NITA PACHECO

FOR a minute Nita, trembling with excitement and terror, stood irresolute. Then, noticing that a few embers still smouldered on the hearth, she found a sliver of fat pine and thrust it among them. As it flared up with a bright blaze, its light disclosed a scene that filled the girl with despair and told the whole sad story — the child with whom her mother was to watch that night lay dead on the only bed in the room. The rest of the scanty furniture was overturned and broken ; while the whole appearance of the place denoted that it had been the scene of a fierce struggle.

In vain did Nita seek for any trace of her mother. It was only too evident that the slave-catchers had been here, made captives of all the living inmates, and removed them to a place of safe keeping before visiting the Pacheco house. Sick at heart and undecided as to her course of action, the poor girl left the cabin. As she emerged from its shattered doorway, she was rudely clasped in a pair of strong arms, and with a hoarse chuckle of satisfaction a voice, that she recognized as belonging to one of the men she had left with Louis, exclaimed :

"So, gal, ye thought ye was gwine to give us the slip, eh ? and maybe bring help to your brother ? We uns is up to them games though, and ye've got to be oncommon spry to git ahead of us. I suspicioned whar ye'd gone the minit I found ye'd lit out without so much as saying by your leave, and I was on to yer trail in less'n no time. Now ye might as well give in and go along quiet with us. We'll find ye a nice easy place whar ye won't hev much to do, and whar ye kin live happier than ye ever could in this here forsaken wilderness."

While thus talking, the man, with a firm grasp of the girl's arm, was leading her back along the trail they had come. She had not spoken since uttering a cry of terror when he first seized her, and she now walked beside him so quietly and unresistingly that he imagined her spirit to be broken beyond further thought of escape.

The darkness of the hammock was intense, and being unaccustomed to the narrow path, Ruffin found difficulty in following it. All at once, as he swerved slightly from the trail, his foot caught in a loose root, and he pitched headlong to the ground, releasing the girl's arm as he fell. In an instant she was gone. Her light footfall gave back no sound to indicate the direction she had taken, and only the mocking forest echoes answered the man's bitter curses which were coupled with commands that she return to him.

Time was precious with the slave-catchers, and to pursue the girl would be a hopeless task. Ross Ruffin realized this, and so, baffled and raging, he made his way to that point on the river where, in a small boat, with Louis still bound and helpless, Troup Jeffers impatiently awaited his coming. The latter upbraided his confederate in unmeasured terms for allowing the girl to escape, and so fierce was their quarrel that it seemed about to result in bloodshed. Finally their interests, rather than their inclinations, led them to control their anger and to reflect that with the captives already secured, including Louis, his mother, and the family of their negro neighbors, the venture promised to be very profitable, after all. So they pulled down the dark river and out to a small schooner that, in charge of two other white men, lay off its mouth, awaiting them.

Louis had listened eagerly to Ruffin's report of his sister's flight, and thus assured of her escape, he became more reconciled to the fate in store for himself. As the boat in which he lay glided from the river's mouth, there came to him the sound of a dear voice that in all probability he would never hear again. It was a passionate cry of farewell from the sister whom he loved better than all the world beside. With a mighty effort the captive raised himself to a sitting posture.

"Good-bye, Nita!" he shouted; "God bless —"

Then he was silenced and struck down by a blow in the face. At the same instant a flash of fire leaped from the boat, and a rifle bullet sped angrily through the forest in the direction from which Nita's voice had come. It did not harm her, but she dared not call again. Nor did she dare remain longer in that vicinity.

Returning to her deserted home, the poor girl hastily gathered a slender store of provisions and then set forth, fearfully and with a breaking heart, to thread the shadowy trails leading to the only place of refuge that she knew, — the village of Philip Emathla the Seminole. For two days she travelled, guided by instinct rather than by a knowledge of the way, and at the end of the second she came to the place where Coacoochee was standing. As her presence was betrayed by Ul-we, and the young Indian sprang to her side, the girl sank into his arms, faint and speechless from exhaustion. Her dress hung in rags, her feet were bare and bleeding, and her tender skin was torn by innumerable thorns.

Filled with wonder and a premonition of evil tidings by this appearance of his friend's sister so far from her home and in so sad a plight, Coacoochee bore her to the open space in which he had stood, and laid her gently down at the base of a great oak. Then, realizing that all his strength would not suffice to carry her over the mile or

more lying between that place and his father's
village, he bade the great staghound stand guard
over the fainting girl, and started off at a speed
that he alone of all his tribe possessed, to seek
assistance.

The peaceful village was startled by his appearance as he dashed breathlessly into it a few minutes
later, and some of the men instinctively grasped
their weapons. With a few words, Coacoochee assured them that there was no immediate cause for
alarm, and then ordering three stalwart young warriors to follow him, he again entered the forest and
hastened back to where he had left the exhausted
girl.

A little later Nita Pacheco was borne into the
village and given over to the skilful ministrations
of the women belonging to King Philip's household.
Under their kindly care the strength of the fugitive
was so restored that within an hour after her arrival
she was able to relate her sad story to the aged chief,
who bent over her and listened to her words with
breathless attention.

When she finished, and Philip Emathla was possessed of all the facts she had to communicate, he drew
himself to his full height and stood for a moment
silent, while his whole frame trembled with anger.

At length he said: " It is well, my daughter. I
have heard thy words, and they have caused my
heart to bleed. From this hour thou shalt be to

Philip Emathla as the child of his old age, and thy sorrows shall be his. Sleep now and regain thy strength while he takes counsel concerning this matter with his wise men, and in the morning he will speak further with thee."

When the old chief repeated Nita Pacheco's story to his warriors assembled about the council fire that night, his words were received in silence, but with fierce scowls, clinched hands, and twitching fingers. At its conclusion the silence was only broken by angry mutterings, but none knew what to advise. At length King Philip addressed Coacoochee, who, youngest of all present, had been allowed a seat at this council for the first time. Calling him by name, the old chief said:

" My son, on account of thy friendship with Louis Pacheco, thy interest in this matter is greater than that of any other among my councillors. What, then, is thy opinion concerning this tale of wrong and outrage ? "

Standing bravely forth in the full glow of fire-light, with his athletic form and proud profile clearly outlined against it, the lad spoke vehemently and from a full heart as he replied :

" The words of my father have made the hearts of his children heavy. They tell us of the wickedness of the white man. That is nothing new. We have heard of it many times before. So many that we are weary with listening. But now this wickedness has fallen on those who have the right to call upon us for vengeance. They are not of our blood, but they lived among us and trusted us to protect them. Louis Pacheco is my friend and brother. This maiden is as a daughter to my father. They were not born slaves. The Great Spirit created them free as the birds of the air or the deer of the forest. Of this freedom, the gift of the Great Spirit, the white man seeks to rob them. Are we dogs that we should suffer this thing? No; the Seminoles are men and warriors. Let the chief send a message to the white man, demanding that these our friends be set free and restored to us. Let him also send out those who will discover whither they have been taken. If they be dead or carried away so far that he cannot find them, then let him lead his warriors to battle with the palefaced dogs, that the fate of our friends may be avenged. Coacoochee has spoken, and to Philip Emathla has he made answer."

This brave speech, delivered with all the fire and enthusiasm of youth as well as with the eloquent gestures that Coacoochee knew so well how to use, was received with murmurs of satisfaction by the younger warriors, whose eyes gleamed with a fierce joy at the thought of battle. The breast of the young orator swelled with pride as, reseating himself in his appointed place, he glanced about him and noted the effect of his maiden effort at public speech-making. His whole soul was enlisted in the cause of those oppressed ones for whom he had just pleaded so earnestly, and he longed with the earnestness of honorable, high-strung, and fearless youth to strike a telling blow in their behalf.

While he with the younger members of the band were thus animated by a spirit of resistance to injustice at any cost, the older warriors shook their heads. They could not but reflect upon their own weakness when they considered the power of the white man and the number of his soldiers.

The old chief who had called forth this manifestation of feeling noted shrewdly the varied expressions of those about him and then dismissed the council, saying that after sleeping he would announce his decision.

D

CHAPTER V

A FOREST BETROTHAL

PHILIP EMATHLA was an old man and a wise one. He had visited the great white Father at Washington, and had thus gained a very different idea of the power and number of the palefaces from that generally held by his tribe. He loved his land and his people. He was determined not to submit to injustice if he could help it, but he shrank from plunging the Seminoles into a war with the powerful and arrogant invaders of their country. He knew that such a war could only result in the utter defeat of the red man, no matter how long or how bravely he might fight. Thus Coacoochee's fiery speech at the council was a source of great anxiety to the old man and caused him to pass a sleepless night. By morning, however, he had decided upon a course of action, and again summoning his councillors, he unfolded it to them.

As the money value of Louis Pacheco and his mother had already been doubly paid by the Indians through the relinquishment of their annuity, Philip Emathla would himself go to the agent at Fort King, claim them as his slaves, and demand their

34

return to him as such. At the same time he would send scouts to St. Augustine to discover if the captives were in that city and what chance there was of rescuing them in case the agent should refuse to recognize his claim. Until these things were done there must be no thought or mention of war. It could only be considered after all else had failed.

As Coacoochee listened to these words, his face assumed a look of resolve, and he eagerly awaited an opportunity to speak. He was no longer content to be considered a dreamer, but was anxious to prove himself the worthy son of a great chief and entitled to the proud rank of warrior. When, therefore, his father finished what he had to say and signified that any who chose might speak, the lad, after waiting for a few minutes out of deference to his elders, rose with a modest but manly bearing and requested that two favors might be granted him. One was that he might be allowed to go alone on the scout to St. Augustine and there learn the fate of his friend. The other, asked with that confusion of manner which all youths, savage as well as civilized, manifest on such occasions, was that he might have his father's permission to make Nita Pacheco a daughter of the tribe, in fact as well as in name, by taking her to be his wife.

After regarding the lad fixedly and in silence for nearly a minute, the old chief made reply as follows:

"My son, although thou hast attained the stature

of a man, and it has been permitted thee to speak in council, thou art still but a boy in knowledge as well as in years. That thou may speedily prove thyself worthy the name of warrior is my hope and desire. Therefore that thou may not lack opportunity for gaining distinction, I hereby grant the first of thy requests on condition that six of my well-tried braves shall go with thee. They may be left in concealment outside the city, and thou may enter it alone ; but it is well to have friends at hand in case of need. It is also well that a young warrior should be guided by the counsel of those who are older and wiser.

"Thy second request will I also grant upon conditions. Gladly will I accept the maiden whom thou hast named, as a daughter in truth as well as in name ; but it seems to have escaped thy mind that no son of the Seminoles may take to himself a wife until he has won the title of warrior and proved himself capable of her support. Again, there is but one time for the taking of wives, which may only be done at the great green corn dance of thy people. If it pleases the maiden to plight thee her troth, to that I will give consent, provided the ceremony shall take place ere the setting of this day's sun. Then when thou art gone on thy mission to discover the fate of her mother and her brother, she will be doubly entitled to the love and protection of thy people. Let, then, a solemn betrothal satisfy thee for the present, and at some future time will the question of thy marriage be considered. Thus speaks Philip Emathla."

Coacoochee had loved the sister of his friend longer than he could remember, and believed that Nita entertained a similar feeling toward him, though no words of love had ever passed between them. Now they were to exchange a promise of marriage! The mere thought gave him a more manly and dignified bearing. And then he was to be immediately separated from her. How hard it would be to leave her! Doubly hard, now that she was in sorrow, and suffering the keenest anxiety. Still, if he could only bring back tidings of the safety of her dear ones, or perhaps even return them to her, how happy it would make her! How proud she would be of him!

To Nita the proposition that she should participate in a ceremony of betrothal to Coacoochee, which among the Seminoles is even more solemn and important than that of marriage itself, was startling but not unwelcome. She loved the handsome youth. In her own mind that had long ago been settled. Now she was homeless and alone. Where could she find a braver or more gallant protector than Coacoochee? Besides, was he not going into danger for her sake, and the sake of those most dear to her? Yes, she would give him her promise in the presence of all his people freely and gladly.

Again the sun was near his setting, and all nature was flooded with the golden glory that waited on his departure. The cluster of palmetto-thatched huts nestled beneath tall trees on the shore of blue Ahpopka Lake wore an expectant air, and their dusky inhabitants, gathered in little groups, seemed to anticipate some event of importance.

At length there came the sound of singing from a leafy bower on the outskirts of the village, and then appeared a bevy of young girls wreathed and garlanded with flowers. In their midst walked one whose face, fairer than theirs, still bore traces of recent suffering. She was clad in a robe of fawn-skin, creamy white and soft as velvet. Exquisitely embroidered, it was fit for the wear of a princess, and had indeed been prepared for the gentle Allala, King Philip's only daughter, shortly before her death. Now, worn for the first time, it formed the betrothal dress of Nita Pacheco. In the tresses of her rippling hair was twined a slender spray of snow-white star jasmine. She wore no other ornament, but none was needed for a beauty so radiant as hers.

So, at least, thought Coacoochee, as, escorted by a picked body of young warriors, gaudy in paint and feathers, he entered the village at this moment, but from its opposite side, and caught a glimpse of her.

Both groups advanced to the centre of the village and halted, facing each other, before the chief's lodge. There for some moments they stood amid an impressive silence that was only broken by the glad songs of birds in the leafy coverts above them. At length the curtain screening the entrance was drawn aside, and Philip Emathla, followed by two of his most trusted councillors, stepped forth. The head of the aged chieftain was unadorned save by a single roseate feather plucked from the wing of a flamingo. This from time immemorial had been the badge of highest authority among the Indians of Florida, and was adopted as such by the latest native occupants of the flowery land. The chief's massive form was set off to fine advantage by a simple tunic and leggings of buckskin. Depending from his neck by a slender chain was a large gold medallion of Washington, while across his breast he wore several other decorations in gold and silver.

Standing in the presence of his people, and facing the setting sun, the chieftain called upon the group of flower-decked maidens to deliver up their sister, and as Nita stepped shyly forth, he took her by the hand. Next he called upon the group of young warriors to deliver up their brother, whereupon their ranks opened, and Coacoochee walked proudly to where his father stood.

Taking him also by the hand, the old chief asked of his son, in a voice that all could plainly hear, if he had carefully considered the obligation he was about to assume. " Do you promise for the sake of this maiden to strive with all your powers to attain the rank of a warrior?   Do you promise, when that time comes, to take her to your lodge to be your squaw? to protect her with your life from harm? to hunt game for her? to see that she suffers not from hunger? to love her and bear with her until the Great Spirit shall call you to dwell with him in the Happy Hunting-grounds?"

"Un-cah" (yes), answered Coacoochee so clearly as to be heard of all.   "I do promise."

Turning to Nita, the chieftain asked: "My daughter, are you also willing to make promise to this youth that when the time comes for him to call thee to his lodge, you will go to him?   Are you willing to promise that from then until the sun shall no longer shine for thee, till thine eyes are closed in the long sleep, and till the music of birds no longer fill thy ears, Coacoochee shall be thy man, and thou shall know no other?   Are you willing to promise that from that time his lodge shall be thy lodge, his friends thy friends, and his enemies thy enemies? Are you willing to promise that from the day you enter his lodge you will love him and care for him, make his word thy law, and follow him even to captivity and death?   Consider well, my daughter, before answering; for thy pledged word may not be lightly broken."

Lifting her head, and smiling as she looked the old man full in the face, Nita answered, in low but distinct tones:

"Un-cah. I am willing to promise."

With this the chieftain placed the girl's hand in that of Coacoochee, and turning to the spectators, who stood silent and attentive, said:

"In thy sight, and in hearing of all men, this my son and this my daughter have given to each other the promise that may not be broken. Therefore I, Philip Emathla, make it known that whenever Coacoochee, after gaining a warrior's rank, shall call this maiden to his lodge, she shall go to him. From that time forth he shall be her warrior, and she shall be his squaw. It is spoken; let it be remembered."

With these words the ceremony of betrothal was concluded, and at once the spectators broke forth in a tumult of rejoicing. Guns were discharged, drums were beaten, great fires were lighted, there was dancing and feasting, and in every way they could devise did these simple-minded dwellers in the forest express their joy over the event that promised so much of happiness to the well-loved son of their chief.

In these rejoicings Coacoochee did not take part, glad as he would have been to do so. He had a duty to perform that might no longer be delayed. The fate of his friend, who was now become almost his brother, must be learned, and it rested with him to discover it.

So on conclusion of the betrothal ceremony he led Nita into his father's lodge, bade her a tender farewell, and promising a speedy return, slipped away almost unobserved.   Followed only by Ul-we, the great staghound, he entered the dark shadows of the forest behind the village, and was immediately lost to view.

CHAPTER VI

CRUEL DEATH OF UL-WE THE STAGHOUND

WHEN Coacoochee left the Indian village on the night of his betrothal and set forth on his journey to St. Augustine, he fully realized that the act marked a crisis in his life, and that from this hour his irresponsible boyhood was a thing of the past. For a moment he was staggered by the thought of what he was undertaking, together with an over-powering sense of his own weakness and lack of worldly knowledge. How could he, a mere lad, educated in nothing save forest craft, hope to compete with the strength, wisdom, and subtlety of the all-powerful white man? His heart sank at the prospect, there came a faltering in his springy stride, he feared to advance, and dreaded to retreat.

As he wavered he became conscious of a presence beside him, and to his ear came the voice of Allala. In tender but reproachful accents it said :

"My brother, to thee are the eyes of our people turning. Philip Emathla is chief of a band; through long strife, bitter trial, and deepest sorrow, Coacoochee shall become leader of a nation. Remember,

43

my brother, that to strive and succeed is glorious; to strive and yield is still honorable; but to yield without striving is contemptible."

The voice ceased, and the young Indian felt that he was again alone, but he was no longer undecided. His veins thrilled with a new life, and his heart was filled with a courage ready to dare anything. In an instant his determination was taken. He would strive for victories, he would learn to bear defeat, but it should never be said of Coacoochee that he was contemptible. Filled with such thoughts, the youth sprang forward and again urged his way along the dim forest trail.

He had gone but a short distance when he came to a group of dark figures evidently awaiting him. They were the six warriors chosen by his father to accompany him on his dangerous mission. As he joined them, a few words of greeting were exchanged, and one of them handed him his rifle, powder-horn, and bullet-pouch. Here he took the lead, with Ul-we close at his heels. The others followed in single file and with long, gliding strides that maintained with slight apparent effort yet bore them over the ground with surprising rapidity.

The night was lighted by a young moon, and such of its rays as were sifted down through the leafy canopy served to guide their steps as truly as though it had been day. When the moon set, the little band halted on the edge of an open glade, and each man

cut a few great leaves of the cabbage palmetto, which
he thrust stem first into the ground to serve as protection against the drenching night dew. Then,
flinging themselves down in the long grass, they
almost instantly fell asleep, leaving only Ul-we to
stand guard.

A brace of wild turkey, shot at daylight a
short distance from where they slept, furnished a
breakfast, and at sunrise they were once more on
their way. That morning they crossed the St.
John's River in a canoe that had been skilfully concealed beneath a bank from all but them, and soon
after sunset they made their second camp within a
few miles of St. Augustine.

Up to this time they had seen no white man, but
now they might expect to see many; for they were
near a travelled road recently opened for the government westward into the far interior, by a man
named Bellamy; thus it was called the "Bellamy
Road," — a name that it bears to this day.

Over it Coacoochee, accompanied only by Ul-we,
walked boldly the next morning until he came to the
city. He did not carry his rifle with him, as he knew
that Indians off their reservation were apt to have all
firearms seized and taken from them. Moreover, he
anticipated no danger. These were times of peace,
in which Indians as well as whites were protected by
treaty. So, cautioning his warriors to remain concealed until his return, the young leader went in

search of the information he had been detailed to obtain.

During his journey he had carefully considered the steps to be taken when he should reach its end. He might easily have slipped into the town under cover of darkness, and, with little chance of being observed, communicated with certain negroes of the place, who would have told him what he desired to know. He might have remained concealed in the outskirts until some of them passed that way. Several other plans suggested themselves, but all were rejected in favor of the one now adopted. Honest and straightforward himself, Coacoochee was disinclined to use methods that might lie open to suspicion. He knew of no reason why he, a free man, should not visit any portion of the land that his people still claimed as their own, and consequently he entered the town boldly and in broad daylight.

The sight of an Indian in the streets of St. Augustine was at that time too common to attract unusual attention. Still, the bearing of the young chief was so noble, and his appearance so striking, that more than one person turned to gaze after him as he passed.

The great dog that followed close at his heels also excited universal admiration, and several men offered to buy him from the youth as he passed them. To these he deigned no reply, for it was part of the Indian policy at that time, as it is now, to feign an ignorance of any language but their own.

Within a few hours Coacoochee had learned all that was to be known concerning the recent expedition of Jeffers and Ruffin. If they were successful in their undertaking, they were to proceed directly to Charleston, South Carolina, and there dispose of their captives. As they had now been absent from St. Augustine for more than a week, this is what they were supposed to have done.

Once during his hurried interviews with those who were able to give him information, but were fearful of being discovered in his company, the young Indian was vaguely warned that some new laws relating to his people had just been passed, and that if he were not careful, he might get into trouble through them.

Several times during the morning one or more of the street dogs of the town ran snarling after Ul-we ; but, in each case, one of his deep growls and a display of his formidable teeth caused them to slink away and leave him unmolested.

Having finished his business, Coacoochee set out on a return to the camp where his warriors awaited him. His heart was heavy with the news that he had just received, and as he walked, he thought bitterly of the fate of the friend who had been dragged into slavery far beyond his reach or power of rescue.

Thus thinking, and paying but slight attention to his surroundings, he reached the edge of the town. He was passing its last building, a low groggery, on the porch of which were collected a group of men, most of them more or less under the influence of liquor.

One of the group was a swarthy-faced fellow named Salano, who had for some unknown reason conceived a bitter hatred against all Indians, and often boasted that he would no more hesitate to shoot one than he would a wolf or a rattlesnake. Beside this man lay his dog, a mongrel cur with a sneaking expression, that had gained some notoriety as a fighter.

As Coacoochee passed this group, though without paying any attention to them, Salano called out to him in an insulting tone :

" Hello, Injun ! whar did you steal that dog ? "

If the young chief heard this question, he did not indicate by any sign that he had done so ; but continued calmly on his way.

Again Salano shouted after him. " I say whar did you steal that dog, Injun ? " then, with an oath, he added : " Bring him here ; I want to look at him."

Still there was no reply.

In the meantime the cur at Salano's feet was growling and showing his teeth as he gazed after the retreating form of Ul-we.

At this juncture his master stopped, and pointing in the direction of the staghound, said, " Go, bite him, sir ! "

The cur darted forward, and made a vicious snap at Ul-we's hind legs, inflicting a painful wound.

The temper of the big dog was tried beyond endurance. He turned, and with a couple of leaps overtook the cur, already in yelping retreat. Ul-we seized him by the back in his powerful jaws. There was a wild yell, a momentary struggle, a crunching of bones, and the cur lay lifeless in the dust. At the same moment the report of a rifle rang out, and the superb staghound sank slowly across the body of his late enemy, shot through the heart.

All this happened in so short a space of time that the double tragedy was complete almost before Coacoochee realized what was taking place.

The moment he did so, he sprang to his faithful companion, and kneeling in the dust beside him, raised the creature's head in his arms. The great, loving eyes opened slowly and gazed pleadingly into the face of the young Indian; with a last effort the dog feebly licked his hand, and then all was over. Ul-we, the tall one, the noblest dog ever owned and loved by a Seminole, was dead.

Over this pathetic scene the group about the groggery made merry with shouts of laughter and taunting remarks. As Coacoochee, satisfied that his dog was really dead, slowly rose to his feet, Salano jeeringly called out, "What'll you take for your pup now, Injun?"

The next moment the man staggered back with

E

an exclamation of terror as the young Indian sprang
to where he stood, and with a face distorted by rage
hissed between his teeth :

"From thy body shall thy heart be torn for this
act!   Coacoochee has sworn it."

Even as he spoke, a pistol held in Salano's hand
was levelled at his head, and his face was burned by
the explosion that instantly followed, though the bullet
intended for him whistled harmlessly over his head.
A young man who had but that moment appeared
on the scene had struck up the murderer's arm at
the instant of pulling the trigger, exclaiming as he
did so :

"Are you mad, Salano!"

Then to Coacoochee he said : "Go now before
further mischief is done.   The man is crazy with
drink, and not responsible for his actions.   I will
see that no further harm comes to you."   Without
a word, but with one penetrating look at the face of
the speaker, as though to fix it indelibly on his
memory, the young Indian turned and walked rapidly away.

He had not gone more than a mile from town, and
was walking slowly with downcast head and filled
with bitter thoughts, when he was roused from his
unhappy reverie by the sound of galloping hoofs
behind him.   Turning, he saw two horsemen rapidly
approaching the place where he stood.   At the same
time he became aware that two others, who had made

a wide circuit under cover of the dense palmetto scrub on either side of the road, and thus obtained a position in front of him, were closing in so as to prevent his escape in that direction. He could have darted into the scrub, and thus have eluded his pursuers for a few minutes; and had he been possessed of his trusty rifle, he would certainly have done so. But unarmed as he was, and as his enemies knew him to be, they could easily hunt him out and shoot him down without taking any risk themselves, if they were so inclined.

So Coacoochee walked steadily forward as though unconscious of being the object toward which the four horsemen were directing their course. He wished he were near enough to the hiding-place of his warriors to call them to him, but they were still a couple of miles away, and even his voice could not be heard at that distance. So, apparently unaware of, or indifferent to, the danger closing in on him, the young Indian resolutely pursued his way until he was almost run down by the horsemen who were approaching him from behind. As they reined sharply up, one of them ordered him to halt.

Coacoochee did as commanded, and turning, found himself again face to face with Fontaine Salano, the man who but a short time before had attempted to take his life.

CHAPTER VII

COACOOCHEE IN THE CLUTCHES OF WHITE RUFFIANS

As the young chief, obeying the stern command to halt, faced about, he found himself covered by a rifle in the hands of his most vindictive enemy. He knew in a moment that a crisis in their intercourse had been reached, and almost expected to be shot down where he stood, so malignant was the expression of the white man's face. Still, with the wonderful self-control in times of danger that forms part of the Indian character, he betrayed no emotion nor trace of fear. He only asked:

"Why should Coacoochee halt at the command of a white man?"

"Because, Coacoochee, if such is your outlandish name, the white man chooses to make you do so, and because he wants to see your pass," replied Salano, sneeringly.

In the meantime the other riders had come up, and two of them, dismounting, now stood on either side of the young Indian. In obedience to an almost imperceptible nod from their leader, these two seized him, and in a moment had pinioned his arms behind

him.   Coacoochee could have flung them from him
and made a dash for liberty even now.   He did make
one convulsive movement in that direction ; but
like a flash the thought came to him that this was
precisely what his enemies desired him to do, that
they might thus have an excuse for killing him.   So
he remained motionless, and quietly allowed himself
to be bound.

At this a shade of disappointment swept over
Salano's face, and he muttered an oath.   The truth
was that, terrified by Coacoochee's recent threat to
have his life in exchange for that of Ul-we, which he
had so cruelly taken, the bully had determined to
get rid of this dangerous youth without delay, and
had hit upon the present plan for so doing.   He had
calculated that his victim would attempt to escape,
or at least offer some resistance.   In either case he
would have shot him down without compunction, and
afterwards if called to account for the act, would
justify himself on the ground that the Indian was
transgressing a law recently passed by the Legisla-
ture of Florida, which he, in his character of Justice
of the Peace, was attempting to enforce.

Still, his plan had not wholly failed, and he now
proceeded to carry it to an extremity.

" So you acknowledge that you hain't got no pass,
do you, Injun ?   And are roaming about the country,
threatening white folks' lives, and doing Lord knows
what other deviltry on your own responsibility," he

said. "Now, then, listen to this." Drawing a paper
from his pocket as he spoke, the man read as follows :

"*An Act to prevent Indians from roaming at large
throughout the Territory :* Be it enacted by the Gov-
ernor and Legislative Council of the Territory, that
from and after the passing of this act, if any Indian,
of the years of discretion, venture to roam or ramble
beyond the boundary lines of the reservations which
have been assigned to the tribe or nation to which
said Indian belongs, it shall and may be lawful for
any person or persons to apprehend, seize, and take
said Indian, and carry him before some Justice of
the Peace, who is hereby authorized, empowered, and
required to direct (if said Indian have not a written permission from the agent to do some specific
act) that there shall be inflicted not exceeding thirty-
nine (39) stripes, at the discretion of the Justice, on
the bare back of said Indian, and, moreover, to cause
the gun of said Indian, if he have any, to be taken
away from him and deposited with the colonel of the
county or captain of the district in which said Indian
may be taken, subject to the order of the Superin-
tendent of Indian Affairs."

"Now, Mr. Injun, what have you got to say to
that?" demanded Salano, as he folded the paper and
restored it to his pocket.

Although Coacoochee had not understood all that
had just been read to him, he comprehended that by
a white man's law, an Indian might be whipped like

a slave or a dog, and his blood boiled hotly at the mere thought of such an outrage. Still he replied to Salano's last question with dignity and a forced composure.

"The Iste-chatte has not been told of this law. It is a new one to him, and he has had no time to learn it. It was not put into the treaty. Coacoochee is the son of a chief. If you lift a hand against him, you lift it against the whole Seminole nation. If you strike him, the land will run red with white men's blood. If you kill him, his spirit will cry for vengeance, and no place can hide you from the fury of his warriors. They will not eat nor drink nor sleep till they have found you out, and torn the cowardly heart from your body."

"Oh come!" interrupted Salano, with an oath, "that will do. We don't want to hear any more from you. This Injun is evidently a dangerous character, gentlemen, and as a Justice of the Peace I shall deal with him according to the law. We'll whip him first, and if that isn't enough, we'll hang him afterwards."

The three men who accompanied Salano were his boon companions, and were equally ready with himself to perform any deed of cruelty or wickedness. They regarded an Indian as fair game, to be hunted and even killed wherever found. Nothing would please them better than a declaration of war against the Seminoles, and they were determined to leave nothing undone to hasten so desirable an event. To whip an Indian under cover of the law was rare sport, and the prospect of hanging him afterwards filled them with a brutal joy. So they readily obeyed the commands of their leader, and after fastening their horses by the roadside, they threw a slip-noose over Coacoochee's head, and drawing it close about his neck, led him a short distance within a grove of trees, to one of which they made fast the loose end of the rope. He was thus allowed to step a couple of paces in each direction. Ripping his tunic from the neck downward with a knife, they stripped it from his back, and all was in readiness for their devilish deed. Their rifles had been left hanging to their saddles, but each man had brought a raw-hide riding-whip with him, and these they now proposed to apply to the bare back of their silent and unresisting victim.

"Ten cuts apiece, gentlemen!" cried Salano, with a ferocious laugh. "That'll make the thirty-nine allowed by law, and one over for good measure. I take great credit to myself for the idea of making the prisoner fast by the neck only, and that with a slip-noose. He's got plenty of room to dance, and if he looses his footing and hangs himself, why, that'll be his lookout and not ours. At any rate, it will be a good riddance of the varmint, and will relieve us from further responsibility in the matter. I claim the first cut at him; so stand back and give me room."

As the others moved back a few paces, the chief ruffian stepped up to the young Indian, and laying the raw hide across the bared shoulders as though to measure the width of the blow he was about to inflict, he lifted it high above his head, saying as he did so :

" You'll cut my heart out, will you, Injun ? We'll see now who is going to do the cutting."

Then with a vicious hiss, the raw hide swept down with the full force of the arm that wielded it.

There was no outcry and no movement on the part of the Indian, only his flesh shrunk and quivered beneath the cruel blow, which left a livid stripe across his shoulders.

That blow was to be paid for with hundreds of innocent lives, and millions of dollars. It was to be felt throughout the length and breadth of the land, and was to be atoned by rivers of blood. In a single instant its fearful magic transformed the young Indian who received it, from a quiet, peace-loving youth, with a generous, affectionate nature, into a savage warrior, relentless and pitiless. It gave to the Seminoles a leader whose very name should become a terror to their enemies, and it precipitated one of the cruellest and most stubbornly contested Indian wars ever waged on American soil.

Again was the whip uplifted, but before it could descend for a second blow, the wretch who wielded it was dashed to the ground, and a white man with blazing eyes stood over his prostrate figure. The newcomer presented a cocked rifle at the startled spectators of the proceedings, who had been too intent upon the perpetration of their crime to take notice of his approach.

"Cowards!" he cried, in ringing tones. "Does it take four of you to whip one Indian? Is this the way you continue a private quarrel and gratify your devilish instincts? Bah! Such wretches as you are a disgrace to manhood! You make me ashamed of my color, since it is the same as your own. Did you not hear me give my word to this youth that he should go in safety? How dared you then even contemplate this outrage? Perhaps you thought that the word of an Englishman might be defied with impunity. From this moment you will know better; for if any one of you ever dares cross my path again, I will shoot him in his tracks as I would any other noxious beast that curses the earth. Now get you gone from this spot ere my forbearance is tempted beyond its strength. Go back to the town, and there proclaim your iniquity, if you dare. You will find few sympathizers in your attempt to precipitate an Indian war, and deluge this fair land with blood. Go, and go on foot. Your horses have already taken the road. Go, and if you even dare to look back until out of my sight, a bullet from this rifle shall spur your lagging pace. And you, Fontaine Salano, you brute of brutes, you pariah dog, do you

THEN WITH A VICIOUS HISS THE RAWHIDE SWEPT DOWN WITH THE
FULL FORCE OF THE ARM THAT WIELDED IT.

СУГЬОРЖПГ
ПИЫ̆ ОЬ.

go with them. Away out of my sight, I say, lest I cause this Indian to flay your bare back with the lashes you intended for him."

Whether the four men imagined that they were confronted by one bereft of his senses, or whether they were indeed the cowards he called them, it is impossible to say. Certain it is that they received the young man's scathing words in silence, and, when ordered to leave, they took their departure with a precipitate haste that would have been comical under less tragic circumstances.

The stranger followed them to the edge of the wood, and watched them until they disappeared in the direction of the town. Then he returned to where Coacoochee, who had not yet seen the face of his deliverer, still remained bound to the tree. As with a keen-edged knife he cut the thongs confining the young Indian's arms, and the rope about his neck, thus allowing the latter to face him, Coacoochee gave a start of surprise. His new friend was the same who, but an hour or so before, had saved him from Fontaine Salano's pistol in the streets of St. Augustine.

CHAPTER VIII

RALPH BOYD THE ENGLISHMAN

THE man who had thus so opportunely come to the rescue of Coacoochee twice in one day was a remarkable character even in that land of adventurers. Descended from a wealthy English family, well educated and accomplished, he had sought a life of adventure, and after spending some years in out-of-the-way corners of the world, had finally settled down on a large plantation in Florida left to him by an uncle whom he had never seen. Here he now lived with his only sister Anstice, who had recently come out to join him.

Filled with a love for freedom and always ready to quarrel with injustice in any form, he had, before even seeing his property, freed his slaves and ordered his attorneys to discharge an oppressive overseer who had mismanaged the plantation for some years. This man, whom Ralph Boyd did not even know by sight, was no other than our slave-catching acquaintance Mr. Troup Jeffers.

In that slave-holding community a man who chose to work his plantation with free labor became immediately unpopular, and some of his neighbors sought quarrels with him, in the hope of driving him from the country. But they had reckoned without their host. Ralph Boyd was not to be driven, as the result of several duels into which they forced him plainly proved. He was a good shot, an expert swordsman, a capital horseman, and was apparently without fear. Therefore it was quickly discovered that to meddle with the young Englishman was to meddle with danger, and that his friendship was infinitely preferable to his enmity. He was of such a sunny disposition that it was difficult to rouse him to anger on his own behalf, but he never permitted a wrong to be perpetrated on the weak or helpless that lay within his powers of redress. Thus a case of cowardly brutality like the present, and one of which the possible consequences were so terrible to contemplate, filled him with a righteous and well-nigh uncontrollable rage.

The Boyd plantation lay some forty miles from St. Augustine, and Boyd had ridden into town that day on a matter of business. He had reached it just in time to witness Salano's shooting of Ul-we. Filled with indignation at the deed, and admiring the manner with which Coacoochee confronted his tormentors, Boyd at once took the young Indian's part and probably saved his life. Then he went about his own business. Some time afterwards he learned by the merest accident of the departure of Salano and his evil associates on the track of the young chief. Fearing that they meditated mischief toward one to whom he had given the promise of his protection, he procured a fresh horse and started in hot pursuit.

Finding the four horses hitched by the roadside, and noting that each man had left his rifle hanging to the saddle, Boyd took the precaution of putting these safely out of the way, by the simple expedient of cutting the horses loose and starting them on the back track before entering the grove. Then, following the sound of voices, he made his way noiselessly among the trees to the disgraceful scene of the whipping. He had not anticipated anything so bad as this, and the sight filled him with an instant fury.

Springing forward, rifle in hand, he stretched Salano on the ground with a single blow, and then confronted the others. They all knew him, and would rather have encountered any other two men. His very presence, in moments of wrath, inspired terror, and when he gave them permission to go, they slunk from him like whipped curs.

If Coacoochee was startled at sight of his deliverer, Boyd was no less so at the frightful change in the face of the young Indian. It was no longer that into which he had gazed an hour before. That was the mobile face of a youth reflecting each passing emotion, and though it was even then clouded by sorrow and anger, a little time would have restored its sunshine. Now its features were rigid, and stamped with a look that expressed at once

intolerable shame and undying hate. The eyes
were those of a wild beast brought to bay and prepared for a death struggle.

The once fearless gaze now fell before that of
the white man. Coacoochee, proudest of Seminoles,
hung his head. This man had witnessed his shame
and had at the same time placed him under an obligation. The young Indian could not face him, and
could not kill him, so he stood motionless and silent,
with his eyes fixed on the ground.

Ralph Boyd appreciated the situation, and understood the other's feelings as though they were his
own, as in a way they were. They would be the
feelings of any free-born, high-spirited youth under
similar circumstances.

"My poor fellow," said Boyd, holding out his
hand as he spoke, "I think I know how you feel,
and I sympathize with you from the bottom of my
heart. You will surely allow me to be your friend,
though, seeing that I have just made four enemies
on your account. Won't you shake hands with me
in token of friendship?"

"I cannot," answered Coacoochee, in a choked
voice. "You are a white man. I have been
whipped by a white man. Not until the mark of
his blow has been washed away with his blood can
I take the hand of any white man in friendship."

"Well, I don't know but what I should feel just
as you do," replied Boyd, musingly. "I have never

before met any of your people, but have been told that you were a treacherous race, without any notions of honor or true bravery. Now it seems to me that your feelings in this matter are very much what mine would be if I were in your place. Still, I hope you are not going to lay up any bitterness against me on account of what was done by another, even though we are, unfortunately, both of the same color. I am curious to know something of you Indians, and would much rather have you for a friend than an enemy."

"Coacoochee will always be your friend," answered the other, earnestly. "Some day he will shake hands with you. Not now. With his life will he serve you. A Seminole never forgives an injury, and he never forgets a kindness. Now I must go."

"Hold on, Coacoochee; you must not go half naked and with that mark on your back," exclaimed Boyd. "Here, I have on two shirts, and I insist that you take one of them. With your permission I will take in exchange this buckskin affair of yours that those villains cut so recklessly, and will keep it as a souvenir of this occasion."

As he spoke, the young Englishman divested himself of his outer garment, a tastefully made hunting-tunic of dark green cloth, and handed it to Coacoochee. Without hesitation the Indian accepted this gift, and put on the garment, which fitted him perfectly.

Then the two young men left the little grove in which events of such grave import to both had just taken place, and walked to where Boyd had left his horse.

Upon Coacoochee saying that he should go but a little further on the road, the other declared an intention to accompany him, and so, leading his horse, walked on beside the shame-faced Indian.

The more Boyd talked with Coacoochee, the more he was pleased with him. He found him to be intelligent and modest, but high-spirited and imbued to an exaggerated degree with savage notions of right and wrong, honor and dishonor. To avenge a wrong and repay a kindness, to deal honorably with the honorable and treacherously with the treacherous, to serve a friend and injure an enemy, was his creed, and by it was his life moulded.

At length they came to the place where the young Indian said he must leave the road. As they paused to exchange farewells, the querulous note of a hawk sounded from the palmetto scrub close beside them. Coacoochee raised his hand, and as though by magic six stalwart warriors leaped into the road and surrounded them.

Boyd made an instinctive movement toward his rifle, but it was checked by the sight of a faint smile on his companion's face. At the same time the latter said quietly:

F

"Fear nothing; they are my friends, and my friends are thy friends."

To the Indians he said in their own tongue, "Note well this man. He is my friend and that of all Seminoles. From them no harm must ever come to him."

Then he waved his hand, and the six warriors disappeared so instantly and so utterly that the white man rubbed his eyes and looked about him in amazement.

Turning, to express his surprise to Coacoochee, he discovered that the young chief had also disappeared, and that he alone occupied the road.

CHAPTER IX

MYSTERIOUS DISAPPEARANCE OF A SENTINEL

FOR a full minute Ralph Boyd stood bewildered in the middle of the road. In vain did he look for some sign and listen for some sound that would betray the whereabouts of those who, but a moment before, had stood with him. The tall grasses waved and the flowers nodded before a gentle breeze, but it was not strong enough to move the stiff leaves of the palmetto scrub, nor was there any motion that might be traced to the passing of human beings among their hidden stalks. From the feathery tips of the cabbage palms came a steady fluttering that rose or fell with the breathings of the wind, and in far-away thickets could be heard the cooing of wood doves, and the occasional cheery note of a quail, but no other sound broke the all-pervading silence.

All at once from a hammock growing at a considerable distance from where the young man stood there came to his ears the thrilling sound of a Seminole war-cry:

" Yo-ho-ee yo-ho-ee yo-ho-ee-che ! "

It was followed by another and another, until the listener counted seven of the ominous cries in as

many distinct voices, and knew that they were
uttered by the seven Indians who had stood with
him in the road.

Unaccustomed to the ways of red men, Boyd could
not understand how they had glided so noiselessly
and swiftly away from him.

"It is like magic," he muttered, "and gives one
a creepy feeling. What a terrible thing a war with
such as they would be in this country, where everything is so favorable to them and so unfavorable to
the movements of troops. And yet war is the very
thing toward which the reckless course of politicians,
slave-hunters, and land-grabbers is hurrying the
government. Well, I shan't take part in it, that's
certain, though my present duty as a white man is
plainly to ride back to St. Augustine and give the
colonel information of this present band of Indians.
I wouldn't think of doing so, only for fear that,
smarting under the insult to that fine young fellow
Coacoochee, they will seek revenge and visit the sins
of the guilty upon innocent heads. If Coacoochee
has only followed my advice and gone directly back
to the reservation, and to his own place, there won't
be any trouble; but if he is going to hang around
here, trying to lift a few scalps, as I am afraid he is,
he may get himself into a fix from which I can't
help him."

It must not be supposed that Ralph Boyd had
been standing in the middle of the road all this

time. He was in the saddle even before the sound of the Indian war-cries informed him of the direction they had taken and where they were. Directly afterwards he put spurs to his horse, and during the latter part of his soliloquy was galloping rapidly back over the road he had just come.

Although Boyd knew Salano to be a bitter and unscrupulous enemy, he had no hesitation in returning to St. Augustine on his account, or for fear of the others with whose cruel sport he had so summarily interfered. He did not believe they would dare publish what they had done, or care to acknowledge that they had been driven off and compelled to forego their intentions by a single man.

To satisfy himself on this point, he made a few inquiries on reaching the city, and finding that nothing was known of the recent adventure, he went to the colonel commanding the small garrison stationed in the city and informed him of the presence near it of an armed band of seven Indian warriors. He also expressed his fear that they intended mischief to some of the plantations along the St. John's.

The colonel listened attentively to all that he had to say and thanked him for the information. Darkness had fallen by this time, and it was too late to do anything that night, but the officer promised to send out a scouting party of twenty troopers at daylight. In the meantime he begged that Boyd would remain as his guest over night, and in the morning consent to guide the troops to the place where he had seen the Indians, which the latter readily agreed to do. He did this the more willingly because he had learned that the scouting party was to be commanded by Irwin Douglass, a young lieutenant with whom he had formed a pleasant acquaintance, and who had already visited him at the plantation.

When, after an early and hurried cup of coffee with the colonel and Douglass the following morning, Boyd joined the soldiers, to whom for a short distance he was to act as guide, he was amazed to find that Fontaine Salano had applied for and received permission to accompany them. He wondered at this as the troop clattered noisily with jingling sabres and bit-chains out of the quiet old town. Was Salano's hatred of the young Indian whom he had so cruelly wronged so bitter that he was determined to seize every opportunity for killing him? Boyd could think of no other reason why the man, naturally so indolent, should undertake this forced march with all the discomforts that must necessarily attend it.

The spring morning was just cool enough to be exhilarating. The fresh air was laden with the perfume of orange groves, and from their green coverts innumerable birds poured forth their choicest melody. The cavalry horses, in high spirits from long idleness, pranced gaily along the narrow streets and were with difficulty reined to a decorous trot.

Once free from the town and out in the broad plain of sand and chaparral that lay beyond, the pace was quickened, and for several miles the troop swung cheerily along at a hand gallop, with polished weapons and accoutrements flashing brightly in the rays of the newly risen sun.

A halt was called at the place where Boyd had encountered the Indians, and scouts were sent in search of signs. These easily found the camp from which Coacoochee had started on his visit to town the morning before, and finally discovered a fresh trail leading to the west or toward the St. John's.

It was not easy for the troops, inexperienced in Indian warfare, to follow this on horseback, and they soon lost it completely. This did not greatly disturb Lieutenant Douglass; for, being satisfied that the plantations along the river were the objective points of those whom he was pursuing, he determined to push on toward them without losing any time in attempting to rediscover the trail.

That evening they reached the great river and encamped near it without having discovered any further Indian sign, or finding that the few widely scattered settlers had been given any cause to suspect the presence of an enemy.

During that night, however, two startling incidents occurred. The first of these was the complete and mysterious disappearance of one of the sentinels who guarded the camp. He had been stationed not far from the edge of the forest, but within easy hail of his sleeping comrades. The sergeant had given him particular cautions regarding the dangers of his post, and warned him to be keenly alert to every sound, even the slightest. He had answered with a laugh, that his ears were too long to permit anything human to get within a rod of him without giving him warning, and he declared his intention of firing in the direction of any suspicious sound.

So they left him, and an hour later the corporal of the guard, visiting the post, found it vacant. In the darkness it was useless to hunt for the missing sentry, and so, without giving a general alarm, the corporal detailed another sentinel to the place of the missing man, and remained with him on the post until morning. They neither saw nor heard anything to arouse their suspicions, but as soon as daylight revealed surrounding objects, they could readily note signs of a struggle at one end of the beat paced by their unfortunate predecessor.

There were no traces of blood, nor in the trail of moccasined feet leading away from the spot could any imprint of the heavy cavalry boots worn by the missing soldier be found. The trail led to a small creek that emptied into the river just above the camp, but there it ended. Both banks of this creek were carefully examined for a mile up and down, but they revealed no sign to denote that they had ever been trodden by human feet.

There was nothing more to be done. The man was reported as missing, and a riderless horse was led by one of the troopers on that day's march, — but this mysterious disappearance and unknown fate of their comrade served to open the eyes of the soldiers to the dreadful possibilities of Indian warfare.

CHAPTER X

FONTAINE SALANO'S TREACHERY AND ITS REWARD

ANOTHER mysterious happening of that first night out was well calculated to exercise a depressing effect on the men and to transform the contempt they had hitherto felt for Indians into a profound respect not unmixed with fear. Fontaine Salano slept rolled in his blanket not far from the lieutenant in command of the party, and within the full light of a camp-fire. Toward morning, however, this fire had burned so low that it shed but little light, and the place where Salano lay was buried in shadow.

When he awoke at the first peep of dawn, he was puzzled by the appearance of a number of strange objects that rose from the ground close by his head. He examined them curiously, but his curiosity was in an instant changed to horror when he discovered them to be seven blood-stained Indian arrows thrust into the ground, three on each side of where his head had lain and one at the upper end of his couch. This one bore impaled on its shaft the bloody heart of a recently killed deer, the significance of which was so plain that no one could fail to understand it.

The mere fact that the Indians had thus been able to penetrate undetected to the very centre of a guarded camp invested them in the eyes of the men with supernatural powers. The effect on Salano was precisely what Coacoochee had intended it should be. To feel that he had been completely within the power of one who had sworn to have his life and had only been spared as a cat spares a mouse, that she may prolong its torture for her own pleasure, filled the wretch with a terror pitiful to behold.

He begged Lieutenant Douglass to return at once to St. Augustine or at least to send him back under escort. The officer politely regretted his inability to comply with either of these requests, saying that it would be contrary to his duty to retire from that part of the country until satisfied that the Indians had left it, and that he dared not weaken his little force by detailing any men for escort duty.

The man displayed such abject cowardice that finally, more out of disgust than pity, Ralph Boyd offered to accompany him back to the city, and to his surprise, Salano accepted the offer eagerly. As they were both volunteers, Douglass had no authority for detaining them, though he protested against the undertaking, and tried to persuade them of its dangers. Ralph Boyd only laughed, and even Salano intimated a belief that the Indians would devote themselves to watching the movements of the scouting party, so that to remain with them would be to remain in the vicinity of greatest danger.

The lieutenant said that he should remove his command only a short distance, to a better and more secure camping-ground that he knew of not very far from Boyd's plantation, over which he promised to keep especial watch. He intended to remain at that place until he learned something definite regarding the movements of the Indians, and there Boyd promised to rejoin him on the following day.

Camp was broken, and the clear bugle notes of " boots and saddles " were ringing on the still morning air as Boyd and Salano rode away from the camp on the return trail to St. Augustine. They rode in silence; for one entertained too great a contempt for the other to care to talk with him, and Salano was perfecting a plan for obtaining one portion of the revenge upon which his mind was intent.

They had not proceeded thus more than two miles, when they came to a narrow gully through which they were obliged to ride in single file, and here Salano, with an exaggerated show of politeness, dropped behind, allowing Boyd to take the lead.

The latter rode unsuspectingly ahead for a few rods, and then, not hearing the sound of the other's horse behind him, turned to see if he were not coming.

The sight that met his eyes was so unexpected

and terrible that for an instant it rendered him incapable of thought or action. Salano, dismounted from his horse, was slowly raising a rifle and taking deliberate aim at him. He could see the cruelly triumphant expression on the swarthy face. In that instant of time he also saw a flashing figure with uplifted arm leap from the underbrush behind Salano. Then all became a blank.

When next Ralph Boyd was able to take an interest in the affairs of this world, he was lying in the shade of a tree, two horses were cropping the grass near him, and a strange, wild-looking figure was dashing water in his face.

"What does this mean? What has happened?" Boyd inquired faintly.

"Wal, cap'n," answered the stranger, in unmistakable English, pausing in his occupation and drawing a long breath. "I'm almighty glad you ain't dead. The Injun said you warn't, but I wouldn't be sure of it myself till this very minute. As to what's happened, I'm a leetle mixed myself, but it's something like this: Some red villians was about to do for me when you come along and stopped 'em. Then a white villian was about to do for you, when one of the red villians stopped him, or at any rate he stopped the worst of it; then the red villian did for the white villian, and did it almighty thorough too."

At this juncture Boyd again closed his eyes and

seemed about to lapse once more into unconscious-
ness, whereupon the stranger began again to dash
water vigorously in his face.

There was a stinging sensation and a loud buzzing
in the young man's head. Salano's murderous aim
had been slightly disconcerted, at the moment of
firing, by a fierce yell in his very ear. At the instant of pulling the trigger Coacoochee's terrible
knife had been buried to the hilt in his body. The
would-be murderer sank dead without a groan, while
his intended victim escaped with a scalp wound
which, though not dangerous, was sufficient to de-
prive him of his senses for some time.

When he had sufficiently recovered his strength to
be able to sit up, and after he had listened to these
details of his own narrow escape, he looked curiously
at his companion and asked him who he was. It is
no wonder that he did not recognize the strange
figure; for though the man wore a pair of army
trousers, he had Indian moccasins on his feet, was
bare-headed, and naked to the waist. Half his face
as well as half of his body was painted red and the
other half black.

In this manner did the Seminoles prepare their
bodies for death, and to those who understood its
meaning, this combination of the two colors had a
very grim significance. Fortunately for the man's
peace of mind, he had not understood why this form
of decoration was applied to him, though his fears

that his life was in danger had been very fully aroused.

In answer to Ralph Boyd's questions, he told his story as follows : " I'm not surprised that you don't recognize me, cap'n ; for I'm not quite sure that I'd recognize myself. Still, whatever I may be to-day, yesterday I was private Hugh Belcher of Company B, Second Regiment United States Dragoons."

" What ! " exclaimed Boyd, " are you the sentry who disappeared last night ? "

" That's who I am, sir," replied the other, " much as my present appearance would seem to point again its being true. How the Reds crept upon me without me hearing a sound of their coming is more than I can tell, for I've always bragged that my ears were as sharp as the next man's. However, they did it, and the first I knew of their presence was when a blanket was flung over my head and I was tripped up. I don't know how many of 'em had me, but there was enough, anyway, to hold me fast, and tie me and get a gag into my mouth, so that I couldn't make a sound. Then they pulled off my boots, put moccasins on my feet, and made me go along with them.

" After awhile we came to this place, and here, as soon as it got light, they stripped me and painted me and tied me to a tree, and was just getting ready to give me a thrashing with a lot of switches they'd cut, though Lord knows I hadn't done nothing to rile 'em, when all of a sudden you and Mr. Salano hove in sight.

"I was faced that way and see Mr. Salano when he dropped off his horse and drawed a bead on you. I'd a hollered, but the gag was still in my mouth, so I couldn't. When the head Injun see what was taking place though, he gave one spring out of the brush, and landed on Mr. Salano's back like a wildcat. At the same time he let loose a yell fit to raise the dead. The gun went off just as he yelled, and you tumbled out of the saddle like you was killed.

"When the head Injun saw that, he run up to you first and dragged you to this place. Then he run back to Mr. Salano and stooped over him like he was feeling of his heart to see if he was dead. When he riz up again, he fetched another yell and called out something in his own lingo about Ul-we. Then the rest crowded around him, and he talked to them for about a minute.

"After that they come back and cut me loose, and the head Injun, pointing to you, said in English, 'You are free. Care for him. He is not dead. Tell him Coacoochee's heart is no longer heavy. He will go to his own people. If the soldiers want him, let them seek him in the swamps of the Okeefenokee.' Then, without another word, they all disappeared, and I set to work to bring you to."

Thus was the death of Ul-we, the tall one, atoned for in heart's blood, and thus was the stripe on

Coacoochee's back washed out with the blood of him who had so wantonly inflicted it. Thus, also, did Coacoochee save the life of his friend and punish the would-be assassin who had so planned his cowardly revenge upon Ralph Boyd that the act would be credited to the Indians.

With the accomplishment of this deed of just retribution, Coacoochee and his warriors disappeared from that part of the country, nor were they again seen there for many months.

G

CHAPTER XI

THE SEMINOLE MUST GO

THE Seminoles must be removed. The clamor of the land-speculator, the slave-hunter, and a host of others interested in driving the Indian from his home had at length been listened to at Washington, and the fiat had gone forth. The Seminoles must be removed to the distant west — peaceably if possible, but forcibly if they will not go otherwise.

A new treaty had been made by which the Indians agreed to remove to the new home selected for them, provided a delegation of chiefs appointed to visit the western land reported favorably concerning it. These went, saw the place, and upon their return reported it to be a cold country where Seminoles would be very unhappy.

Upon hearing this, the Indians said that they would prefer to remain where they were. Thereupon the United States Government said through its commissioners that it made no difference whether they wanted to go or not ; they must go.

In the meantime, outrages of every kind were perpetrated upon the Indians. The whipping of those discovered off the reservation, that was begun with Coacoochee, was continued. Several Indians were thus whipped to death by the white brutes into whose cowardly hands they fell. The system of withholding annuities and supplies was continued, and the helpless Indians were recklessly plundered right and left.

General Andrew Jackson, who was now President, had no love for Indians. He had in former years wronged them too cruelly for that, while teaching them lessons of the white man's power. He therefore appointed General Wiley Thompson of Georgia, as the Seminole agent, and ordered him to compel their removal to the far west without further delay. He also sent troops to Florida, and these began to gather at Fort Brooke and Tampa Bay under command of General Clinch.

It was evident that the Seminoles must either submit to leave the sunny land of their birth, their homes, and the graves of their fathers, or they must fight in its defence, and for their rights as free men. If they consented to go west to the land that those chiefs who had seen it described as cold and unproductive, they would find already established there their old and powerful enemies, the Creeks, who were eagerly awaiting their coming, with a view to seizing their negro allies and selling them into slavery. It was evident that a fight for his very existence was to be forced upon the Seminole in either case, and it only remained for him to choose whether he would fight in his own land, of which he knew every swamp, hammock, and glade, and of which his enemy was ignorant, or whether he should go to a distant country, of which he knew nothing, and fight against an enemy already well acquainted with it.

This was the alternative presented to the warriors of Philip Emathla's village assembled about their council fire on a summer's evening a few weeks after that with which this history opens.

On Coacoochee, now sitting in the place of honor at the right hand of the chief his father and earnestly regarding the speaker who laid this state of affairs before them, the weeks just passed had borne with the weight of so many years. During their short space he had passed from youth to manhood. Having directed the search for himself that followed the death of Salano, toward the Okeefenokee, while his village lay in exactly the opposite direction, he had escaped all intercourse with the whites from that time to the present. But from that experience he had returned so much wiser and graver that his advice was now sought by warriors much older than he, while by those of his own age and younger he was regarded as a leader. Thus, though still a youth in years, and though he still reverenced and obeyed his father, he was to all intents the chief of Philip Emathla's powerful band.

It was in this capacity that the speaker, to hear

whom this council was gathered, evidently regarded
him, and it was to Coacoochee that his remarks were
especially directed.

This speaker was a member of a band of Seminoles
known as the Baton Rouge or Red Sticks, who occupied a territory at some distance from that of King
Philip. His father, whom he had never known, was
a white man, but his mother was the daughter of
a native chieftain, and though he spoke English
fluently, he had passed all of his twenty-eight years
among the Seminoles, and they were his people.
Although not a chief, nor yet regarded as a prom-
inent leader, he was possessed of such force of character and such a commanding presence that he had
acquired a great influence over all the Indians with
whom he was thrown in contact. His name was
Ah-ha-se-ho-la (black drink), generally pronounced
Osceola by the whites, who also called him by his
father's name of Powell.

This dauntless warrior was bitterly opposed to the
emigration of his tribe, and was anxious to declare
war against the whites rather than submit to it.
He believed that the Seminoles, roaming over a vast
extent of territory abounding in natural hiding-
places, might defend themselves against any army
of white soldiers that should undertake to subdue
them for at least three years. Could the conflict be
sustained for that length of time without the whites
gaining any decided advantages, he declared they

would then give up the struggle and allow the Indians to retain their present lands unmolested.

Osceola was now visiting the different bands of the tribe, preaching this crusade of resistance to tyranny. As he stood before Philip Emathla and his warriors, with his noble figure and fine face fully displayed in the bright firelight, they were thrilled by his eloquence. With bated breath they listened to his summing up of their grievances, and when he declared that he would rather die fighting for this land than live in any other, they greeted his words with a murmur of approving assent.

Never had Coacoochee been so powerfully affected. The sting of the white man's whip across his shoulders was still felt, and he was choked with the sense of outrage and injustice inflicted upon his people. His fingers clutched nervously at the hilt of his knife and he longed for the time to come when he might fight madly for all that a man holds most dear.

As his gaze wandered for a moment from the face of the speaker, it fell on a group just visible within the circle of firelight. There sat the beautiful girl to whom he had so recently plighted his troth, and beside her Chen-o-wah, the daughter of a Creek chief and his quadroon squaw. She was the wife of Osceola, and the one being in all the world whom the fierce forest warrior loved.

For a moment Coacoochee's determination wavered as he reflected what these and others equally helpless would suffer in a time of war. There came a memory of the manner in which Nita's mother and brother had been consigned to slavery by the white man. No word had come from them, but he could imagine their fate. Might not the same fate overtake her most dear to him and hundreds of others with her? Would it not be better for them to incur the dangers and sufferings of war rather than those of slavery? Yes, a thousand times yes.

And then, perhaps the whites were not so very powerful, after all. Their soldiers, so far as he had seen them, were but few in number, and moved slowly from place to place. He and his warriors could travel twenty miles to their five. Besides, there were the vast watery fastnesses of the Everglades and the Big Cypress in the far south, to which the Indians could always retreat and into which no white man would ever dare follow them. Yes, his voice should be raised for war, no matter how long it might last, nor how bloody it might be, and the sooner it could be begun, the better. But he must listen, for Philip Emathla was about to speak.

CHAPTER XII

CHEN-O-WAH IS STOLEN BY THE SLAVE-CATCHERS

THE aged chieftain rose slowly and for a moment gazed lovingly and in silence at those gathered about him; then he said: " My children, we have listened to the words of Ah-ha-se-ho-la, and we know them to be true. But he has spoken with the voice of a young man. He sees with young eyes. My eyes are old, but they can look back over many seasons that a young man cannot see. They can also look forward further than his, and see many things. I have seen the great council of the white man, and his warriors. I have seen his villages. His lodges are more numerous than the trees of the forest, and his numbers are those of the leaves of countless trees. To fight with him would be like fighting the waves of the great salt waters that reach to the sky. If we should kill one, ten would spring up to take his place. For a hundred who may fall, a thousand will stand. He is strong, and we are weak. Let us then live at peace with him while we may. Let us meet him in council and tell him how little it is that we ask. There is a land beyond Okee-chobee, the great sweet water, that the white man can never want, but where the red man could dwell in peace and plenty. Let him leave this to us, and we will ask no more.

"If he will not do this, then let us fight. Never will Philip Emathla consent to go to the strange and distant land of the setting sun. If it is a better land than this, as the white man tells us, why does he not go there himself and leave us alone? It is a cold country. My people would die there. It is better to die here and die fighting.

"The white chief at Fort King calls us together for one more talk with him. Philip is old. He cannot travel so far, but Coacoochee shall go in his place. He will speak wisely, and if peace can be had, he will find it. If there is no peace, if the Seminole must fight, then who will fight harder or more bravely than Coacoochee? At his name the white man will tremble, and his squaws will hide their faces in fear. The enemies of Coacoochee will fall before him as ripe fruit falls before the breath of Hu-la-lah (the wind). He will kill till he is weary of killing. His footsteps will be marked with blood. Rivers of blood shall flow where he passes. I am old and feeble, but Coacoochee is young and strong. From this day shall he be a war-chief of the Seminoles. Philip Emathla has spoken."

At this announcement there came a great shout of rejoicing, and as the council broke up, the warriors crowded about Coacoochee to tell him how proud they would be to have him lead them in battle.

After the tumult had somewhat subsided, Osceola, who had not hitherto spoken directly to Coacoochee, stepped up to him. The two young men grasped each other's hands, and gazed earnestly in each other's face. Finally Osceola, apparently satisfied with what he saw, broke the silence, and said:

"We are brothers?"

"We are brothers," answered the young war-chief, and thus was made a compact between the two that was only to be broken by death.

The following morning, Coacoochee, with a small escort of warriors, set forth, in company with Osceola and Chen-o-wah, to travel to the village of Micanopy, head chief of the Seminoles, there to hold another council before going to Fort King for a talk with the agent.

In Micanopy's village they found assembled a large number of Seminole warriors, and many of the sub-chiefs of the tribe. This council was a grave and momentous affair. It was to decide the fate of a nation, and its deliberations were prolonged over two days. Micanopy, the head chief, was old, corpulent, and fond of his ease. He loved his land and hated the thought of war. He was greatly disinclined to remove to the west, but it was not until urged and almost compelled by the younger men, especially Coacoochee and Osceola, that he finally declared positively that he would not do so.

His utterance decided the majority of the council. They would fight before submitting to removal, but on one pretext and another they would gain all possible time in which to prepare for war.

It was also announced at this council that any Seminole who should openly advocate removal, and should make preparations for emigrating, should be put to death.

In all the council there was but one dissenting voice. It was that of a sub-chief named Charlo, who had been raised to the head of a small band by the agent, in place of an able warrior who was an uncompromising enemy of the whites. This petty chief spoke in favor of removal, and ridiculed the suggestion that the tribe could hold out for any length of time against the overwhelming power of the white man. He was listened to with impatience, and many dark glances were cast at him as he resumed his seat.

Three days later some fourteen chiefs, accompanied by a large number of their people, were encamped near Fort King, and active preparations were going forward for the great talk that was to be held that afternoon.

On the morning of that day, a thick-set, evil-looking man, whom the reader would at once recognize as his old acquaintance Mr. Troup Jeffers the slave-trader, sat in the agent's office engaged in earnest conversation with General Wiley Thompson.

"Thar ain't no doubt about it, gineral," he was saying. "She's easy enough identified, and I'll take my affidavy right here that she's the gal Jess who run away from old Miss Cooke's place two year ago. You've got a list of all them niggers and their description, as well as the order from Washington for their capture and deliverin' up. You know you have, and when I tell you what this gal looks like, you see if she don't answer the description exactly."

"Yes, sir, I've no doubt," answered the agent, wearily, for of the many trials of his difficult position, the importunities of the slave-hunters who besieged him at all hours were the greatest. "I don't doubt what you say, and I'll give you an order for the girl which you can present to the chiefs. If they give her up, well and good ; but if they won't, why they won't, that's all, and matters are too critical just now for us to attempt to force them."

"All right, gineral," replied Mr. Jeffers, with a triumphant glitter in his cruel little eyes. "The order is all I want, and I'll get the gal without putting you or anybody else to a mite of trouble."

Thus saying, the trader took the slip of paper handed him by the agent, and left the office.

Like a vulture scenting the carnage from afar, the slave-trader hearing that the Seminoles and their

negro allies were about to be removed, had hastened
to the scene of action, determined in some way to
secure a share of the peculiar property in which
he dealt, before it should be placed beyond his
reach.

In the Indian camp he had seen several good-
looking young women in whose veins he was convinced flowed negro blood, and he decided that his
purpose would be served by securing one or more of
these. Going to the agent with the trumped-up
story of having thus discovered a runaway slave girl,
he obtained the coveted order for her restoration to
her lawful owner. Armed with this, he proceeded
to carry out his wicked design.

His plan was very simple, and to put it into operation, he repaired to the store of the post trader. It
was located in a grove of live oaks, some distance
beyond the stockade, and was hidden from view of
those in or near the fort. To it, groups of Indians,
men, women, and children, found their way at all
times for the purchase of such supplies as they
needed and could afford.

Rogers, the storekeeper, whose conscience from a
long dealing with and cheating of Indians was as cal-
loused and hardened as that of Mr. Jeffers himself,
was not above turning what he called an honest
penny by any means that came in his way. Therefore when the slave-trader explained his business,
showed the agent's order, and offered Rogers ten

dollars to assist him in recapturing his alleged property, the latter readily consented to do so.

Troup Jeffers was almost certain that one or more of the young women whom he had noticed in the Indian camp would visit the store at some time during the day, and so he waited patiently the advent of a victim.

At length, late in the afternoon, when most of the Indians were attracted to the scene of the council, then in session, a squaw was seen to approach the store. She was one of those whom Mr. Jeffers had selected as suitable for the slave market, and the instant he observed her he exclaimed to the storekeeper:

"Here comes the very gal I'm after — old Miss Cooke's Jess. I'll just step into the back room, and if you can persuade her to come in there to look at something or other, we'll have her as slick as a whistle."

"All right," responded Rogers, who a minute later was waiting on his customer with infinitely more politeness than he usually vouchsafed to an Indian.

She desired to purchase some coffee and sugar with which to surprise and please her husband when he returned to his lodge after the council should be ended, and the storekeeper easily persuaded her to enter the other room, where he said his best goods were kept.

As the unsuspecting woman bent over a sugar barrel, she was seized from behind, and her head was enveloped in a shawl, by which her cries were completely stifled.

A few minutes later, bound and helpless, she was lifted into a light wagon and driven rapidly away.

Half an hour afterwards, a boy who worked for the storekeeper remarked to his employer:

" I should think you would be afraid of Powell."

" What for? " asked Rogers.

" Why, for letting that man carry off his wife," was the reply.

Thus did the storekeeper receive his first intimation that the alleged runaway slave girl was Chen-o-wah, the adored wife of Osceola.

CHAPTER XIII

"WILEY THOMPSON, WHERE IS MY WIFE?"

WHILE the wife of Osceola was thus being kidnapped and consigned to slavery, he, ignorant of the blow in store for him, was participating in a far different scene. Just outside the gateway of the fort, in an open space of level sward, the great council upon which so much depended was assembled. At one side of a long table sat General Clinch, commanding the army in Florida, with the officers of his staff standing behind him. Beside him sat General Wiley Thompson, the agent, red-faced and pompous, Lieutenant Harris, the United States disbursing agent, who was to conduct the Indians to their western homes, and several commissioners. All the officers were in full uniform, and presented a brave appearance. Behind them were two companies of infantry, resting at ease on their loaded muskets, but ready to spring into action at a moment's notice. Just inside the gateway of the fort the guns of its light battery were charged to the muzzle with grape and canister, ready for instant service. This was one side of the picture.

On the opposite side of the table from the whites sat or stood a group of Indian chiefs, sullen, determined, and watchful. Too many times already had the white man cheated them. They would take care that he should not do so again. They had learned by bitter experience how lightly he regarded such treaties as conflicted with his interests. They knew the value of his false promises and fair words.

A little in front of the others sat Micanopy, head chief of the tribe, and close behind him, so that they could whisper in his ear, stood Coacoochee and Osceola. Grouped about them were Otee the Jumper, Tiger Tail, Allapatta Tustenugge, the Fighting Alligator, Arpeika, or Sam Jones, Black Dirt, Ya ha Hadjo, the Mad Wolf, Coa Hadjo, Halatoochee, Abram, the negro chief, Passac Micco, and many others. Behind them stood one hundred warriors, tall, clean-built fellows, lithe and sinewy, their bare legs as hard and smooth as those of bronze statues. Concealed in a hammock, but a short distance away, was another body of warriors held in reserve by Coacoochee, who had thought it best not to display the full strength of his force at once.

The old men, women, and children had been left in camp not far from the trader's store. Here everything was prepared for instant flight in case the council should terminate in an outbreak.

The proceedings were opened by General Thompson, who stated that he had thus called the Indians

H

together that they might decide upon a day when they would fulfil their promise contained in the treaty of Payne's Landing, and set forth for their new home in the west. He had prepared a paper setting forth the conditions of removal, which he now wished all the chiefs to sign.

Then Otee the Jumper, who was one of the most fluent speakers of the tribe, arose and calmly but firmly stated that his people did not consider themselves as bound by that treaty to remove from their country, and had decided in solemn council not to do so.

At this point the Seminole speaker was rudely interrupted by General Thompson, who, flushed and furious, sprang to his feet and demanded by what right the Indians interpreted the treaty differently from the whites by whom it was drawn up. He accused them of treachery and double-dealing, and ended by declaring that it made no difference whether they were willing to remove or not, for they would be made to go, alive or dead, and he for one did not care which.

This speech drew forth angry replies from the chiefs, and to these the agent retorted with such bitterness that General Clinch was finally obliged to interpose his authority to calm both sides. He told the Indians how useless it would be for them to struggle against the power of the United States, and how greatly he would prefer that they should remove peaceably rather than oblige him to remove them by force.

At this the Indians smiled grimly and exchanged contemptuous glances. They knew that there were only seven hundred soldiers in all Florida, and the idea of compelling them to do anything they did not choose, with a little army like that, was too absurd. It almost made them laugh, but their native dignity prevented such a breach of decorum.

General Clinch talked long and earnestly and was listened to with respect and close attention. The agent regarded his arguments as so unanswerable that at their conclusion he called on the chiefs by name to step forward and sign the paper he had prepared.

"Micanopy, you are head chief. Come up and sign first at the head of the list."

"No, Micanopy will never sign."

"Then Coacoochee may sign first. He comes, I believe, as representative of the wise and brave King Philip."

"No, Coacoochee will not sign either for his father or himself."

"Jumper, then; and when he signs, I will make him head chief."

"No."

"Alligator?"

"No."

"Sam Jones?"

"No."

" Abram ? "

" By golly.   No."

At these repeated refusals to comply with his request, and the evident contempt with which his offers of promotion were regarded, the fat agent became so angry as to entirely lose his self-control.

" If you will not sign," he shouted, " you are no longer fit to hold your positions.   I therefore declare that Micanopy, Coacoochee, Jumper, Alligator, Sam Jones, and Abram, shall cease from this minute to be chiefs of the Seminole nation, and their names shall be struck from the roll of chiefs."

At this an angry murmur ran through the ranks of the Indians, who considered that a grievous insult had thus been offered them.   Those chiefs who had been sitting sprang to their feet and fell back a few paces.   The warriors behind them moved up closer, and Coacoochee, slipping unnoticed through the throng, hurried back to the hammock to direct the flight of the women and children, and bring up his reserve force of warriors.

In the meantime an Indian who had come from the camp was talking with low, hurried words to Osceola, who listened to him like one in a dream or who does not fully comprehend what he hears.

Suddenly he sprang forward, his face livid with passion, and crying in a loud voice, " I will sign !

IT SUNK DEEP INTO THE WOOD OF THE TABLE AND STOOD QUIVERING AS THOUGH WITH RAGE.

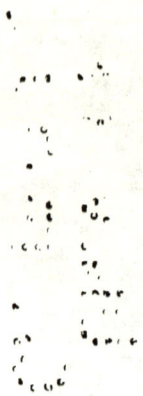

I, Osceola the Baton Rouge, will sign this paper of the white man."

Then stepping up to the table, while both whites and Indians watched him with breathless interest, the fierce warrior plucked the scalping-knife from his girdle and drove it with furious energy through the outspread paper. It sunk deep into the wood of the table, and stood quivering as though with rage.

"There is my signature, General Wiley Thompson," he cried in a voice that trembled with the intensity of his emotion. "There is the signature of Osceola, and I would that it were inscribed on your cowardly heart. Where is my wife? What have you done with her? Give her back to me, I say, and as safe as when I left her in yonder grove. If you do not, I swear by the white man's God, and by the Great Spirit of my people, that not only your own vile life, but that of every white man who comes within reach of Osceola's vengeance, shall be forfeited. As you have shown no mercy, so shall you receive none. The word shall be unknown to the Seminole tongue. You taunt me with being a half-blood. I am one ; but I am yet a man, and not a slave. With my white blood I defy you, and with my Indian blood I despise you. Wiley Thompson, where is my wife ? "

CHAPTER XIV

OSCEOLA SIGNS THE TREATY

THE group of white men on the opposite side of the table had left their seats before Osceola stepped toward it. General Clinch exchanged a few words with the agent and gave an order to the officer in command of the troops. These were moved forward a few paces, though, blinded by the intensity of his feelings, the half-breed failed to notice their change of position.

Now, in obedience to a signal from the agent, they sprang forward with fixed bayonets, and in an instant Osceola, cut off from his friends, was hedged in by a wall of glittering steel. At the same moment a sharp rattle of drums was heard within the fort, and the light battery, dashing out from the gateway in a cloud of dust, was wheeled into position with its murderous muzzles trained full on the startled Indians.

With one forward movement the pitiless storm of death would have swept through their crowded ranks. They knew this and stepped backward instead.

Within two minutes after the council was so summarily dissolved, not an Indian was to be seen. Within five minutes Osceola, heavily ironed, was thrust into the strongest cell of the guard-house and the door locked behind him. By this time, also, the troops had retired, and General Thompson was inquiring in every direction what the crazy half-breed meant by demanding a wife from him. He knew nothing about the fellow's wife. Did not even know he had a wife, and was inclined to think that Osceola was drunk, or else had trumped up this demand for the purpose of exciting the Indians to resistance.

Finally, however, through Rogers, the trader, he discovered the real facts of the case. Then he realized the awkward position in which his careless giving of an order for the recovery of a runaway slave had placed not only himself, but all the whites in that part of the country.

He visited the prisoner in his cell, and tried to quiet him by explaining that it was all a mistake, and by assuring him that every effort should be made to recover Chen-o-wah and bring her back; but all to no purpose.

Osceola replied that his wife alone had been seized of all those who visited the trader's store. Moreover, she had been seized upon a written order from himself, for the paper had been read aloud in the presence of several persons. No, there was no mistake, and as for the agent's promise to restore Chen-o-wah to him, he would believe it when he saw her, but not before.

For six days the forest warrior who had been struck this deadly blow paced hopelessly up and down his narrow cell, dragging his clanking chains behind him. During this time he hardly touched food nor would he speak to a human being. No one save himself knew the bitterness of his heart, or the terrible thoughts that seethed in his mind during those six days. He appeared like one consumed by an inward fire, and it even seemed as though his haughty spirit was about to escape from the imprisoned body.

At length he sent for General Thompson, and expressed a willingness to sign the paper that should commit him to emigration. "My spirit is broken," he said; "your irons have entered my soul. I can hold out no longer. By these chains I am disgraced in the eyes of my people, and my influence over them is gone. It is better that I should go away and die in a strange land. Bring me your paper; I will sign it."

But that was not sufficient. The paper must be signed in the presence of other Seminoles, that they might be witnesses to the act, and spread the great news abroad throughout the nation. Even to this humiliation Osceola consented, and a messenger was despatched to bring in the first band of Indians he should meet. This messenger was given a token by

Osceola, and thus provided, he had no difficulty in persuading Coacoochee and some forty warriors, thirty of whom belonged to the captive's own band, to again visit the fort.

Although they came to the fort, Coacoochee's caution would not allow them to pass within its gates, and so the ceremony of signing was of necessity performed outside.

General Clinch and his staff had returned to Tampa, but there still remained enough of officers at Fort King to escort the agent and lend an imposing effect to the ceremony.

Osceola was led to the place of signing, under guard and with the irons still upon his ankles. He approached the table with downcast eyes, apparently unmindful of the presence of either friends or foes. As he took the pen preparatory to signing, the agent asked :

" Powell, do you acknowledge in the presence of these witnesses, that you are about to sign this paper of your own free will, without fear or compulsion ? "

The half-breed regarded his questioner with a curious expression for a moment, and then answered :

" I have no fear. No one could compel me. I sign because it pleases me to do so."

Thus saying, he affixed his signature to the hated paper, with a steady hand. Immediately afterwards his irons were struck off, and he was once more a free man.

The agent now asked Coacoochee if he would not also sign, but that wily young Indian refused to do so at that time. " When I have spoken with Ah-ha-se-ho-la, and learned his reasons for signing, perhaps I may also touch the white man's talking stick," he said.

When Osceola had retired with his friends to their camp, General Thompson turned to one of his companions, and rubbing his hands complacently, remarked :

" That is a capital stroke of business. I have been all along regretting the unfortunate affair of that fellow's wife. Now, though, I begin to think it was one of the best things that could have happened for us. It has brought him to terms as I don't believe anything else would, and though he is not a chief, his influence is the most powerful in the tribe."

" You may be right," replied Lieutenant Smith, the young army officer to whom this remark was addressed, " but it was an outrageous thing, all the same, to steal the poor chap's wife. It makes me feel ashamed to be mixed up in this wretched business, and if I were not dependent on my profession for a living, and so forced to obey the orders of my superiors who have sent me here, I'd have nothing more to do with it. The idea of stealing a man's wife and selling her into slavery ! I don't wonder it drove him so nearly crazy that he was willing to sign or do anything else.   Under the circumstances I wouldn't give a fig for his signature."

"Nonsense!" replied the agent; "you don't know these people as I do.   He is only an Indian in spite of his mixture of white blood, and they don't feel about such things as we do.   I'll guarantee that in less than a month he will have forgotten all about this wife and will have taken another or maybe two of them, in her place."

At this same time Coacoochee and Osceola were walking apart from the other Indians and talking earnestly.

"Was there no way for my brother to save his life but by signing the white man's paper?" inquired the former.

At this Osceola broke into a hard and bitter laugh. "Does my brother regard me so meanly as to think that to save my life alone, or to save a thousand lives such as mine, I would have signed?" he asked.   "No. It was not to save life that Osceola put pen to paper, but to take it.   It was that he might be revenged on those who have wronged him far deeper than by killing him, that he did it.   When his vengeance is accomplished, then will he gladly die; but he will never go to the western land."

"Listen," he continued, noting the other's look of bewilderment at these words: "once the Indian fought with bows and arrows, while the white man fought with guns.   Did he continue to do this when he found that his weapons were no match for those of the white man? No; he threw away his bows and arrows, and got guns in their place. Once Osceola was honest, his tongue was straight, he would not tell a lie. Are the white men so? No, their tongues are crooked; they say one thing and mean another; they have cheated the Indian and lied to him from the first day that they set foot on his land. They have laughed at his honesty and said, 'The Indian is a fool who knows no better.' Now Ah-ha-se-ho-la is fighting them with their own weapons. For them his tongue is no longer straight. It is as crooked as their own. Does my brother now understand why I signed?"

This style of reasoning was new to Coacoochee, and he pondered over it for a minute before replying. "It is true," he thought, "that the white man gains many advantages over the Indian by cheating and lying to him. If they do those things, why should not the Indian do them as well? In the present instance how could Osceola have gained his liberty by any other means? Yes, it must be right to fight the white man with his own weapons."

So Coacoochee acknowledged that Osceola was justified in the course he had pursued, and congratulated him on his escape from the white man's prison. He was also rejoiced to learn that his friend was to remain and aid them in the coming war rather than to leave them and go to the far-off western land.

Thus answered Coacoochee. At the same time deep down in his heart the young war-chief hoped that he might never find it necessary to fight any enemy with so dangerous a weapon as a crooked tongue.

Now the two young men laid their plans for the future. They agreed that as much time as possible should be gained before open hostilities were declared, in order that the Indians might make all possible preparations for war. With this end in view, Osceola was to remain near the fort, and while still expressing a willingness to emigrate whenever the others of his tribe should come in, was to procure such supplies as he could, especially ammunition, that might be stored for the coming struggle.

Coacoochee was to visit the scattered bands and induce them to provide safe hiding-places for their women and children, that the warriors might be free to fight.

While confined in the fort, Osceola had learned that the chief Charlo, who styled himself "Charlo Emathla," was disposing of his cattle preparatory to emigrating, and now the young men agreed that in his case it was necessary to show both whites and Indians the earnestness of their purpose by carrying out the decisions of the chiefs and putting him to death.

This, Osceola undertook to do, and Coacoochee was glad to be relieved of the unpleasant duty.

Thus matters being arranged, the friends separated; and while Coacoochee with his ten warriors took their departure, Osceola with his thirty followers remained near the fort, to carry out his plan for averting war as long as possible, and to watch for the revenge against those who had robbed him of his wife, that had now become the object of his most intense desire.

Thus matters stood for several months. At the end of that time, the agent becoming suspicious of the Indians on account of their purchasing such quantities of powder, peremptorily forbade the further sale of ammunition to them. Thereupon Osceola sent out runners to carry the news to every Seminole band from the Okeefenokee to the Everglades, and from the Atlantic to the Gulf, that the time for action had arrived, and that the first blow of the war was about to be struck.

CHAPTER XV

LOUIS PACHECO BIDES HIS TIME

TAMPA BAY was filled with transports waiting to carry the Seminoles to New Orleans on their way to the Indian Territory. On shore, the soldiers' encampment beneath the grand old live-oaks of Fort Brooke swarmed with troops, newly arrived from the north, and hoping that the Indians would at least make a show of resistance. Of course, no one wanted a prolonged war; but a brisk campaign with plenty of fighting, that would last through the winter, would be a most pleasing diversion from the ordinary monotony of military life. It was not supposed, however, that the Seminoles would fight. Major Francis Dade was so certain of this, that he volunteered to march across the Indian country with only a corporal's guard at his back.

Among those who prayed most earnestly for a taste of fighting, in which they might prove the metal of which they were made, were several lieutenants recently emancipated from West Point and ordered to duty on this far southern frontier.

A few days before Christmas, 1835, a jovial party of three young officers was assembled in the hospi-

table house of a planter, a few miles from Fort
Brooke. They were to dine there, and at the dinner table the sole topic of conversation was the impending war. The Indians had been given until the
end of December to make their preparations for emigration, and to assemble at the appointed places of
rendezvous. On the first day of January, 1836,
their reservation was to be thrown open to the
throngs of speculators already on hand, and with
difficulty restrained from rushing in and seizing the
coveted lands without waiting for the Indians to
vacate them. .

General Clinch had decided to send Major Dade,
not, indeed, with a corporal's guard, but with two
companies of troops, to reinforce the garrison at Fort
King. From that post, which was well within the
reservation, he was to move against the Indians and
compel them to move promptly on January 1, if
they showed a disinclination to do so of their own
accord.

Several of the young officers assembled about the
planter's dinner table were to accompany this expedition, and their anticipations of the pleasures of the
campaign were only equalled by the regrets of those
who were to be left behind.

Some one suggested that there might be some
fighting before the troops returned, and that their
march might be attended with a certain amount of
danger.

"Danger?" cried Lieutenant Mudge, the gayest spirit of the party, and the most popular man at the post. "Let us hope there will be some danger. What would a soldier's life be without it? A weary round of drill. Hurrah, then, for danger! say I. Louis, fill the glasses. Now, gentlemen, I give you the toast of 'A short campaign and a merry one, with plenty of hard fighting, plenty of danger, and speedy promotion to all good fellows.'"

The toast was hailed with acclamation and drunk with a cheer; while after it the calls for Louis grew louder, more frequent, and more peremptory than ever. It was "Here, Louis!" "Here, you nigger!" "Step lively now!" from all sides, and the bewildering orders were so promptly obeyed by the deft-handed, intelligent-appearing young mulatto, who answered to the name of Louis, that he was unanimously declared to be a treasure. Those of the officers who were to remain at Fort Brooke, envied the planter such a capital servant, and those who were to accompany the expedition to Fort King, wished they might take him with them to wait on their mess.

"Well, I don't know but that can be arranged," remarked the planter, thoughtfully. "Major Dade was asking me to-day where he could obtain a reliable guide, and Louis, who overheard him, has since told me that he is intimately acquainted with the country between here and Fort King. Isn't that so, boy?"

I

" Yes, sir," replied the mulatto; " I was born and brought up in this country, and I know every foot of the way from here to Fort King like I know the do-yard of my ole mammy's cabin."

This answer was delivered so quietly, and with such an apparent air of indifference, that no one looking at the man would have suspected the wild tumult of thought seething within his breast at that moment. For months he had waited, planned, hoped, and endured, for such an opportunity as this. At last it had come. He was almost unnerved by conflicting emotions, and to conceal them, he flew about the table more actively than ever, anticipating every want of his master's guests, and waiting on them with an assiduity that went far to confirm the good impression already formed of him.

Once, Lieutenant Mudge, happening to glance up at an instant when Louis was intently regarding him, was startled by a fleeting expression that swept across the man's face. For a second his eyes glared like those of a famished tiger, and his lips seemed to be slightly drawn back from the clinched white teeth. Although the devilish look vanished as quickly as it came, leaving only the respectful expression of a well-trained servant in its place, it gave the young soldier a shock, and filled him with a vague uneasiness that he found hard to shake off. He spoke of it afterwards to his host, but the latter only laughed and said:

"Nonsense, my dear boy ! It must have been the champagne. I have had that nigger for nearly a year now, and a more honest, faithful, intelligent, and thoroughly reliable servant I never owned. If Dade will pay a fair price for him, I will let him go for a few months, and thus you will secure a reliable guide and a capital table servant, both in one."

In answer to some further inquiries concerning Louis, he said : "I'd no idea he was born in this part of the country or knew anything about it, but as he says he does, it must be so, for I have never known him to tell a lie. He knows it would not be safe to lie to me. I got him from a trader in Charleston last spring, and only brought him down here a couple of months ago, when I came to look after this plantation. But you can depend on Louis. He don't dare deceive me, for he knows if he did I'd kill him. I make it a rule to have none but thoroughly honest servants about me, and they all know it."

The reader has doubtless surmised ere this that the servant whom his master praised so highly was no other than Louis Pacheco, friend of Coacoochee, the free dweller beside the Tomoka, whom the slave-catchers had kidnapped and carried off.

Inheriting the refinement of his Spanish father, well educated, and accomplished, Louis would have killed himself rather than submit to the degradation of the lot imposed upon him, but for one thing — the same spirit that actuated Osceola during his imprisonment restrained Louis from any act against his own life. He lived that he might obtain revenge. So bitter was his hatred of the whole white race, that at times he could scarcely restrain its open expression.

He managed, however, to control himself and devoted his entire energies to winning the confidence, not only of the man who had bought him, but of all the other whites with whom he was thrown in contact. Thus did he prepare the more readily to carry out his plans when the time came. He saw his aged mother die from overwork in the cotton-fields, without betraying the added bitterness of his feelings, and was even laughingly chided by his master for not displaying greater filial affection. He planned a negro insurrection, but could not carry it out. Then he conceived the project of inducing a great number of negroes to run away with him, and join his friends the Seminoles, but this scheme also came to naught. He was planning to escape alone and make his way to Florida, where he hoped to find some trace of the dearly loved sister from whom he had been so cruelly separated, when chance favored him, and his master brought him to the very place where he most desired to be.

In Tampa, he quickly learned of the condition of affairs between the Indians and whites, and he looked eagerly about for some means of aiding his friends in their approaching struggle.

The proposed expedition of Major Dade, for the relief and reinforcement of Fort King, was kept a secret so far as possible, for fear lest it should delay the coming in of numbers of Indians, who were supposed to be on their way to the several designated* points of assembly. It was, however, freely discussed in the presence of Louis Pacheco, for he was supposed to be so well content with his present position, and to have so little knowledge of Indian affairs, that it could make no difference whether he knew of it or not.

So Louis listened, and treasured all the stray bits of information thus obtained, and put them together until he was possessed of a very clear idea of the existing state of affairs, and of what the whites intended doing.

Through the field hands of the plantation he opened communication with the free negroes who dwelt among the Indians. Thus he soon learned that his friend Coacoochee was now a war-chief and an influential leader among the Seminoles.

Now the hour of his triumph, the time of his revenge, had surely come. If he could only obtain the position of guide to Major Dade's little army, what would be easier than to deliver them into the hands of Coacoochee? What a bitter blow that would be to the whites, and how it would strengthen the Seminole cause! How far it would go toward repaying him for the death of his mother, the loss of his beautiful sister, his own weary slavery, and the destruction of their happy home on the Tomoka! Yes, it must be done.

The day after that of the dinner party his master concluded arrangements with Major Dade, by which Louis was engaged as guide to the expedition and steward of the officers' mess. So the slave was ordered to hold himself in readiness to start on Christmas Day.

CHAPTER XVI

OSCEOLA'S REVENGE

In the meantime, Osceola had carried out his part of the arrangement with Coacoochee in regard to the traitor, Charlo Emathla. Although warned of the fate in store for him in case he persisted in disregarding the wishes of his people and the commands of the other chiefs, this Indian, dazzled by sight of the white man's gold, flattered by his praise, and assured of his protection, persisted in his course.

Osceola waited until certain that he had accepted a considerable sum of money from the agent, and then prepared an ambush beside a trail along which the doomed man must return to his camp. It was completely successful; the victim fell at the first fire, and covering his face with his hands, received the fatal blow without a word. Tied up in his handkerchief was a quantity of gold and silver. This, Osceola declared was the price of red men's blood, and, sternly forbidding his followers to touch it, he flung it broadcast in every direction.

When news of this summary punishment of a renegade was received at Fort King, it created a serious feeling of anxiety and alarm for the future.

This was shared by all except the agent, who declared, in his pompous manner, that he knew the Indians too well to fear them. They might murder one of their own kind here and there, but they would never muster up courage to attack a white man. Oh no! the rascals were too well aware of the consequences of such an act.

Another report that reached the fort about the same time increased the uneasiness of its inmates. It was of six Indians who had been brutally and wantonly set upon by a party of white land-grabbers. The Indians were in camp, quietly engaged in cooking their supper, when the whites rode up, made them prisoners, took away their rifles, and examined their packs, appropriating to their own use whatever they fancied, and destroying the rest. Then they tied the Indians to trees and began whipping them.

While they were thus engaged, four other Indians appeared on the scene and opened an ineffective fire upon the aggressors. The whites answered with a volley from their rifles that killed one Indian and wounded another. Both parties then withdrew from the field, the whites carrying with them the rifles and baggage that they had stolen.

This outrage was termed an Indian encroachment, and a company of militia was at once ordered out to chastise the Indians and protect citizens.

By such acts as these the land-grabbers hoped to

hasten the movements of the Seminoles and compel
them to evacuate the coveted territory the more
rapidly.

It was with gloomy forebodings that the little
garrison of Fort King, who, from long experience,
had gained some knowledge of the Indian character,
heard of these and similar brutalities. They knew
that such things would drive the savage warriors to
acts of retaliation, and precipitate the crisis that now
appeared so imminent. Their fears were heightened
by the fact that early in December the Indians ceased
visiting the fort, and it was reported that all their
villages in that part of the country were abandoned.

So the month dragged slowly away. Christmas
Day was passed quietly and without the usual festivities of the season. The anxiety of the garrison
would have been still further increased had they
known that on that very day Osceola and a band of
picked warriors took up a position in a dense hammock from which they could watch every movement
in and about the fort.

Osceola's object was the killing of the agent,
whom he believed to be directly implicated in the
abduction of Chen-o-wah. So determined was he to
accomplish this, that he had decided if no better
opportunity offered to venture an attack against the
fort itself, desperate as he knew this measure to be.

Coacoochee at this time was gathering the warriors
of the tribe and preparing them for battle in the

depths of the great Wahoo Swamp, the hidden mysteries of which no white man had ever explored. It lay a day's journey from Fort King, and to it were hastening many chiefs with their followers.

On the morning of Christmas Day a negro runner, well-nigh exhausted with the speed at which he had travelled, reached the swamp encampment and asked to be led at once to Coacoochee, the war-chief. The moment he had delivered his message the young warrior, trembling with excitement, sought the other chiefs and made known to them the wonderful news he had just received.

"This very day," he said, "the white soldiers have left Tampa to march through the Seminole country. At the end of four days they hope to reach Fort King. They are guided by one whom I thought dead, but who sends word that he is alive. He is my friend and may be trusted. He will bring them by this road. Shall we allow them to pass by us and join their friends? Or shall we meet them in battle and prove to them that our words were not empty boastings, when we said the Seminole would fight for his land? The white man laughs at us and whips us as though we were dogs. He takes from us that which pleases him, and gives us nothing but blows in return. The Indian and the wolf together are marks for his rifle. Let us show him that we are men and warriors. Let us strike a blow that he will never forget. It may be that when he

finds the Seminole ready to fight, he will let us alone
to dwell peaceably in our own land. Are the words
of Coacoochee good in the ears of the tribe? Are
his warriors glad when they hear them?"

A long discussion followed; but when it was
ended, the counsel of the young war-chief had been
accepted.

Then through the dim forest aisles echoed the
hollow booming of the kasi-lalki, or great war-drum.
Fleet runners were despatched in all directions,
some to hasten the incoming bands, and some to
watch the movements of the advancing troops.
One was sent to bear the great news to Osceola,
and bid him hasten if he would take part in the
first battle of the war.

When this messenger reached those secreted in
the hammock near Fort King, and delivered his
tidings, Osceola bade him return and tell Coacoochee that if at the end of one more day his purpose
had not been accomplished, he would abandon it
for the present and hasten to join him.

On the following afternoon two figures were seen
by the eager watchers to leave the fort and stroll
toward the trader's store a mile away. Osceola's
keen eye was the first to recognize them, and he
knew that the hour of his vengeance had arrived.

The two who strolled thus carelessly, apparently
unconscious of danger, were the agent, General
Wiley Thompson, and his friend, Lieutenant Con-

stantine Smith. They were smoking their after-
dinner cigars and talking earnestly. Their subject
was the rights and wrongs of the Indian. As they
reached the crest of a slight eminence, these words,
uttered in Wiley Thompson's most emphatic tone,
reached the ears of Osceola, who, with flashing eyes
and compressed lips, peered at the speaker from a
thicket not ten yards away.

"I tell you, sir, the Indian is no better than any
other savage beast, and deserves no better treatment
at our hands."

They were the last words he ever spoke; for at
that instant there burst from the thicket a blind-
ing flash and the crashing report of thirty rifles,
discharged simultaneously. Both men were instantly killed, and with yells of triumph the Indians
rushed from their hiding-place, each intent upon
procuring a scalp or some other trophy of the first
event of the contest so long anticipated and now so
sadly begun.

But Osceola's vengeance did not rest here.
There were others within reach who had aided in
the stealing of his wife, and he bade his warriors
follow him to the store of the trader. A few minutes later Rogers and his two clerks had been added
to the list of victims. After helping themselves to
all the goods they could carry, the Indians set fire
to the store and started toward the Wahoo Swamp,
where they hoped to join Coacoochee in time to

participate in the battle of which he had sent them notice.

The little garrison of fifty men at Fort King heard the firing and the war-cries, and saw the smoke from the blazing store rise above the hammock. They knew only too well what these things meant; but supposing the Indians to be in force and about to attack the post, they dared not venture beyond its limits. They waited anxiously for the coming of the promised reinforcements from Tampa, but weary days passed, and no word came from them.

CHAPTER XVII

ON THE VERGE OF THE WAHOO SWAMP

On the afternoon of Christmas Day, Major Dade's little command of two companies of troops, numbering one hundred and ten souls, marched gaily out from Fort Brooke on Tampa Bay and started for Fort King, one hundred miles away, near where the city of Ocala now stands. Both officers and men were in the highest spirits, and regarded their present expedition as a pleasant relief from the monotony of garrison life. It was not at all likely they would be called upon to do any fighting; for, although the Indians had been acting suspiciously for some time, nobody believed they would dare come into open conflict with the whites. And what if they did! Was not one white man equal to five Indians at any time? To be sure, the soldiers were unfamiliar with the country, but then they had a guide who knew every foot of it.

Louis Pacheco was one of the most popular members of the expedition. He was not only a good guide, but he was polite, obliging, and attentive to the wants of the officers. He certainly was a treasure, and they were fortunate to have secured his services. So the lieutenants said to one another.

For two days the command moved steadily forward, its one piece of light artillery and its one baggage wagon bumping heavily over the log-like roots of the saw-palmetto, and threatening to break down with each mile, but never doing so. They experienced no difficulty in crossing the dark, forest-shaded Withlacoochee ; for Louis led them to the best ford on the whole river, and the officers agreed that they were making much better progress than could have been expected.

On the third night they had skirted the great Wahoo Swamp and were camped near its northern end. As this place was known to be a favorite Indian resort, the sentinels of that night were cautioned to be unusually vigilant. The corporal of the guard was instructed to inspect every post at least once an hour, and oftener than that towards morning, when an attack was supposed to be most imminent. As the officer of the day was equally on the alert, and visited the sentries many times during the night, the camp was deemed securely guarded.

All that day Louis, the guide, had been unusually silent. More than once he was observed to direct long, penetrating glances toward the dense forest growth of the great swamp, as though it held some peculiar fascination for him. It seemed as though he were conscious of the keen eyes, that, peering from its dark depths, watched so exultingly the march of the troops. It seemed as though he must see the lithe figures that, gliding silently from thicket to thicket, or from one mossy covert to another, so easily kept pace with the slow-moving column.

In waiting on the officers' mess that evening, Louis was so absent-minded that he made innumerable blunders, and drew forth more than one angry rebuke from those whom he served.

At last one of these remarked that, if the nigger was not more attentive to his duties, he would be apt to make an acquaintance with the whipping-post before long.

Then there flashed into the man's face for an instant the same look that Lieutenant Mudge had detected once before, and from that moment his demeanor changed. He was no longer absent-minded. He was no longer undecided. The time of his irresolution was passed.

That night he slept apart from any other occupant of the camp, beyond the line of tents and on the side nearest the swamp hammock. For hours after rolling himself in his blanket the man lay open-eyed and thinking. This was either the last night of his life or the last of his slavery, he knew not which. On the morrow he would be either dead or free. On the morrow, if he lived, he would learn the fate of the dear sister from whom he had heard no word since that terrible night on the Tomoka. On the morrow would be struck a blow for liberty that should be felt throughout the length and breadth of the land, and on the morrow his score against the white man would be wiped out.   The account would be settled.

Louis had expected the attack to be made that day, and from each hammock or clump of timber they passed, had dreaded, and hoped to hear, the shrill war-whoop mingled with the crack of rifles. Now, he thought it might be made during the night or just at dawn.   At all events, it must be made, if made at all, before the following sunset, for at that hour the command expected to reach Fort King.

As he lay thinking of these things, the querulous cry of a hawk suddenly broke the stillness of the night.   It came from the swamp.   Again it sounded, and this time with a slight difference of tone.   The weary sentinels wondered for a moment at the strangeness of such a cry at that hour, and then dismissed it from their minds.

Not so with Louis Pacheco.   The second cry had confirmed the suspicion aroused by the first.   It was long since he had heard the signal of Coacoo-chee; but he recognized and answered it.   The gentle, quavering cry of a little screech owl, though coming from the camp, alarmed no one.   It went straight to the ears of Coacoochee, however, as he lay hidden in the saw-palmettoes, only a few rods beyond the tents, and he was content to wait

K

patiently, knowing that his friend had heard and understood his signal.

All the old forest instincts, long suppressed and almost forgotten, were instantly aroused in Louis. No Indian could have crept more cautiously or silently toward the line of sentries than he, and none could have slipped past them more deftly. A few minutes later the owl's note was sounded at the edge of the hammock and immediately answered from a spot but a short distance away. Then there came a rustle beside the motionless figure and a whispered :

"Louis, my brother ? "

"Coacoochee, is it you ? "

For a few minutes they whispered only of their own affairs, and Louis learned of Nita's escape from the slave-catchers, of her flight to Philip Emathla's village, and of her betrothal to Coacoochee, all in a breath. He longed to fly to her at that very moment; but a weary journey lay between them, and before he could undertake it a stern and terrible duty remained to be performed. He must return to the camp of soldiers and remain with them to the bitter end. Otherwise the plan for their destruction might yet miscarry.

Coacoochee told him the reason why the attack had not already been made was that the Indians had awaited the arrival of Osceola and Micanopy. The latter had come in that evening, and it was decided to wait no longer, but to begin the fight at daylight.

Louis opposed this plan, saying that Major Dade expected an attack to be made at daylight, if made at all, and would be particularly on guard at that time. He also seemed to feel that if he were attacked, it would be from that swamp. Therefore, the mulatto advised that the attack be made at a point some miles beyond the swamp, where nothing of the kind would be anticipated.

Coacoochee acknowledged the soundness of this advice, and agreeing to follow it, the two separated, one to lead his warriors to the appointed place and prepare them for battle, the other to work his way with infinite caution back into the camp of sleeping soldiers. Fortunately for him the night was intensely dark, and though at one time a sentry passed so close that he could have touched him, by lying flat and almost holding his breath he escaped discovery.

He had barely reached his sleeping-place and rolled himself again in his blanket, when an officer came along, and stumbling over his prostrate form, exclaimed:

"Hello, Louis! Is that you?"

Upon receiving an affirmative answer, he continued: "Well, I must confess that it is a great relief to find you. I missed you, and have been searching for you. I really began to think you had deserted and left us to find our own way out of this wilderness. Where have you been?"

"The major's horse got loose, sir, and came very near stepping on me," replied Louis. "And I just took him over to the cart, where I tied him up again. Sorry to have caused you any anxiety, sir."

"Oh, that's all right," answered the officer. "I'm glad your excuse is such a good one, for these are times when we can't be too careful, you know."

With this he walked away to visit the line of sentries, while Louis, bathed in a profuse perspiration in spite of the chill of the night, shuddered as he realized the narrowness of his escape.

CHAPTER XVIII

COACOOCHEE'S FIRST BATTLE

The next morning's sun ushered in one of the fairest of Floridian days ; the air was clear, cool, and bracing. It was filled with the aromatic odors of pines and vibrant with the songs of birds. All was life and activity in the camp of soldiers, who were preparing for an early start on the long day's march that they hoped would bring them to their destination that same evening.

"We are past all the bad places now, boys," cried Major Dade, cheerily, as he rode to the head of the column. "This swamp is our last danger point, and beyond this there is nothing to apprehend. The cowardly redskins have let a good chance slip by, and it will be long before they will be given another."

Then the bugles sounded merrily, and with light hearts the command resumed its march. But the Indians had moved earlier than they.

At daylight that morning one hundred and eighty warriors glided like shadows out from the dark recesses of the swamp, and, following the lead of Coacoochee, advanced some four miles beyond it. Where they finally halted in the open pine woods there was a thick growth of scrub or saw-palmetto.

A pond bounded the road on the east at this point, and the entire body of Indians took positions on the opposite or western side. Each warrior selected his own tree or clump of palmetto, and sank out of sight behind it. Three minutes after their arrival nothing was to be seen nor heard save the solemn pines and the sighing of the wind through their branches.

There was so little to arouse suspicion that a small herd of deer fleeing before the advancing troops and coming down the wind dashed in among the Indians before discovering their presence. Even then the hidden warriors made no sign, and the terrified animals pursued their flight unmolested.

Besides Coacoochee, the chiefs in command of the Seminole force were Micanopy, Jumper, and Alligator. It had been determined that Micanopy, as head chief, should fire the first shot of the contest, and as the old man was timid and undecided, Coacoochee stood beside him to strengthen his courage.

At length about nine o'clock the troops appeared in view. They marched easily in open order, the bright sunlight glinted bravely on their polished weapons, and many were the shouts of light-hearted merriment that rose from their ranks. Louis, the guide, was not to be seen, as on some trifling pretext he had dropped behind the column.

The advanced guard reached the pond and passed

it unmolested.   It was not until the main body was directly abreast the Indian centre that the wild war-whoop of Otee the Jumper rang through the forest. The next instant Micanopy's trembling fingers, guided by Coacoochee's unflinching hand, pulled the trigger of the first rifle. With its flash a great sheet of flame leaped from the roadside, and half of Major Dade's command lay dead, without having known from where or by whom the fatal blow was struck.

The survivors, confused and demoralized by the suddenness and unexpectedness of this attack from an unseen foe, still made a brave effort to rally and return the pitiless fire that seemed to leap from every tree of the forest.   Their one field-piece, a six-pounder, was brought up and discharged several times, but its gunners presented an attractive target to the hidden riflemen, and it was speedily silenced.

A small company of soldiers managed to fell a few trees in the form of a triangular barricade.   Behind this they took shelter, and from it maintained a stout fire for some hours ; but early in the afternoon their last gun was silenced, and only the shadows of death brooded over the terrible scene.

During the fight the Indians had kept up an incessant yelling, but now they appeared stunned at the completeness of their success and contemplated their victory in silence.

With Louis Pacheco, who had joined the Indians immediately after the first fire, Coacoochee walked slowly and thoughtfully over the battle-field. He sternly forbade his warriors to mutilate or rob the dead, and speedily withdrew them to their encampment in the great swamp, from which they had emerged with such mingled hopes and apprehensions that morning.

Soon after their departure a band of fifty negroes, who had been summoned from a distance to take part in the battle, rode up to the scene of slaughter. Disappointed at having arrived too late to participate in it, they made an eager search among the heaps of slain, for any who should still show signs of life. If such were discovered, they were immediately put to death, while even the dead bodies were mutilated and stripped. After thus gratifying their blood-thirsty instincts, these, too, laden with scalps and plunder of every description, followed their Indian allies to the swamp, and on the blood-soaked field an awful stillness succeeded the wild tumult of battle.

As darkness shrouded the pitiful scene, two human figures, the only living survivors of " Dade's Massacre," slowly disengaged themselves from the dead bodies by which they were surrounded. They were wounded, and faint from the loss of blood, but they dragged themselves painfully away and were lost in the night shadows of the forest. Five days later they reached Fort Brooke and there gave the first notice of the terrible blow by which the despised Seminole had defied the power of the United States.

The Indian loss in this battle was three killed and five wounded.

That same night, Osceola and his warriors, laden with trophies and plunder, reached the encampment ·in the Wahoo Swamp. They had much to tell as well as much to hear, and the whole night was devoted to feasting, dancing, drinking, and every species of savage rejoicing over their successes.

Coacoochee, though filled with a sense of exultation, took no part in these excesses. He preferred talking with Louis and several of the graver chiefs regarding the future conduct of the war, and the chances for its speedy termination. All were agreed that there would be no further fighting for some time, and as both the young men were most anxious to visit Philip Emathla's village, they determined to do so at once.

At daylight, therefore, they left the swamp and started on their journey. By noon they were threading an open forest many miles from their point of departure. They were proceeding in silence, with Louis following Coacoochee, and stepping exactly in his tracks. This precaution was taken as a matter of habit, rather than from any idea that there was an enemy within many miles of them.

Suddenly Coacoochee stopped, held up his hand in warning, and listened intently, with his head inclined slightly forward. "Does my brother hear anything?" he asked.

No; Louis heard nothing save the sound of wind among the tree-tops. His ears were not so sharp as those of Coacoochee, nor, for the matter of that, was any other pair in the whole Seminole nation. So marvellously keen was the young war-chief's sense of hearing, that his companions deemed it unsafe to utter a word not intended for his ears within sight of where he stood. They believed him to be able to hear ordinary conversation as far as he could see. Although this was undoubtedly an exaggeration, his powers in this respect were certainly remarkable, and excited astonishment in all who were acquainted with them.

Now, after standing and listening for a moment with bent head, he threw himself to the ground, and placing one ear in direct contact with the earth, covered the other with his hand. He also closed his eyes, the better to concentrate all his powers into the one effort of hearing.

He lay thus for several minutes, and then slowly regained his feet. There was now an anxious expression on his face. Louis could no longer restrain his curiosity. "What is it, Coacoochee? What do you think you hear?"

The asking of this question would have at once betrayed Louis to be of other than Indian blood; for no Seminole would have exhibited the slightest curiosity until the other was ready to disclose his secret of his own accord.

So Coacoochee smiled slightly at his comrade's impatience as he answered :

"I hear more white men coming from that way "— here he pointed to the north; "they are many. Some of them are soldiers, and some are not. They travel slowly, for they have much baggage. They fear no danger and are careless. They have no cannon, but they have many horses. They know nothing of yesterday's battle. Let us go and look at them, where my brother will see that Coacoochee has heard truly."

Louis gazed at his companion, in amazement. "How is it possible for you to hear these things when I can hear nothing at all ? " he asked. "I am not deaf. My ears are as good as those of most men, but they detect no sound. You must be making game of me. Is it not so ? "

For answer Coacoochee persuaded him to lay his ear to the ground and listen as he had done a moment before.

When Louis rose, he said : "I do indeed hear something in the ground, but it is only a confused murmur. I cannot tell what it is or where it comes from."

Coacoochee smiled, and said : "My brother's ears are good. He has heard more than would most men ; but Coacoochee's are better. No sound is withheld from them. He can hear the grass grow and the flowers unfold. The murmur that my

brother hears is the sound of an army marching.
They are white men because they tread so heavily.
Some of them are soldiers because they blow bugles
and because they keep step in their marching. More
of them are not, for they walk as they please, and
many of them ride on horses. They have much
baggage, for I hear the sound of many wagons.
They fear no danger and are careless, for they run
races with their horses and fire pistols. They have
not learned of yesterday's battle, or they would be
sorrowful and quiet. Now they laugh and are
merry."

Half an hour later, as Coacoochee and Louis
occupied positions among the spreading, moss-
enveloped limbs of a large tree, the eyesight of the
latter confirmed all that his comrade's marvellous
hearing had already told them.

From their perch they could overlook a broad
savanna, across which slowly moved a small army of
white men. They counted nearly one thousand, two
hundred of whom were regular troops ; the rest were
ununiformed militia, many of them mounted and
exhibiting but little discipline. These rode hither
and thither, as they pleased, ran races, fired
their pistols at stray birds, and shouted loudly.
They were a cruel, rough set, and the heart of
Coacoochee grew heavy with the thought of such
a powerful and merciless invasion of the Seminole
country.

CHAPTER XIX

RALPH BOYD AND THE SLAVE-CATCHER

The army so unexpectedly discovered by Coacoochee was under the immediate command of General
Clinch, and was largely composed of Florida volunteers. Most of these were land-hunters, slave-hunters,
or other reckless adventurers, who had taken advantage of this opportunity for gaining a safe entrance
into the Indian country and examining its best lands
before it should be thrown open to general occupation. The majority of them had no idea that the
Indians would dare resist this occupation by the
whites, or that they would be called upon to do
any fighting. At the same time they expressed a
cheerful willingness to kill any number of redskins, and loudly declared their belief in the policy
of extermination.

This motley throng of freebooters, together with
four companies of regular troops, having been collected
at Fort Drane, some twenty-five miles from Fort
King, General Clinch decided to march them into
and through the Indian country for the purpose
of hastening the movements of the Seminoles, and
show them how powerful a force he could bring

against them.   Even he had no idea that any armed resistance would be offered to his progress.

While Coacoochee and Louis watched in breathless silence the passing of this army of invaders, whose openly declared object was to rob them of their homes, they were startled by the sound of voices immediately beneath their tree.   Looking down, they saw two men who had straggled from the main body and sought relief from the noontide heat of the sun, in the tempting shade.

At first our friends did not recognize the new-comers ; but all at once a familiar tone came to the ears of Louis Pacheco ; then he knew that the man whom he hated most on earth, the man who had sold him and his mother into slavery, the dealer, Troup Jeffers, had once more crossed his path.

The two men had not ridden up to the tree in company, but had approached it from different divisions of the passing column, though evidently animated by a common impulse.   It was quickly apparent that they did not even know each other ; for Mr. Troup Jeffers, who reached the tree first, greeted the other with:

"Good-day, stranger.   Light down and enjoy the shade.   Hit's powerful refreshing after the heat out yonder."

As the other dismounted from his horse, and, still retaining a hold on the bridle, flung himself at full length on the scanty grass at the foot of the tree, Jeffers continued :

"This appears to be a fine bit of country."

"Yes."

"But they tell me it ain't a circumstance to the Injun lands on the far side of the Withlacoochee."

"No ? "

"No. Them is said to be the best lands in Floridy. I reckin you're land-hunting. Ain't ye, now ? "

"No."

"Must be niggers, then ? "

"No sir. I am after neither land nor negroes ; I have come merely to see the country."

"Wal, that seems kinder curious," remarked Jeffers, reflectively. "Strange that a man like you should take all this trouble and risk his life — not that I suppose there's a mite of danger — just to look at a country that he don't kalkilate to make nothing out of."

"Yet some people have the poor taste to enjoy travel for travel's sake," replied the other. "But I suppose you have come on business? "

"You bet I have," answered Mr. Jeffers. "I've come after niggers, and I don't care who knows it. Hit's a lawful business, and as good as another, if I do say it. You see, thar's lots of 'em among the Injuns, and they're all described and claimed. Now I've bought a lot of these claims cheap, and the gineral has promised that jest as soon as the Injuns is corralled for emigration, all the claimed niggers shall be sorted out, and restored to their lawful owners. Owing to my claims, I'm the biggest lawful owner there is. So I thought I'd jest come along with the first crowd, and be on hand early to see that I wasn't cheated."

"A most wise precaution," remarked the stranger, sarcastically.

"Yes," continued Jeffers, unmindful of his companion's tone; "you see there is niggers *and* niggers. While some of them is worth their weight in silver as property, I wouldn't have some of the others as a gift. There's Injun niggers, for instance — half-bloods, you know; they're so wild that you have to kill 'em to tame 'em. Why, I lost more'n a hundred dollars in cash, besides what I reckoned to make, on a half-blood that I got up to Fort King a few months ago. She was wild as a hawk, and fretted, and wouldn't eat nothing, and finally died on my hands afore I got a chance to sell her."

"Certainly a most inconsiderate thing to do," remarked the stranger.

"Wasn't it, now? The only kind I want to deal with is the full bloods or them as is mixed with white. The best haul I ever made from the Injuns was about a year ago over on the east coast. He was wild and ugly as they make 'em when I first got him, but I soon tamed him down and sold him for one thousand dollars. I've heard that he hain't never showed a mite of spirit since I broke him in, and he makes one of the best all-round servants you ever see.   Louis is his name, and I'd like to get hold of a dozen more just like him. What! you ain't going to start along so soon, be ye?"

From the moment that Louis recognized this man and realized that his cruellest enemy was at last completely within his power, it had been difficult to refrain from sending a rifle bullet through the brute's cowardly heart.   It is doubtful if he could have withheld his hand had it not been for a warning look from Coacoochee and a gentle pressure of his hand.   The young Indian himself was visibly affected as he listened to the cold-blooded tone with which the ruffian told of the death of Chen-o-wah, the beautiful wife of Osceola, and his hand twitched nervously as he fingered the handle of his scalping-knife; but he was able to restrain his own inclinations, even as he had restrained those of his companion. He knew that he had a duty to perform vastly more important than the punishment of the slave-catcher, and that for its sake even this enemy must be allowed to escape for the present.

In reply to Mr. Jeffers' exclamation of surprise at his sudden departure from the cool shade in which they rested, the stranger answered :

"Yes, Mr. Slave-catcher, I am going; for I have no desire to cultivate the further acquaintance of a

L

scoundrel.   You are therefore warned to keep your
distance from me so long as we both accompany
this expedition."

With this, the speaker sprang into his saddle, and
as his horse started, he took off his hat with a profound bow of mock courtesy, saying : " I am very
sorry to have met you, sir, and I hope I may never
have the misfortune to do so again."

As the young man dashed away, the slave-trader
gazed after him in open-mouthed amazement.   Then
he muttered, loud enough for Coacoochee to hear :
" Wal, if that don't beat all !   You're a nice, re-
spectable, chummy sort of a chap, ain't you, now ?
Jest a leetle too nice to live, and I shouldn't be surprised if you was to get hurt by some one besides
Injuns, if ever we have the luck to get into a
scrimmage with the red cusses."

These remarks were particularly interesting to
Coacoochee ; for, as the stranger removed his hat on
riding away, the mystery of his voice, which had
haunted the young chief with a familiar sound, was
explained.   The face, as revealed by the lifting of
the drooping sombrero, was that of his acquaintance
and preserver, Ralph Boyd the Englishman.

It is more than likely that Coacoochee would
have seized the present opportunity for rendering
Mr. Troup Jeffers forever powerless to injure any
man, white, red, or black, but for an interruption
that came just as he was contemplating a sudden

descent from the tree. It appeared in the form of a lieutenant of regulars, who commanded the rear guard of the little army, and whose duty it was to drive in all stragglers.

So Mr. Troup Jeffers rode away, utterly unconscious of the imminent danger he had just escaped. He was, however, full of an ugly hate against the man who a few minutes before had treated him with such scorn, and was determined to discover his identity at the first opportunity.

As the rear guard of the army disappeared from the view of the two watchers, they slipped to the ground from their hiding-place, more than glad of an opportunity to stretch their cramped limbs. Coacoochee was the first to speak, and he said :

"They go to the Withlacoochee, and will seek to cross at Haney's ferry. They must be delayed until our warriors can be brought to meet them. We are two. One must return to the Wahoo Swamp, tell Osceola of this thing, and bid him hasten with all his fighting men to the ford that is by the Itto micco [magnolia tree]. This shall be your errand, Louis my brother, and I pray you make what speed you may, for our time is short. I will hasten to reach the ferry before the soldiers, and in some way prevent their using the boat. Then must they go to the ford, for there is no other place to cross."

CHAPTER XX

AN ALLIGATOR AND HIS MYSTERIOUS ASSAILANT

LATE that same evening the watchers of Osceola's camp in the great swamp were startled by the sudden appearance of a human form almost within their lines. He was instantly surrounded and led to the camp-fire in front of the chieftain's lodge, that his character might be determined. The surprise of the Indians upon discovering him to be Louis Pacheco, whom they supposed to be a long day's journey from that place, was forgotten in that caused by his tidings.

It seemed incredible that, while they had just destroyed one army of white men, another should already be on the confines of their country and about to invade it. But Louis had seen and counted them Coacoochee's plan was a wise one, and they would follow it. So the bustle of preparation was immediately begun. The fight of the day before had nearly exhausted their ammunition. Bullets must be moulded, and powder-horns refilled from a keg brought from a distant, carefully hidden magazine, a supply of provisions must be prepared, for on the war-trail no fires could be lighted and no game could be hunted.

When all was ready, Osceola caused his men to take a few hours' sleep; but with the first flush of daylight they were on the march, swiftly but silently threading the dim and oftentimes submerged pathways of the swamp. There were two hundred and fifty in all, of whom the greater number were warriors under Osceola, and the balance were negroes led by Alligator.

On the following morning they reached the appointed place, and concealed themselves in the forest growth lining the bank on the south side of the ford. As this was the only point along that part of the river at which it was possible to cross without boats, they were satisfied that the attempt to enter the Indian country would be made here, and that here the expected battle must take place.

Still, the troops should have arrived by this time, and as yet there was no sign of them. Neither had Coacoochee appeared, though this was where he had promised to meet them. Osceola had just decided to send a scouting party to the ferry to make sure that Coacoochee had completed his self-imposed task, when a remarkable incident arrested his attention and caused him to withhold the order.

A green bush was floating slowly down the river toward the ford, and several of the Indians were commenting on a peculiarity of its motion. Instead of floating straight down with the current of the stream, it was unmistakably moving diagonally across the river toward them. When first noticed it had been in the middle of the channel, but now it was decidedly nearer their side.

The Withlacoochee abounded in alligators that grew to immense size, and just at this time one of the largest of these seemed strangely attracted toward the floating bush. His black snout, and the protruding eyes, set back so far from it as to give proof of his great length, were all that he showed above the surface. These, however, were observed to be moving cautiously nearer and nearer to the bush, until finally they almost touched it.

All at once the monster sprang convulsively forward, throwing half his length from the water. For a moment his huge tail lashed the waves into a foam that appeared tinged with red. At the same time, a hideous bellowing roar of mingled rage and pain woke the forest echoes. Then, with a sullen plunge, the brute sank and was seen no more.

The strangest thing of this whole remarkable performance was not the disappearance of the great reptile, but the sudden appearance close beside it, at the very height of the flurry, of a round black object that looked extremely like a human head.

It was only seen for a second; then the sharp report of a rifle rang out from across the river, and the object instantly disappeared. With this, a white man, tall, gaunt, and clad in the uniform of a United States dragoon, stepped from the thick growth, and scanned intently the surface of the water as he carefully reloaded his rifle. He stood thus for several minutes, and then, apparently satisfied that his shot had been effective, he turned and vanished among the trees.

It would have been an easy matter for the concealed warriors to kill him while he stood in plain view, and several guns were raised for the purpose, but Osceola forbade the firing of a shot. The appearance of that one soldier satisfied him that the others would soon arrive, and he did not wish to give them the slightest intimation of his presence until they should begin crossing the river.

Suddenly he and those with him were startled by the cry of a hawk twice repeated in their immediate vicinity. They recognized it as the signal of Coacoochee; but where was he? As they gazed inquiringly about them, there was a rustling among the flags and lily-pads growing at the river's edge. Then, so quickly that he was exposed to view but a single instant, Coacoochee, naked except for a thong of buckskin about his waist, sprang from the water to the shelter of the bushes on the bank and stood among them.

The young war-chief had taken a long circuit around General Clinch's army, and reached the ferry toward which they were evidently marching, well in advance of them, the evening before. He already knew that the ferryman, alarmed by the impending Indian troubles, had abandoned his post and removed with his family to a place of safety.

What he did not know, however, was that the great scow used as a ferryboat lay high and dry on the bank, where a recent fall in the waters of the river had left it. He had expected to find it afloat and to either set it adrift, or sink it in the middle of the stream.

Now he was at a loss what to do. He could not move the clumsy craft from its muddy resting-place. His time was limited, and he had no tools, not even a hatchet, with which to destroy it. There was but one thing left, and that was fire. As he looked at the massive, water-soaked timbers of the scow, Coacoochee realized that to destroy it by fire would be a tedious undertaking. However, he set resolutely to work, and within an hour flames were leaping merrily about the stranded boat. He had torn all the dry woodwork that would yield to his efforts from the ferryman's log cabin which stood at some distance back from the river. He had gathered a quantity of lightwood from dead pine trees, and had built three great fires, one at each end of the scow and one in the middle.

When all this was accomplished to his satisfaction, the youth became conscious that he was faint and weak from hunger, as he had eaten nothing that day. Visiting the ferryman's deserted cabin, he finally discovered half a barrel of hard bread and a small quantity of uncooked provisions secreted in a dark corner of the little loft that had served the family as a storeroom.

As he was selecting a few articles of food to carry away and eat at his leisure in some snug hiding-place from which he might also watch the operations of the expected troops, the young chief was alarmed by the sound of voices.

The next moment several soldiers entered the cabin, calling loudly upon its supposed occupants, of whose recent departure they were evidently unaware. Receiving no reply to their shouts, they ransacked the two lower rooms. One even climbed the rude ladder leading to the little loft and peered curiously about him. Crouched in its darkest corner and hardly breathing, Coacoochee escaped observation, and the trooper descended to report that no one was up there. "It's clear enough that the folks have lit out," he added.

"There must be somebody around to start that smoke down by the river," said another voice.

"Well, I reckon we'd best go and see what's burning as well as who's there," was the reply.

With this they left the house, and Coacoochee heard some one order two of them to stay and look after the horses; while the others went to ascertain the cause of the fire.

He determined to make a bold dash for liberty, and risk the shots that the two men would certainly fire at him ; but when he was half-way down the ladder, the sound of fresh voices caused him hurriedly to regain his hiding-place. Now there was much talking, and he knew that the main body of troops had arrived.

As it was nearly sunset, the soldiers went into camp between the house and the river, and a number of them took possession of the house itself. Fortunately the hot, stuffy little loft did not offer sufficient attractions to tempt any of them to occupy it, though several peered into its gloom from the ladder. As they did not discern the crouching form in the corner, the young Indian began to fancy that he might remain there in safety so long as he chose.

He was rejoiced to learn, from fragments of conversation that his fires had rendered the scow useless. He also learned to his dismay that an old canoe had been discovered, and was even then being patched up so that it would float. In it the troops would cross the river, a few at a time, on the following morning.

Coacoochee passed a weary night, not daring to sleep, lest he should make some movement that would betray his presence to those in the rooms below. Occasionally he was forced by the pains in his cramped limbs to change his position, but he did this as seldom as possible and with the utmost caution.

At length, just as daylight was breaking, and certain sounds indicated that the camp was waking up, one of these cautious movements dislodged a hard biscuit that lay on the floor beside him. Slipping through a crevice in the rude flooring, it fell plump on the face of one of the sleepers below.

The man thus suddenly wakened sprang up with a cry of alarm. He laughed when he discovered the cause of his fright, and exclaimed in Ralph Boyd's well-remembered voice :

" Hello ! There's hard bread up-stairs, boys, and the rats are at work on it. I'm going to stop their fun, and secure my share."

With this he started toward the ladder, and Coacoochee nerved himself for the discovery that he knew was now unavoidable.

CHAPTER XXI

BATTLE OF THE WITHLACOOCHEE

THE man who had been so rudely roused from his sleep slowly climbed the ladder leading to the loft, and began cautiously to feel his way across the uneven flooring. The place in which the Indian crouched and awaited his coming was still shrouded in utter darkness; but by the uncertain light coming up from below, the approaching figure was faintly outlined.

This man had proved himself Coacoochee's friend, and the young chief had no intention of harming him. Still, he could not allow himself to be captured, even by Ralph Boyd. He dared not trust himself in the hands of the whites after what had so recently happened. Besides, it was now more than ever necessary that he should be at liberty to communicate with Osceola and inform him of the proposed movements of the troops. These thoughts flashed through his mind during the few seconds occupied by Boyd in groping his way toward the dark corner.

Suddenly from out of it a dim figure sprang upon the white man, with such irresistible force that he

156

was hurled breathless to the floor. With one bound it reached the aperture through which the ladder protruded, and slid to the room below. The half-awakened men who occupied this, startled by the crash above them, were scrambling to their feet, and, as Coacoochee dashed through them toward the open door, several hands were stretched forth to seize him. They failed to check his progress, and in another moment he was gone.

With the swiftness of a bird he darted across the open space behind the house, and disappeared in the forest beyond. So sudden and unexpected was this entire performance that not a shot was fired after him, and the young Indian could hardly realize the completeness of his escape as he found himself unharmed amid the friendly shadows of the trees.

Had he chosen to continue his flight directly away from the river, it would have been an easy matter to gain a position of absolute safety, so far as any pursuit was concerned. But he must reach the ford and those whom he supposed to be there awaiting him. Therefore, after making a long detour through the forest, he again approached the Withlacoochee, at a point several miles above where he had left it.

In the meantime, the presence of an Indian in the very heart of their camp had occasioned the greatest excitement throughout General Clinch's army. He was the first they had encountered, and his boldness, together with the manner in which he had eluded them, invested him with an alarming air of mystery. It was the general opinion that there must be others on that side of the river in the immediate vicinity, and scouts were sent out in all directions to ascertain their whereabouts. At the same time the crossing of the Withlacoochee by means of the single canoe was begun and prosecuted with all possible rapidity.

Coacoochee was greatly embarrassed in his attempt to gain the ford by the presence of the scouting parties, and was more than once on the eve of being discovered by them. Even though he might reach the river without attracting their notice, he feared they would detect him in the act of crossing it.

Finally he hit upon an expedient that he believed might prove successful. Cautiously gaining the bank at some distance above the ford, he hastily bound together four bits of dry wood in the form of a square by means of slender withes of the wild grape. For this purpose he choose green vines that were covered with leaves. He also cut a number of leafy twigs, and inserting their ends beneath the lashing of vines produced a fair imitation of a green bush. The deception was heightened as he carefully placed his rude structure in the water, where it floated most naturally.

Then concealing his rifle and clothing, and thrusting the trusty knife, which was now to be his only weapon, into the snakeskin sheath that depended from a buckskin thong about his waist, the youth slipped gently into the water and sank beneath its surface. When he rose, his head was inside the little square of sticks and completely screened from view by its leafy canopy. Thus floating, and paddling gently with his hands, he caused the mass of foliage to move almost imperceptibly out from the shore, while at the same time he and it were borne downward with the sluggish current.

Coacoochee had no fear of alligators. He had been familiar with them ever since he could remember anything, and was well acquainted with their cowardly nature. Thus when he had successfully passed the middle of the river, and was gently working his way toward its opposite bank, the near approach of one of these monsters did not cause him any uneasiness. He knew that he could frighten the great reptile away, or even kill it, though he feared that by so doing he might expose himself to a shot from those who still scouted along the bank he had so recently left.

Finally the monster approached so close that he was sickened by its musky breath, and it became evident that he was about to be attacked. Drawing his long knife, the young Indian allowed himself to sink without making a sound or a movement. A single stroke carried him directly beneath the huge

beast, and a powerful upward thrust plunged the
keen blade deep into its most vulnerable spot through
the soft skin under one of the fore-shoulders.

In spite of the danger from the creature's death
flurry, Coacoochee was compelled to rise for breath
close beside it.

This was the moment waited for by a white scout
on the further bank, who had for some time been
directing keenly suspicious glances at the mysterious
movements of the floating bush.   More than once his
rifle had been raised for the purpose of sending an
inquiring leaden messenger into the centre of that
clump of foliage, but each time it had been lowered
as its owner determined to watch and wait a little
longer.

Now the bullet was sped, and only the great com-
motion of the water caused it to miss its mark by an
inch.   As the head at which he had fired immediately
disappeared, and was seen no more, the rifleman fancied that his shot had taken effect, and that there was
one Indian less to be removed from the country.

Swimming under water with the desperation of
one conscious that his life depends upon his efforts,
Coacoochee did not again come to the surface until
he touched the stems of the great "bonnets," or
leaves of the yellow cow-lily on the further side
of the river, and could rise for a breath of the
blessed air beneath their friendly screen.

Here he lay motionless for several minutes, recovering from his exhaustion. At length he ventured to give the hawk's call as a warning to his friends of his presence. Then, gathering all his strength, he made the quiet rush for safety that carried him among them.

It did not take many seconds to inform them that the enemy for whom they were watching so anxiously was even then crossing the river, unconscious of danger, a mile below that point.

The report had hardly been made before the eager warriors who crowded about the speaker were in motion. Coacoochee was quickly provided with clothing, a rifle, and ammunition, and fifteen minutes later the entire Indian force was within hearing of the sounds made by the soldiers as they crossed the river. Here a halt was made while Osceola himself crept forward with the noiseless movement of a serpent to discover the enemy's exact location and disposition.

To his dismay, he found that a force equal in number to his own had already crossed the river, with others constantly coming. There must not be a minute's delay if he would fight with the faintest hope of checking their advance.

Hastily the forest warriors chose their positions, and a crashing volley from their rifles was the first announcement given the soldiers of their presence. Although staggered for a moment, the regulars quickly recovered, fixed their gleaming bayonets, and

M

with a wild yell charged into the cloud of smoke.
The Indians fell back; but only long enough to
reload their guns, when they advanced in turn, pouring such a deadly fire into the white ranks that
their formation was broken, and the soldiers were
driven back to the river's bank.

Here they were reformed by the general himself,
and led to a second charge with results similar to
the first. This time the Indians did not give way
so readily, nor fall back so far. Under the frenzied
leadership of Alligator and Osceola, who urged them
with wild cries and frantic gestures to stand firm,
they contested with knives, hatchets, and clubbed
rifles each step of the way over which they were
slowly forced.

In order to shelter themselves against the Indian
fire, the soldiers adopted their plan of fighting, and
each, selecting a tree, took his position behind it.
Here an exposure of the smallest portion of a body
was certain to draw a shot, and the whites were soon
made aware by their rapidly increasing number of
wounded, that at this game they were no match for
the Indian marksmen.

Coacoochee and half a dozen warriors had concealed themselves on the river bank above the ferry,
so that their rifles commanded it, and their fire so
effectually dampened the ardor of the five hundred
volunteers remaining on the other side that not one
of them crossed or took part in the battle, except

by firing a few scattering shots from their own side of the river.

For more than an hour the battle raged. Osceola was wounded, and the Indian ammunition was giving out. They were becoming discouraged and were about to retire. All at once Coacoochee, who, on hearing of Osceola's wound, had left his little band of sharpshooters to guard the crossing, appeared among them. The effect of his presence and inspiring words was magical. Loud and fierce rang out his battle cry:

" Yo-ho-ee yo-ho-ee yo-ho-ee-chee! "

With the last grains of powder in their rifles and led by their dauntless young chief, the entire body of warriors, yelling like demons, dashed madly through the forest toward the line of troops.

" They must have been heavily reinforced," shouted the bewildered soldiers to each other. " There are thousands of them ! "

From every bunch of palmetto, from every tuft of grass, and from behind every tree, a yelling, half-naked, and death-dealing Indian seemed to spring forth. A heavy but ill-aimed fire did not check them in the slightest. The soldiers began to fall back from one tree to another. Some of them ran. The wounded were hurriedly removed to the river bank. Perhaps some were overlooked. There was no time to search for those who were not in plain view. The dead were left where they had fallen.

With the first sign of this yielding, the frenzied yelling of the Indians increased, until the whole forest seemed alive with them. The retreat of the soldiers became a flight. A scattering volley from behind hastened their steps. The battle of the Withlacoochee was ended.

CHAPTER XXII

THE YOUNG CHIEF MAKES A TIMELY DISCOVERY

WITHOUT ammunition the warriors of Coacoochee could not be persuaded to remain on the field of battle, and the frightened soldiers had hardly reached the river bank before the Indians were also in full retreat toward their strongholds in the great swamp.

Of this the soldiers knew nothing, nor did they stop to inquire why they were not pursued. They were thankful enough to be allowed to re-embark, a dozen at a time, in their one canoe and recross the river without molestation. They imagined the forest behind them to be swarming with Indians, and they trembled beneath the supposed gaze of hundreds of gleaming eyes with which their fancy filled every thicket.

Late that afternoon General Clinch and his terrified army were in full retreat toward Fort Drane, with their eyes widely opened to the danger and difficulty of invading an enemy's country, even though that enemy was but a band of despised Indians. They carried with them fifty wounded men and left four dead behind them, besides several others reported as missing. They had killed three of the

enemy and wounded five. When they reached the
safe shelter of the fort, they reported that they had
gained an important victory.

Upon the retreat of the Seminoles, Coacoochee
and Louis, who had rejoined him that day, remained behind to watch the troops and discover
what they might of their plans for the future.
They supposed, of course, that with the cessation
of the Indian fire, the soldiers would again advance,
and finding no further opposition offered, would
proceed with their invasion of the country. They
could hardly believe their own eyes, therefore, when
they saw that the troops were actually recrossing
the river, as evidently in full retreat as were the
Seminole warriors in the opposite direction at that
very moment.

Upon beholding this marvellous sight, Louis was
in favor of hastening after their friends and bringing them back to follow and harass General Clinch's
retreating army ; but Coacoochee said that without
ammunition they could do nothing, and that it was
better, under the circumstances, to let affairs remain
as they were. At the same time, he desired Louis
to hasten up to the ford, cross the river at that point,
and, coming cautiously down on the other side, discover if the soldiers were really in retreat, or if
they still had their position near the ferryman's
house. While the mulatto was thus engaged, he
himself would remain where they were, to follow the

troops, should they recover from their panic, and decide, after all, to continue their invasion of the Indian country.

After Louis had been despatched on this mission, Coacoochee, satisfied that the soldiers were too intent upon recrossing the river and gaining a place of safety to disturb him, ventured to revisit the battle-field, in the hope of finding a stray powder-flask or pouch of bullets.

So successful was his search, that he not only found a number of these, but several rifles that had been flung away by the soldiers in their hurried flight.

While busy collecting these prizes, the young chief was startled by hearing a faint groan. He looked about him. There was nobody in sight; but again he heard a groan. This time he located it as proceeding from a clump of palmettoes a few paces distant.

Approaching these, and cautiously parting their broad leaves, he discovered the body of a white man lying face downward. The man was evidently severely wounded, for he lay motionless in a pool of blood, but that he was also alive was shown by his occasional feeble groans.

Coacoochee's first impulse was to leave him where he lay. He would soon die there. At any rate, the wolves would make short work of him that night. It was contrary to the policy of the Indians to take prisoners, and he certainly could not be burdened with one, — a wounded one, at that.

His second impulse, which was urged by pity, of which even an Indian's breast is not wholly void, was to put the wretch out of his misery by means of a mercifully aimed bullet. He knew that his savage companions would ridicule such an act. They would either leave the man to his fate, after making sure that he could not possibly recover, or they would revive him sufficiently to comprehend their purpose and then kill him. They would never be so weak as to kill an unconscious man merely to save him from suffering. Still this was what Coacoochee was about to do, and he felt a kindly warming of the heart, as one does who is about to perform a generous deed.

Slowly he raised his rifle and took a careful aim at the head of the motionless figure before him. His finger was on the trigger. An instant more and the deed would have been accomplished.

But there is no report. The brown rifle is slowly lowered, and the young Indian's gaze rests as though fascinated upon something that caught his eye as it sighted along the deadly tube.

It is only a peculiar seam in the white man's buckskin hunting-tunic, but it runs down the middle of the back from collar to the bottom of the shirt. There are other noticeable features about that hunting-shirt. The little bunches of fringe at the shoulders are of a peculiar cut, and all of its stitching is in yellow silk.

With a low cry of mingled horror and anticipation, Coacoochee dropped his rifle, and springing forward, turned the unconscious man over so that his face was exposed. It was that of Ralph Boyd, the man who had twice saved his life; the man to whose noble scorn of one of the cruellest enemies of an oppressed race he had listened with such pleasure only two days before.

Indian and stern warrior though he was, Coacoochee turned faint at the thought of how nearly he had taken this precious life, for the saving of which he would willingly risk his own. The hunting-shirt worn by Boyd was the very one in which Coacoochee had paid his last memorable visit to St. Augustine. It was the one that had been slit from top to bottom by Fontaine Salano's knife, and stripped from him, in preparation for the whipping the brute proposed to administer. The thought of that shameful moment caused Coacoochee's blood to boil again with rage. At the same time the sight of this noble-hearted stranger who had saved him from that bitter indignity moved him to greatest pity.

Kneeling beside the unconscious man, the young Indian sought to discover the nature of his wound. To his amazement, it was caused by a bullet that had been fired from *behind*. How could such a thing be? None but white men were behind Boyd during the battle. Suddenly the muttered words of Troup Jeffers flashed into his mind. Now all was clear. To gratify his own petty revenge the slave-catcher had committed this cowardly act.

The young chief was busily engaged in stanching the flow of blood, and binding a poultice of healing leaves, mixed with the glutinous juice of a cabbage palm, on the wound, when Louis returned and stood beside him.

The whites were in full retreat from the scene of their recent discomfiture, and Louis had returned in the very canoe they had used and abandoned. Now he and Coacoochee bore the wounded man tenderly to it, crossed the river, and carried him to the ferryman's cabin, where both he and the young chief had passed the previous night, unconscious of each other's presence. Here they made him as comfortable as possible, and here for awhile we must leave them.

CHAPTER XXIII

SHAKESPEARE IN THE FOREST

LIKE a fire sped by strong winds across a prairie of brown and sun-dried grasses, so did the flames of war sweep across the entire breadth of Florida. For a year had the Indians been preparing for it. Now they were ready to gather in numbers, and fight armies, or scatter in small bands, to spread death and destruction in every direction. The Seminole was about to make a desperate defence of his country, and to teach its invaders that they might not steal it from him with impunity.

Express riders carried news of the war in every direction. Everywhere cabins, farms, and plantations were abandoned, while their owners flocked into forts and settlements for mutual protection and safety.

One day, some two weeks after the events narrated in the preceding chapter, a novel procession was to be seen wending its slow, dusty way along one of the few roads of those times that led from the St. John's River to St. Augustine. The procession presented a confused medley of horsemen, pedestrians, wheeled vehicles, and cattle, and might

171

have reminded one of the migration of a band of Asiatic nomads.

It was indeed a migration, though one directed rather by force of circumstances than by choice. It was a white household, with its servants, cattle, and readily portable effects, fleeing from an abandoned plantation towards St. Augustine for safety against the Indians. None of the party had seen an Indian as yet, but they were reported to be ravaging both banks of the river from Mandarin to Picolata.

At first the young mistress of this particular estate had discredited the reports, for it was only rumored as yet that the Seminoles had really declared war. Her brother being absent from home, she for some time resolutely declined to abandon the house in which he had left her. The neighboring places on either side had been deserted for several days, and their occupants had entreated her to fly with them, but without avail.

"No," she replied; "here Ralph left me, and here I shall stay until he comes again, or until I am driven away by something more real than mere rumors."

At length that "something" came. All night the southern sky was reddened by a dull glow occasionally heightened by jets of flame and columns of sparks.

At daylight a frightened negro brought word that the Indians were but a few miles away, and had burned the deserted buildings on three plantations during the night.

Now was indeed time to seek safety in flight, and "Missy" Anstice, as the servants called her, ordered a hurried departure. Her own preparations were very simple. A small trunk of clothing and a few precious souvenirs were all that she proposed to take. With only herself, Letty her maid, and these few things in the carriage that old Primus would drive, and the servants in carts or on muleback, they ought to travel so speedily as to reach St. Augustine some time that same night.

But while Anstice was quite ready to start, she found to her dismay that no one else was. Confusion reigned in the quarters; there was a wild running hither and thither, a piling on the carts of rickety household furniture, bedding, and goods of every description; a loud squawking of fowls tied by the legs, and hung in mournful festoons from every projecting point, and a confused lowing, bleating, and grunting from flocks and herds.

In vain did the young mistress command and plead. All the servants on that plantation were free. Many of them owned the carts they were loading, and nothing short of the appearance of Indians on the spot could have induced them to relinquish their precious household treasures. "Lor, Missy Anstice!" one would say reproachfully, "yo wouldn' tink ob astin' a ole ooman to leab behine de onliest fedder bed she done got?"

"But I am going to leave all mine, aunty."

"Yah, honey; but yo'se got a heap ob 'em, while I've ony got jes' dis one."

And so it went. Useless articles taken from overloaded carts, at Anstice's earnest solicitation, were slyly added to others when she was not looking. Her brother acted as his own overseer, so there were no whites on the plantation to aid her. She alone must order this exodus, and beneath its responsibilities she found herself well-nigh helpless.

At length, in despair, and having wasted most of the morning in useless expostulations, she entered the heavy, old-fashioned coach, with Letty the maid, and gave Primus the order to set forth.

As the carriage passed the quarters, there was a great cry of:

"Don' yo leab us, Missy Anstice! Don' yo gway an' leab us to de Injins! We'se a comin'."

So Primus was ordered to drive slowly, and under other circumstances the English girl would have been vastly amused at the motley procession that began to straggle along behind her; but the danger was too imminent and too great to admit of any thoughts save those of anxiety and fear.

An hour or more passed without incident. The sun beat down fiercely from an unclouded sky, and the shadows of the tall pines seemed to nestle close

"TO LEAB BEHINE DE ONLIEST FEDDER BED SHE DONE GOT."

to the brown trunks in an effort to escape his scorching rays. A sound of locusts filled the air. The grateful sea-breeze that would steal inland an hour later was still afar off, and but for the urgency of their flight, the slow-moving cavalcade would have rested until it came. The tongues of the cattle hung from their mouths, and a cloud of dust enveloped them. The heads of horses and mules were stretched straight out, and their ears drooped. Old Primus nodded on the carriage seat. Letty was fast asleep, and even her young mistress started from an occasional doze.

Unobserved by a single eye in all that weary throng, another cloud of dust, similar to that hanging above and about them, rose in their rear. It approached rapidly, until it was so close that the clouds mingled. Then from out the gray canopy burst a whirlwind of yells, shots, galloping horses, and human forms with wildly waving arms.

In an instant the fugitives were roused from their drowsiness to a state of bewildered terror. Men shouted and beat their animals, women screamed, horses plunged, mules kicked, and carts were upset.

The first intimation of this onset that reached the occupants of the carriage, was in the form of madly galloping cattle that, with loud bellowings, wild eyes, and streaming tails, began to dash past on either side. Then their own horses took fright, and urged on by old Primus, tore away down the road.

All at once the terrified occupants of the flying vehicle looked up at the sound of a triumphant yell, only to behold fierce eyes glaring at them from hideously painted faces at either door. The muzzle of a rifle was thrust in at one of the open windows, and at sight of it Anstice Boyd hid her face in her hands, believing that her last moment had come.

When she recovered from her terror sufficiently to look about her once more, Letty was sobbing hysterically on the floor, but there was no motion to the carriage, and all was silent around them. Primus was no longer on the box, and the carriage was not in the road.

Determined to discover their exact situation, Anstice opened one of the doors, with a view to stepping out. At that moment a loud and significant "ugh!" coming from beneath the carriage, caused her to change her mind and hastily reclose the door, as though it were in some way a protection.

A few moments later two mounted Indians rode up to the carriage, and each leading one of its horses, it began to move slowly through the trackless pine forest. As it started, the Indian who had been left to guard it sprang to the seat lately occupied by old Primus.

For hours the strange journey was continued, and it was after sunset when it finally ended near the great river at a place some miles below the plantation they had left that morning. Now the wearied prisoners were allowed to leave their carriage, and were led to where several negro women were cooking supper over a small fire.

Anstice was provided with food, but she could not eat. Terror and anxiety had robbed her of all appetite, and she could only sit and gaze at the strange scene about her, as it was disclosed by the fitful firelight.

Piles of plunder were scattered on all sides. A lowing of cattle, grunting of hogs, cackling and crowing of fowls, the spoils of many a ravaged barnyard, rose on the night air. There was much laughing and talking, both in a strange Indian language that still seemed to contain a number of English words, and in the homely negro dialect.

As the bewildered girl crouched at the foot of a tree, and recalling tale after tale of savage atrocities, trembled at the fate she believed to be in store for her, she started at the sound of a heavy footfall close at hand.

"Bress yo heart, honey! hit's ony me!" exclaimed the well-known voice of old Primus, who, after a long search, had just discovered his young mistress. "Hyar's a jug o' milk an' a hot pone, an' I'se come to 'splain dere hain't no reason fo' being scairt ob dese yeah red Injuns. Ole Primus done fix it so's dey hain't gwine hut yo. Dey's mighty frienly to

N

de cullud folks, and say ef we gwine long wif 'em,
we stay free same like we allers bin; but ef we
go ter Augustine, de white folks cotch us an' sell
us fo payin de expenses ob de wah.

"Same time I bin makin' 'rangement wif 'em dat
ef we'se gwine long er dem, dey is boun ter let
yo go safe to Augustine, whar Marse Boyd'll be
looking fer yo. Yes'm, I'se bin councillin' wif 'em
an' settle all dat ar."

"But, Primus, I thought you were scared to death
of the Indians, and didn't understand a word of
their language," interrupted Anstice.

"Who? me! Sho, Missy Anstice, yo suttenly don't
reckin I was scairt. No'm, I hain't scairt ob no
red Injin, now dat I onerstan'in deir langwidge an'
deir 'tenshuns. Why, missy, deir talk's mighty nigh
de same as ourn when yo gits de hang ob hit. So,
honey, yo want to chirk up and quit yo mo'nin', an'
eat a bit, and den come to de theayter, foh it sholy
will be fine."

"What do you mean by the theatre?" asked the
bewildered girl; whereupon Primus explained that at
one of the plantations raided by the Indians a company of actors on their way to St. Augustine had
been discovered, captured, and brought along with
all their properties. These people were at first
informed that they were to be burned to death at
the stake. Afterwards it was decided that they
should be given their lives and freedom if they

would entertain their captors with an exhibition of their art that very evening. This contract stipulated that the performance should be as complete and detailed as though given before a white audience, and that any member of the company failing to act his part in a satisfactory manner would render himself liable to become a target for bullets and arrows.

Under the circumstances it is doubtful if a play was ever presented under more extraordinary conditions, greater difficulties, or by actors more anxious to perform creditably their respective parts, than was this one given in the depths of a Florida wilderness. The stage was an open space, roofed by arching trees, and lighted by great fires of pine knots constantly replenished. The wings were two wagons drawn up on either side.

The play selected for this important occasion was Hamlet, and for awhile everything proceeded smoothly. Then the audience began to grow impatient of the long soliloquies, and to the intense surprise of the captives, a gruff voice called out :

"Oh, cut it short an' git to fightin'! "

"No, give us a dance," shouted another, "an' hyar's a chune to dance by."

With this a pistol shot rang out, and a ball struck the ground close to Horatio's feet. The frightened actor bounded into the air, and as he alighted, another shot, coupled with a fierce order to *dance*, assured him that his tormentors were in deadly earnest. So he danced, and the others were compelled to join him. To an accompaniment of roars of laughter from the delighted savages, the terrified actors, clad in all the bravery of tinsel armor and nodding plumes, were thus compelled to cut capers and perform strange antics until some of them fell to the ground from sheer exhaustion.

The humor of the savages now took another turn, and with fierce oaths, mingled with threats of instant death if the players were ever seen in that country again, they drove them from camp and bade them make their way to St. Augustine.

As these fugitives disappeared in the surrounding darkness, a big, hideously painted savage who wore on his face the uncommon adornment of a bristling beard, advanced to Anstice Boyd, and in a jargon of broken English bade her follow them if she valued her life.

As the frightened girl started to obey this mandate, old Primus interfered and began to remonstrate with the savage, whereupon he was struck to the ground with so cruel a blow that blood gushed from his mouth. Filled with horror at these happenings, and believing her life to be in peril if she lingered another minute, the fair English girl sprang away, and was quickly lost to sight in the black forest shadows.

CHAPTER XXIV

BOGUS INDIANS AND THE REAL ARTICLE

As Anstice Boyd fled blindly from the presence of the savage who had just struck down her faithful servant, she had no idea of the direction she was taking, nor of what haven she might hope to reach. She knew only that she was once more free to make her way to friends, if she could, and her greatest present fear was that the savages might repent their generosity, and seek to recapture her. So, as she ran, she listened fearfully for sounds of pursuit, and several times fancied that she heard soft footfalls close at hand, though hasty glances over her shoulder disclosed no cause for apprehension.

At length, she came to the end of her strength, and sank wearily to the ground at the foot of a giant magnolia. Almost as she did so, a low cry of despair came from her lips, for with noiseless step the slender form of a young Indian stood, like an apparition beside her. She had not then escaped, after all, but was still at the mercy of the savages whose cruelty she had so recently witnessed. This one had doubtless been sent to kill her. Thus thinking, the trembling girl covered her face with her hands, and, praying that the fatal blow might be swift and sure, dumbly awaited its delivery. Seconds passed, and it did not fall. The agony of suspense was intolerable. She was about to spring up as though in an effort to escape, and thus precipitate her fate, when, to her amazement, she became aware that the Indian was speaking in a low tone, and in her own tongue.

"My white sister must not be afraid," he said. "Coacoochee has come far to find her and take her to a place of safety. Ralph Boyd is his friend, his only friend among all the millions of white men. He is wounded, and lies in a Seminole lodge. After a little we will go to him. There is no time now to tell more. I have that to do which must be done quickly. Let my sister rest here, and in one hour I will come again."

As he concluded these words, which had been uttered hurriedly, and in a voice but little above a whisper, the Indian turned and disappeared as noiselessly as he had come, seeming to melt away among the woodland shadows.

The bewildered girl, thus again left alone, tried to collect her dazed senses and fix upon some plan of action. Should she still attempt to escape, or should she trust the youth who had just announced himself to be Coacoochee, the friend of her brother? Of course, he must belong to the band that had recently held her captive, though she had not seen him among them. What should she do? Which way should she turn?

In her terror, Anstice was unconsciously asking these questions aloud, though her only answers were the night sounds of the forest. Suddenly there came to her ears the crash of rifles, accompanied by the blood-chilling Seminole war-cry, and followed by fierce yells, shrieks of mortal agony, and the other horrid sounds of a death-struggle between man and man, that was evidently taking place but a short distance from her.

The girl sprang to her feet, but, bound to the spot by the horror of those sounds, she listened breathlessly and with strained ears. Had the savages been attacked by a party of whites? It might be. She knew that troops of both regulars and militia were abroad in every direction. Had not she and her brother entertained one of these small war-parties hastening from St. Augustine to join the western army only a short time before? It had been commanded by their friend, Lieutenant Irwin Douglass, who had easily persuaded Ralph Boyd to accompany him as far as Fort King, that he might learn for himself the true state of affairs in the Indian country. Might it not be that one of these detachments, even, possibly, that of Douglass himself, had tracked this band of savages to their hiding-place, and were visiting upon them a terrible but well-merited punishment?

In that case, to fly would be folly; for, with the
Indians defeated, as of course they must be, she
would find safety among the victors.

Thus thinking, and filled with an eager desire to
learn more of the tragedy being enacted so near her,
the girl began to advance, fearfully and cautiously,
in the direction of those appalling sounds. As she
approached the scene of conflict, its noise gradually
died away, until an occasional shout and a confused
murmur of voices were borne to her on the night air.
The short battle was ended, and one side or the other
was victorious; which one, she must discover at all
hazards. A gleam of firelight directed her steps,
and she continued her cautious advance to a point
of river bank, from which, though still concealed by
dark shadows, she could command a full view of the
beach below. There, by the light of the rising
moon, aided by that of the fires, she beheld a scene
so strange that for some minutes she could make
nothing of it.

Two large flat-boats, such as were used by plant-
ers along the river for the transportation of produce
to waiting vessels at its mouth, lay moored to the
bank. One of them seemed to be piled high with
plunder, while the other was filled with a dark mass
of humanity, from which came a medley of voices
speaking with the unmistakable accent of negroes.
Anstice could see that these had been captives, as,
two at a time, they stepped ashore, where the ropes

confining them were severed by flashing knives in the hands of dusky figures, apparently Indians. A number of motionless forms lay on the beach, and some of the others seemed to be examining these, going from one to another, and spending but a few moments with each one.

The girl gazed anxiously, but full of bewilderment and with a heavy heart, at these things. Where were the whites she had so confidently expected to see? She could not discover one. All of those on the beach, dead as well as living, appeared to be either Indians or negroes. What could it mean? Did Indian fight with Indian? She had never heard of such a thing in Florida.

As she looked and wondered with ever-sinking heart, and filled with despairing thoughts, she was attracted by the voice of an Indian who, near one of the fires, was evidently issuing an order to the others. She imagined him to be the one who had appeared to her a short time before, and called himself "Coacoochee," but she could not be certain. In striving to obtain a better view of his face, she incautiously stepped forward to a projecting point of the bank. In another moment the treacherous soil had loosened beneath her weight, and with frantic but ineffective efforts to save herself, she slid down the sandy face of the bluff to its bottom.

At her first appearance, the startled savages seized their guns, and nerved themselves for an attack;

but, on discovering how little cause there was for
alarm, they remained motionless, though staring
with amazement at the unexpected intruder.

Poor Anstice was not only filled with fresh ter-
rors, but was covered with confusion at the absurd-
ity of her situation.   Ere she could regain her feet,
the Indian who seemed to be in command sprang
forward and assisted her to rise.

"My white sister came too quickly," he said
gravely; "she should have stayed in the shadow of
the itto micco [magnolia] till the time for coming.
It is not good for her to see such things."   Here
the speaker swept his arm over the battle-ground.
"Since she has come," he continued, "Coacoochee
will deliver the words of Ralph Boyd —"

At this moment he was interrupted by a joyful
cry, a rush of footsteps, and Letty, the maid, sobbing and laughing in a breath, came flying up the
beach, to fling her arms about the neck of her
beloved young mistress.   She was followed by old
Primus, hobbling stiffly, and uttering pious ejacula-
tions of thankfulness.   Behind him crowded the
entire force of the plantation, men, women, and children, all shouting with joy at the sight of "Missy
Anstice."

The stern-faced warriors watched this scene with
indulgent smiles, for they knew that the sunny-
haired girl, looking all the fairer in contrast with
the sable-hued throng about her, was the sister of

the white man who had so befriended their young war-chief.

"What does it all mean?" cried Anstice, at length disengaging herself from Letty's hysterical embrace. "What was the cause of the firing I heard but a short while since? Who are those yonder?" Here she pointed with a shudder at the motionless forms lying prone on the sands. "Surely they must be Indians, and yet, I knew not that the hand of the red man was lifted against his fellows."

"They are not of the Iste-chatte [red man], but belong to the Iste-hatke [white man]," answered Coacoochee, gravely.

"Dey's white debbils painted wif blackness," muttered old Primus.

"They are white men, Miss Anstice, disguised like Injuns," explained Letty, whose style of conversation, from long service as lady's maid, was superior to her station. "And oh, Miss Anstice! they were going to take us down the river to sell us into slavery. We wouldn't believe they could be white men, but the paint has been washed from the faces of some of them, and now we know it is so."

Gradually, by listening to one and another who volunteered information, Anstice Boyd learned that the supposed savages, whose prisoner she had been, were indeed a party of white slave-catchers, disguised in paint and feathers, so that their deeds of

rascality might be laid to the Seminoles. Coacoochee, to relieve the anxiety of Ralph Boyd, who lay
wounded and helpless in an Indian village, had set
forth with a small band of warriors to escort his
friend's sister to a place of safety, among people of
her own race. He found the plantation deserted,
and, coming across the trail of the marauders who
had captured its occupants, quickly discovered their
true character by many unmistakable signs.

When they encamped for the night, the vengeful
eyes of his warriors were upon them; and when, for
their own safety, they freed their white prisoners and
drove them away to spread the report of this fresh
Indian outrage, these were allowed to pass through
the Seminole line without molestation. Coacoochee
alone followed Anstice Boyd beyond ear-shot of the
camp, to assure her of friendly aid and safety; then
he returned to deal out to the white ruffians their
well-deserved punishment.

He would not fire on them while they and the
blacks whom they proposed to turn into property
were mingled together; but when the latter were
bound and driven into the boats, he gave the terrible
signal. More than half the painted band fell at the
first fire; the remainder, with the exception of the
leader and two others, who escaped in a canoe, were
quickly despatched, and the deed of vengeance was
completed.

In view of these occurrences, and with the cer-

tainty that troops would be sent in pursuit of Coacoochee's band, to which all the recent aggressions
would of course be credited, the young chief no
longer deemed it prudent to attempt to escort his
friend's sister to the vicinity of any white settlement.
He proposed instead to carry her to her brother.

The girl accepted this plan, provided she might be
accompanied by her maid Letty, a condition to which
the young Indian readily agreed.

During the few hours that remained of the night,
Anstice and her maid slept the sleep of utter weariness in the carriage that had brought them to that
place, and with the earliest dawn were prepared to
start toward the Seminole stronghold, deep hidden
among Withlacoochee swamps.

CHAPTER XXV

On the morning following that midnight tragedy of the wilderness, the Indians made haste to retreat to that portion of the country which they still called their own. The flat-boats were used to carry themselves, their negro allies, and such of the plunder as could be readily transported to the opposite side of the river; the cattle and horses were made to swim across. Such of the plunder collected by the white renegades as must be left behind was burned. Among all the property thus acquired by the Indians, none was more highly prized than the gorgeous costumes of the theatrical company. The unfortunate actors had been forced to abandon these in their hurried flight, and now Coacoochee's grim-faced warriors wore them with startling effect.

Anstice Boyd could not help smiling at the fantastic appearance thus presented by her escort, though feeling that the circumstances in which she was placed warranted anything rather than smiles or light-heartedness. Was her brother really wounded, and was she being taken to him, or were those only

190

plausible tales to lure her away beyond chance of rescue?

"Can we trust him, Letty? Has he told us the truth?" she asked of her maid, indicating Coacoochee with a slight nod.

"Law, yes, Miss Anstice! You can always trust an Injun to tell you the truth, for they hasn't learned how to lie; that is, them as has kept away from white folks hasn't. As for that young man, he has an honest face, and I believe every word he says. He'll take us straight to Marse Ralph, I know he will."

Comforted by this assurance, Anstice crossed the river with a lighter heart than she had known for days. When, on the other side, and mounted on a spirited pony she was allowed to dash on in advance of the strange cavalcade that followed her, she began to experience an hitherto unknown thrill of delight in the wild freedom of the forest life unfolding before her.

Soon after leaving the river, the Indians began to divide into small parties, each of which took a different direction, thus making a number of divergent trails well calculated to baffle pursuit. The negroes also separated into little companies, all of which were to be guided to a common rendezvous, where, under the leadership of old Primus, they promised to remain until "Marse" Boyd should again return to the plantation and send for them.

Thus Anstice and her maid finally found themselves escorted only by Coacoochee and two other warriors. Pushing forward with all speed, this little party reached, at noon of the second day, the bank of a dark stream that flowed sluggishly through an almost impenetrable cypress swamp. One of the Indians remained here with the horses, while the rest of the party embarked in one of several canoes that had been carefully hidden at this point.

Urged on by the lusty paddles of Coacoochee and his companion, this craft proceeded swiftly for nearly a mile up the shadowy stream. Not even the noonday sun could penetrate the dense foliage that arched above them. Festoons of vines depended like huge serpents from interlacing branches, and funereal streamers of gray moss hung motionless in the stagnant air. The black waters swarmed with great alligators, that showed little fear of the canoe, and gave it reluctant passage. Strange birds, water-turkeys with snake-like necks, red-billed cormorants, purple galinules, and long-legged herons, startled from their meditations by the dip of paddles, flapped heavily up stream in advance of the oncoming craft, with discordant cries.

Upon such slender threads hang the fate of nations and communities as well as that of individuals, that, but for these brainless water-fowl, flying stupidly up the quiet river and spreading with harsh voices the news that something had frightened them, the whole course of the Seminole war might have been changed. As it was, a single Indian, who was cautiously making his way down stream in a small canoe, hugging the darkest shadows, and casting furtive glances on all sides, was quick to make use of the information thus furnished.

As the squawking birds redoubled their cries at sight of him, he turned his canoe quickly and drove it deep in among the cypresses at one side, so that it was completely hidden from the view of any who might pass up or down the river.

This Indian, who was known as Chitta-lustee (the black snake), had hardly gained the hiding-place from which he peered out with eager eyes, before the craft containing Coacoochee and his little party swept into view around a bend, and slipped swiftly past him. The keen eye of the young war-chief did not fail to note the floating bubbles left by the paddle of the spy, but attributed them to an alligator, or to some of the innumerable turtles that were constantly plumping into the water from half-submerged logs as the canoe approached. So he paid no attention to them, but a minute later guided his slender craft across the river, and into an opening so concealed by low-hanging branches, that one unfamiliar with its location might have searched for it in vain.

This was what Chitta-lustee had been doing, and for the discovery, made now by accident, he had

o

been promised a fabulous reward in *whiskey*. There were renegades among the Seminoles as well as among the whites, and of these the Black Snake was one. Seduced from his allegiance to those of his own blood by an unquenchable thirst for the white man's fire-water, he had sold himself, body and soul, to the enemies of his race.

General Scott, who had succeeded to the command of the army in Florida, was bending all his energies toward breaking up the Indian strongholds amid the swampy labyrinths of the Withlacoochee. Of these, the most important was that of Osceola. No white man had ever seen it, and but few Seminoles outside of the band occupying it had penetrated its mysteries. Therefore the entire force of renegades, *friendly Indians* the whites called them, some seventy in number, drawn from the band of that traitor chief who had been bribed to agree to removal, were now engaged in a search for these secluded camps, while liberal rewards had been promised for the discovery of any one of them. Goods to the amount of one hundred dollars, and one of the chiefships from which General Wiley Thompson had deposed the rightful holders, would be given to him who should lead the troops to the stronghold of Osceola. Chitta-lustee cared little for the honor of chiefship, but dazzled by a vision of one hundred dollars' worth of fire-water, which was the only class of white man's goods for which he longed, he made up his mind to discover the hidden retreat of the Baton Rouge, or perish in the attempt.

For many days had he skulked in the swamps, repeatedly passing the concealed entrance to which Coacoochee had now unwittingly guided him, without seeing it. As he noted the marks by which it might be identified, he gloated over the prize that seemed at length within his grasp and awaited impatiently the evening shadows that should enable him to make further explorations.

In the meantime, the canoe from which Anstice Boyd was casting shuddering glances at the sombre scenes about her, continued for a short distance up a serpentine creek, so narrow as to barely afford it passage, and was finally halted beside a huge, moss-grown log. This, half-buried in the ooze of the swamp, afforded a landing-place, at which the party disembarked. As they did so, Coacoochee turned to the English girl, and said:

"The eye of the Iste-hatke has never looked upon this place. Ralph Boyd knows it not, for he was brought here in darkness. Will my sister keep its secret hidden deep in her own bosom, where no enemy of the Iste-chatte shall ever find it?"

To this query Anstice replied: "Coacoochee, as you deal with me, so will I deal by you. Take me in safety to my brother, and your secret shall be safe with me forever."

"Un-cah! It is good," replied the young Indian.

"Now let us go. Step only where I step, and let
the black girl step only where you step, for the trail
is narrow."

And narrow it proved. Other logs, felled at
right angles to the first, and sunk so deep in treacherous mud that their upper surface was often under
water, formed a precarious pathway to a strip of
firmer land. This natural causeway, to step from
which was to be plunged in mud as black and soft
as tar, besides being almost as tenacious, led for
nearly half a mile to an island that rose abruptly
from the surrounding swamp.

This island was apparently completely covered
with an impenetrable growth of timber and underbrush laced together by a myriad of thorny vines.
The only trail by which the formidable barricade
might be penetrated was not opposite the end of the
causeway, but lay at some distance, to one side, where
it was carefully concealed from all but those who
would die rather than reveal its secret. Even when
it was once entered, its windings were not easy
to trace. But its perplexities were short, and
after a few rods the pathway ended abruptly in a
scene so foreign to that from which it started, that
it seemed to belong to another world. Instead of
the funereal gloom, the slime, the rank growth, and
crowding horrors of the great swamp, here was a
cleared space, acres in extent, bathed in sunlight,
and alive with cheerful human activity.

On the highest point of land, beneath a clump of stately trees, stood a cluster of palmetto-thatched huts, some open on all sides, and others enclosed; but all raised a foot or two from the ground, so as to allow of a free circulation of air beneath them. In and about these swarmed a happy, busy population. Warriors, whose naked limbs exhibited the firm outlines of bronze statues, cleaned or mended their weapons. Groups of laughing women, cleanly in person, attractive to look upon, and modestly clad, prepared food or engaged in other domestic duties; while rollicking bands of chubby children shouted shrilly over games that differed little from those of other children all over the world. Stretching away from the village were broad fields of corn and cane, amid which yams, pumpkins, and melons grew with wonderful luxuriance. These fields were cared for by negroes, who dwelt in their own quarters, and worked the productive land on shares, that frequently brought larger returns to them than to the red-skinned proprietors of the soil.

This was the swamp stronghold of Osceola, to which Coacoochee and Louis had retreated after the battle of the Withlacoochee, bringing with them the unconscious form of Ralph Boyd, the Englishman friend of the enslaved and champion of the oppressed.

In common with most of the whites, this young man had underrated both the numbers and courage of the Seminoles, and had not believed they would dare fight, even for their homes, against United States troops. It was only upon penetrating their country with General Clinch's army that Ralph Boyd realized how bitter was to be the struggle and that it was already begun. He had been shot down quite early in the battle at the river-crossing and lay on the field unnoticed until found by the one Indian who was inclined to save his life rather than take it.

When the wounded man next opened his eyes, he found himself lying on a couch of softest skins, amid surroundings so foreign to anything he had ever known that for awhile he was confident he was dreaming. Then as the well-remembered form of Coacoochee bent anxiously over him, a memory of recent events flashed into his mind. He realized that an Indian war with all its attendant horrors was sweeping over the land, and recalled the fact that his sister Anstice was alone and unprotected on the plantation by the St. John's. Weakly he strove to rise, but fell back with a groan.

"My brother must rest," said Coacoochee, chidingly. "He is among friends, and there is no cause for uneasiness. Here there is no white man to shoot him from behind."

"I care not for myself," murmured the sufferer. "It is my sister, left without one to protect her or guide her to a place of safety. I must go to her."

Again he attempted to rise, but was gently restrained by the young Indian, who said :

"Let not my brother be troubled. Coacoochee
will go in his place and guide the white maiden to
a safe shelter."

"Will you, Coacoochee? Will you do this thing
for me?" exclaimed Boyd, a faint color flushing his
pale cheeks.

"Un-cah," answered the young war-chief. "This
very hour will I go, and when I come again I will
bring a token from the white maiden who dwells
by the great river."

CHAPTER XXVI

TWO SPIES AND THEIR FATE

COACOOCHEE had fulfilled his promise, and conducted the sister of his friend to a place of safety. As he entered the village followed closely by the first white girl that many of its inmates had ever seen, they gazed wonderingly and in silence at the unaccustomed spectacle. Even the voices of the children were so suddenly hushed that Ralph Boyd, tossing wearily on his narrow couch in one of the enclosed huts, noted the quick cessation of sounds to which he had become wonted, and awaited its explanation with nervous impatience. The old Indian woman who acted as his nurse stepped outside, and for the moment he was alone. Filled with an intense desire to know what was taking place, the wounded man strove to rise, with the intention of crawling to the door of the hut; but ere he could carry out his design, the curtain of deerskins that closed it was thrust aside, and Coacoochee stood before him.

With a feeble shout of joy at sight of his friend, the sufferer exclaimed tremulously: " Is she safe ? Have you brought a token from her ? "

"The white maiden is safe, and I have brought a token," answered the young Indian, proudly.

As he spoke, he moved aside, and in another moment Anstice Boyd, sobbing for joy, was kneeling beside her brother, with her arms about his neck.

From that moment Ralph Boyd's recovery was sure and rapid, for there are no more certain cures for any wound than careful nursing and a relief from anxiety. Within a week he was not only able to sit up, but to take short walks about the village, the strange life of which he studied with never-failing interest. So well ordered and peaceful was it, so filled with cheerful industry, that it was difficult to believe it a dwelling-place of those who were even then engaged in fighting for their homes and rights. But evidences that such was the case were visible on all sides. War-parties were constantly going and coming. Osceola, now head chief of this particular band, and one of the leading spirits of the war, was away most of the time, hovering about the flanks of some army, cutting off their supplies, killing, burning, and destroying; here to-day, and far away to-morrow, spreading everywhere the terror of his name.

Coacoochee would fain have been engaged in similar service; but his own band of warriors under the temporary leadership of Louis Pacheco, was operating far to the eastward, between the St. John's and the coast, while he felt pledged to remain with his

white friends until Ralph Boyd could be removed to
a place of greater safety.   He feared to leave them ;
for among the inmates of the camp were certain
vindictive spirits who so hungered for white scalps
that they made frequent threats of what would hap-
pen to the brother and sister, whom they regarded
as captives, in case they had their way with them.
So the young war-chief restrained his longings for
more active service, and devoted himself to collecting
great quantities of corn and other supplies, which he
stored in this swamp stronghold for future use.

When not waiting on her brother, Anstice amused
herself by observing the domestic life of the village
and in cultivating an acquaintance among its women
and children. · The former were so shy that she
made but little headway with them.   In fact, her
maid Letty was far more popular among the Indian women than she.   With the children, however,
Anstice became an object for adoration almost from
the moment of her appearance among them.   So
devoted were they to her that she could not walk
abroad without an attendant throng of sturdy ur-
chins or naked toddlers.   .

One drowsy afternoon, leaving her brother asleep
in a hammock woven of tough swamp grasses, Anstice, accompanied by her usual escort of children
and with a slim little maiden clinging to each
hand, visited a dense thicket near the pathway
leading out to the great swamp, in search of bead-

like palmetto berries, which she proposed to string into necklaces. Seating herself on the edge of the forest growth, she despatched several of the children in search of the coveted berries. Diving under the bushes and threading their tangled mazes like so many quail, these quickly disappeared from view, though shouts of laughter plainly indicated their movements.

Suddenly a scream of childish terror was uttered close at hand, and a little lad, trembling with fright, came running back to where Anstice was sitting. Filled with a dread of wild beasts or deadly serpents, the girl sprang to her feet, and making use of the few Seminole words she had acquired while in the village, called loudly :

"At-tess-cha, che-paw-ne ! At-tess-cha, mastchay !" (Come here, boys! come here quickly!)

The quality of terror in her voice rather than the words themselves must have attracted attention, for while there came no answer, the children's shouts were suddenly hushed. Each embryo warrior dropped to the ground where he was, and like hunted rabbits, lay motionless, but keenly alert, until they should learn from which direction danger might be expected. Those who had remained with Anstice clung to her skirts, and the urchin who had given the alarm glanced fearfully behind him.

As the girl stood irresolute, there came a movement in the bushes close at hand. Then to her amazement, her name was called softly, but in a voice whose accents she would have recognized anywhere and under all circumstances. It needed not the parting of the leafy screen and a glimpse of the anxious face behind it, to tell her that Irwin Douglass, the lieutenant of dragoons, who had so often shared the hospitality of her brother's table, had, by some inconceivable means, penetrated the secrets of this Indian stronghold and ventured within its deadly confines.

"Oh, Mr. Douglass!" she cried, in a voice trembling with apprehension. "How came you here? Do you not realize your awful peril? You will be killed if you stay a minute longer! Fly, then! Fly, I beg of you, while there is yet time."

"But, Miss Boyd! Anstice! why are you here instead of safe in Augustine as we thought? Are you not in equal, or even in greater, peril? Come with me, and I will gladly beat a retreat, but I cannot leave you to the mercy of the savages. This place is infested by an overwhelming force of troops, who only await my return to make an attack. The Indians will surely kill you rather than allow you to be rescued."

"No! No! I am in no peril!" replied the agitated girl. "I am here of my own free will, and shall be safe in any event. But you! If you value your life! If you love — "

Just then two grim warriors appeared as though they had dropped from the sky, one on either side of Douglass, and in spite of a mighty struggle for freedom, made him their prisoner. One of the children had sped to the village. Coacoochee, with several followers, had taken the trail, and closed in from two sides on Anstice and the lieutenant, while they were too full of amazement at each other's presence in that place to note the stealthy approach.

As two of the Indians seized the young officer, the others sprang after a retreating form they had just discovered skulking through the forest. It was that of Chitta-lustee, the spy, who had carried the news of his finding of this stronghold to Fort King. From there he had guided a body of troops back to the log landing, whence he had been sent, in company with Lieutenant Douglass, to note the exact state of affairs in the village before an attack should be ordered. Together they had crept undetected to a place from which they could command a fair view of the village, and estimate the force of its defenders, which at that moment did not number more than a dozen warriors.

The spies were about to retire from their dangerous position when prevented by the approach of Anstice and her retinue of children. One of these had chanced upon their hiding-place, and while Douglass pleaded with the English girl to seize this opportunity for escape from what he imagined to be a terrible captivity, his companion was trying to secure his own safety by slowly and noiselessly creeping away. He had gained a fair distance, and was beginning to move more rapidly, when discovered by Coacoochee, who, followed by the other warriors, immediately sprang in pursuit.

Down to the edge of the swamp and out on the narrow causeway fled the spy, and after him, like hound in full view of his quarry, leaped the avenger. It was a terrible race along that slender path, slippery with slime and water. Chitta-lustee flung away his rifle, and, with breath coming in panting gasps, ran for his life. A few rods more, and he would be safe.

Coacoochee, reckless of consequences, and filled with a fierce determination to destroy, at all hazards, this most dangerous enemy of his people, only clenched his teeth more tightly, and leaped forward with an increase of speed, as he detected a glint of weapons directly ahead, and realized that the farther end of the causeway was already occupied by troops. He bore only a light spear that he had snatched up at the first alarm, and, with all his skill, he must be at least within twenty yards of a mark ere he could hurl it effectively.

He was still one hundred yards away, and now he could distinguish the uniforms of those who were advancing to meet the panting fugitive. Those who followed the young chief were halting doubtfully. To them it seemed that he was rushing toward certain destruction. They could not restrain him. To follow his example and throw their lives away uselessly would be worse than folly. So they stayed their steps, and watched the fearful race with fascinated gaze.

Only for a moment, and then all was over. Chitta-lustee slipped and stumbled on one of the water-soaked logs at the end of the causeway. As he recovered himself, there came a flash of darting steel, and the keen blade of a hurtling spear, flung with the utmost of Coacoochee's nervous strength, sunk deep between his shoulders. With a choking cry, and out-flung arms, the traitor pitched headlong into the black waters, and disappeared forever, while cries of horror came from the advancing soldiers whose protection he had so nearly gained.

Even as the young war-chief delivered his deadly blow, and without waiting to note its effect, he turned and fled toward his own people. A dozen angry rifles rang out behind him, and the whole swamp echoed with fierce yells from the enraged soldiers, but no bullet struck him, and no taunt served to stay his steps.

The three Indians fled swiftly as hunted deer, back along the treacherous trail, while the troops followed with what speed they might. It was so difficult a path, and so dangerous, and the heavy-booted soldiers slipped from its narrow verge so often, that

those whom they pursued reached the island and
disappeared among its thickets ere they had more
than started. Then back through the heavy air
came mockingly and defiantly the Seminole war-
cry:

"Yo-ho-ee yo-ho-ee yo-ho-ee-chee!"

Thus they knew that a surprise of the stronghold they had so labored to gain was no longer
possible.

Still with a courage worthy of a nobler cause
the troops pushed forward, unguided save by instinct and a burning desire to avenge the death of
their well-loved lieutenant, whom they supposed the
savages had already killed. With all their efforts it
was a full half-hour ere the advance drew near to
the wooded island that rose silent and mysterious
before them, and they began to feel firmer ground
beneath their feet.

Before they reached its encircling forest wall,
flashes of flame began to leap from the dark thickets,
and before the deadly fire of an unseen foe the advance was staggered and halted. It was only for a
moment, and then they sprang forward with a cheer
to charge the fatal barricade.

A dozen troopers had fallen ere the Indian fire
was silenced, and as yet the soldiers had not caught
a glimpse of their foe. In the thickset undergrowth
they were tripped and flung to the ground by snake-
like roots, encircled and held fast by tough vines,

clutched and drawn backward by stout thorns curved and sharp as a tiger's claws. No human being save a naked Indian could thread that forest maze, and as the soldiers could discover no opening through it, they decided to make one. Swords, axes, and knives were called into requisition. Every now and then a rifle shot from the unseen foe proved the Indians to be still watchful and defiant.

It was not until another half-hour had been expended in this exhausting effort at road-cutting that the trail lying well to one side was discovered.

Wearied by their futile efforts, made furious by opposition, and galled by the fire from unseen rifles that had been steadily thinning their numbers ever since they reached the island, the troops rushed with fierce shouts to the opening, streamed through it, and gained the central, cleared space in which stood the Seminole village. Here, for a moment, the tumultuous advance was checked, and each man clutched his weapon with a closer grip, in expectation of an attack.

But none was made. The peaceful village, all aglow with the light of a setting sun, was silent and deserted. No voices came from it, nor from the broad fields that lay clothed in luxuriant verdure beyond. There was no sound of busy workers, no laughter of children. A raven with glossy plumage, iridescent in the sunlight, croaked a hoarse challenge from a lofty tree-top, and a solitary buzzard circled

P

overhead on motionless pinions, but no other signs of life were to be detected.

After a minute of irresolution Captain Chase, the officer in command of the expedition, deployed his men as skirmishers, and was about to give the order "Forward!" when this strange thing happened:

From one of the thatched huts of the village three human beings emerged and advanced slowly toward the motionless line of soldiers. Two were men, evidently white men, and one of these wore a uniform. Between them walked a young girl whose shapely head was crowned with a mass of gold-red hair. As she drew near, a murmur of admiration at her beauty passed along the stern line of blue-coated troops. Then an irrepressible tumult of cheers rent the air, for in one of the girl's companions the soldiers recognized their own beloved lieutenant, Irwin Douglass. But curiosity got the better of enthusiasm, and as the noise subsided, each trooper waited in breathless silence for an explanation of this strange encounter.

CHAPTER XXVII

ANSTICE BOYD SAVES THE LIFE OF A CAPTIVE

WHILE Coacoochee was engaged in his fierce pursuit of the traitor Seminole across the black causeway, Irwin Douglass was led to the village, where he was securely bound to one of the great trees by which it was shaded. Here his captors left him, and seizing their rifles hastened back to the edge of the swamp.

The moment Anstice realized that the young soldier, though a captive, was not doomed to instant death, she flew back to the hut occupied by her brother, whom she found still quietly sleeping in his grass-woven hammock. Roused into a startled wakefulness by her abrupt entrance, the convalescent was for some moments at a loss to comprehend what she was saying or what had caused her excitement.

"Who do you say is captured? and what has happened, dear, to frighten you?" he asked, in a bewildered tone.

"Irwin Douglass, and they are going to kill him, and the village is about to be attacked, and we shall all be murdered!" cried the terrified girl.

"Douglass captured and about to be killed? Impossible!" exclaimed Boyd, rising and starting toward the doorway. "But I will go and see. Surely Coacoochee would never murder a prisoner in cold blood. As for ourselves, you know we are safe so long as we are his guests. Wait here, sister, and I will bring Douglass back with me, if, as you say, he is in the village."

But the frightened girl clung to him and would not be left. So they set forth together, and had hardly gained the outer air before a sound of firing from the causeway warned them that fighting of some sort was begun. The same sounds created vast excitement among the inmates of the village, and the crowd of negroes, who, at the first note of alarm, had come swarming up from the fields. These so occupied the entire foreground that the brother and sister could get no sight of him whom they sought. Neither was their friend the young war-chief to be seen. They attempted to make way through the throng, but were impatiently pushed back, the crowd scowling and muttering at them angrily.

One huge, coal-black negro even advanced upon them with a drawn knife and so ugly an expression, that Ralph Boyd instinctively thrust his sister behind him, and nerved himself to receive an attack. Unarmed and weakened by illness as he was, the outcome of such a struggle could readily be foreseen, and the white man cast a despairing glance about him in search of some weapon. There was none, and the gleaming knife was already uplifted for a deadly stroke, when, with a shrill cry, a black woman sprang betwixt the two, snatched the knife from the negro's hand, and flourishing it in his face, poured out such a furious torrent of angry, scornful, and threatening words, that the brute slunk away from her, completely cowed.

Now, turning and almost pushing Boyd and his sister before her, Letty — for the black Amazon was no other than Anstice's own maid — succeeded in getting them back inside the hut before their assailant had time to rally from his discomfiture. Then, still clutching the knife she had so adroitly captured, the black girl stood guard before the entrance, deaf alike to those of her own color, who taunted her with being a traitor to her race, and to the entreaties of her young mistress, that she should attempt a rescue of the prisoner about whom the crowd of Indian women and negroes still swarmed.

"Cayn't do it, Miss Anstice," replied the black girl, firmly, but without turning her head. "I'se powerful sorry for Marse Douglass, but when it's him or you, I know which one I'se bound to look after."

"But, Letty, they will murder him!"

"No, Miss Anstice, not till Coacoochee says so. They das'n't kill him, not till the chief gives the word."

"But supposing Coacoochee does not come? He may be killed or captured himself, you know."

"There ain't no use speculating on that, Miss Anstice, because he's come already. I can see him out there now, talking to the crowd. Looks like he's in a powerful hurry, too, and I spec's the end of time has come for poor Marse Douglass. Oh Lord, Miss Anstice! Stop up your ears, quick!"

At these ominous words, the brave English girl, instead of complying, darted from the hut so swiftly, that ere Letty could interfere to prevent her, she had gained the centre of the village. There she came upon a scene well calculated to freeze the blood in her veins. Irwin Douglass, bound to a tree, with his pale, resolute face turned toward the setting sun, gazed with unflinching calmness into the black muzzles of four levelled rifles, that in another moment would pour their deadly contents into his body. The pitiless warriors who held them, and only awaited a signal from their young chief to press the fatal triggers, scanned the face of their victim in vain for the faintest trace of fear. There was none; and they were filled with regrets that so brave a man could not be reserved for a more lingering and trying form of death. But there was no time to spare. The soldiers were even now upon them, and whatever was to be done must be done quickly. Already murmurs of impatience could be heard among the spectators.

As Coacoochee was about to give the dread command, there came a quick rush, and the girlish figure of Anstice Boyd stood full in front of the cruel rifles, between them and their human mark. Her wonderful hair, half loosed from its coil, glinted like spun gold in the red sunlight. Her eyes were big with terror, and her face was bloodless, but her voice rang out clear and strong, as she cried:

"Coacoochee, you must not do this thing! You dare not!"

"He is an enemy," answered the young chief, calmly; and without betraying his annoyance at this interruption. "If we should not kill him, he would kill us."

"He might in battle or in fair fight, but he would never shoot down a helpless prisoner," replied the girl, in scornful tones. "Set him free, place a weapon in his hands, and fight him man to man, if you dare."

"Gladly would I," answered the young Seminole, "if there was time, but there is not. Thy people have hunted us like wolves to our den, and even now are upon us. In another minute must we fly for our lives. Our friends we can leave to their friends. Our captive we cannot take, and dare not release. He is a spy. The white man puts a spy to death; why should not the Indian? Coacoochee has spoken. The spy must die. Let my white sister stand aside."

Very stern was the young war-chief, and very determined. A murmur of approbation rose from the dusky throng about him as his words fell upon their ears.

A wave of despair surged over Anstice Boyd. Her face flushed, then became deadly pale. Her voice was well-nigh choked as she answered:

"Then, oh, Coacoochee, if you will not yield to the dictates of humanity, still listen to me. In the name of Allala, thy spirit sister, in the name of her who still lives, and is most dear to thee, in the name of Ralph Boyd, who, by his deeds, has proved himself thy friend, I plead for this man's life. If this is not enough, I demand it for yet another reason." Here, with face crimsoned like the rising sun, the girl stepped close to the young chief, and spoke a few words in a tone so low that none but he could catch their import.

His stern face softened, and for a moment he looked curiously at her. Then drawing his own silver-mounted knife from its sheath, he handed it to her, saying:

"The words of the white maiden have sunk deep into the heart of Coacoochee. Let her lead him whom she has saved to the lodge of her brother. Keep him there, close hidden from my people, so long as a voice is heard in this place. Then, and not till then, will it be safe for the Iste-hatke to venture forth. Farewell, my sister! Thank not

THE GIRL STEPPED CLOSE TO THE YOUNG CHIEF AND SPOKE A FEW WORDS.

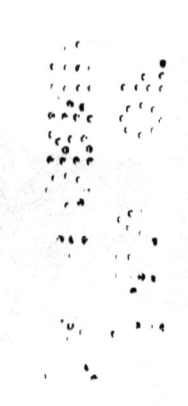

the wild cat that his claws are sheathed. Thank
rather Allala, Nita, and Ralph Boyd. *Hi-e-pas!*
Hi-e-pas!"

The last two words were uttered in ringing tones
of command to his own people, and, supplemented
as they were by a crashing volley of musketry from
the edge of the swamp, they produced an instant
effect.

Although many glances of hate were flashed at
the white girl and the prisoner, whom she freed
from his bonds with two strokes of Coacoochee's
keen knife, they were allowed to pass unharmed to
the hut occupied by Ralph Boyd. He walked with
them ; for, without his sister's knowledge, he had
stood close by her side while she pleaded for the
life of Irwin Douglass, ready to strike a blow in
her defence, or to share her fate.

The three entered the hut together, and as its
curtain of deerskin was drawn so as to exclude all
prying eyes, the overwrought girl fell into her
brother's arms, weeping hysterically. The young
soldier, who but a moment before stood within the
shadow of death, gazed curiously and awkwardly
for a second on this scene, and then turning away,
sat down with his face buried in his hands.

Ralph Boyd sought to calm his brave sister
with loving words. So filled was each of the three
with crowding emotions that they took no note of
time nor of outside sounds, until at length the girl

ceased her sobbing and gazed with a smile into her
brother's face. Then, with a weight lifted from
his heart, he began to talk to her in a cheerful
strain.

"It was nobly done, sister mine," he said, "and
as a special pleader I will name you before any
barrister in the land. What argument, though, was
it you used at the last? I failed to catch the words,
but they must have been of powerful force."

Again a tide of crimson mantled the girl's fair
cheeks, as she replied: "Coacoochee knows, and I
know; but let it suffice you, brother, that they
were effective; for more than that I can never
tell."

At this juncture, the young soldier, looking as
guilty as though he had been caught at eavesdrop-
ping, rose, drew aside the curtain at the entrance,
and stepped outside. As he did so, he uttered an
exclamation that quickly brought the others to his
side.

The village, recently so populous and filled with
busy life, was deserted. Not a soul was to be seen.
Even the pigs and chickens had disappeared. An
unbroken silence, as of an impending doom, brooded
over the place, and, as the three who were now its
sole occupants walked among the vacant habitations,
they felt impelled to lower their voices, as though
in presence of the dead. They had gone but a
short distance when their attention was attracted by

the sound of many voices and the tramp of armed men.   Turning in that direction, they beheld a body of troops pouring from the pathway leading to the swamp, and toward these they at once directed their steps.

As the three whose recent experiences had been so thrilling walked slowly down the grassy slope, Douglass strove to find words with which to thank Anstice Boyd for the gift of his life; but the girl interrupted him at the outset, and begged him never to mention the subject again.

"Very well," he replied, "since that is your desire, I will strive to obey.   I do so the more readily that mere words fail to express my feelings; but I shall live in hope of the time when by some service I may be able to indicate my gratitude."

Whatever else the grateful young soldier might have said was interrupted by cheers from the troops, who at that moment recognized the comrade whom they had mourned as lost to them forever.   As quiet was restored, his brother officers crowded about him with a hearty welcome and an avalanche of questions.

"That will do for the present, gentlemen," interposed Captain Chase.   "Excuse a soldier's abruptness, madam," he added, bowing to Anstice, "but in this stern business of war, duty must precede even the ordinary courtesies of life.   Now, Mr.

Douglass, since you are so happily restored to us, please tell me what to expect in yonder den of swamp devils? Are we to be attacked? Shall we charge. What force opposes us? What is the meaning of this ominous silence?"

"I hardly know how to answer you, sir," replied the lieutenant, "for I am as ignorant concerning the enemy's movements as yourself. So far as I know, there is not a soul in yonder village, though but a few minutes ago it was swarming with life."

"What has become of them, then?" demanded the officer, impatiently.

"I do not know, sir."

"You can at least tell in which direction they went."

"No, sir, I cannot even do that; for I did not see them go, nor do I know when they departed."

"Upon my soul, this is a most extraordinary state of affairs!" exclaimed the officer, flushing angrily. "I must confess that I had not heretofore credited you with blindness. Perhaps, sir, you can give us the desired information?" he added, turning to Ralph Boyd.

Upon the young Englishman claiming an equal ignorance with the lieutenant, the irate captain said in a tone of suppressed anger: "This matter shall be investigated at a more convenient time, but at present it seems that we must make discoveries for ourselves.   To your places, gentlemen. Forward !   Double quick !   March ! "

With this the line of blue-coated troops advanced swiftly up the slope and charged the empty huts of the deserted village.

CHAPTER XXVIII

THE MARK OF THE WILDCAT

In vain did the soldiers ransack the empty huts of the village, and scour the island from end to end. Not a single human being or evidence of life did they discover, nor were they fired upon from the belt of timber surrounding the cleared fields. The hundreds of men, women, and children, Indians and negroes, who had been at home in this place less than an hour before, had vanished as mysteriously and completely as though the earth had opened and swallowed them. Even the secret place of exit through the swamp, provided for just such an emergency as the present, had not been discovered when darkness put an end to the search, and the troops camped in and about the Indian village for the night.

The officer commanding the expedition was furious. He had expected to destroy or capture the entire force of the enemy gathered at this point. Instead of so doing, he had not only failed to capture a single prisoner, but could not discover that his fire had resulted in the killing or even wounding of a single warrior. On the other hand, the dead of his own command numbered seven,

while a score of others were more or less severely
wounded. His anger was in nowise diminished
by what he was pleased to term the culpable ignorance of Lieutenant Douglass concerning the strength
and movements of the Indians.

When questioned on these points, the young
officer, with a delicacy that forbade the part taken
by Anstice Boyd in his rescue becoming common
talk of the camp, would only say that, having been
confined in a closed hut, he had no opportunity of
knowing what was taking place outside.

"Were you bound, blind-folded, or in any other
way deprived of the use of your faculties?" demanded the commander.

"No, sir, I was not."

"In that case it is incredible that you could not
have found some opportunity for making observa-
tions of what was taking place about you ; and that
you failed to do so, must be regarded as a grave
neglect of duty. The very fact that the savages,
having you in their power, presented you with both
life and liberty, would seem to argue a closer sympathy between you and them than is permissible
between an officer of the United States army and
the enemies of his Government. Therefore, sir, I
shall take it upon myself to suspend you from duty,
and shall prefer charges against you which you will
be allowed to meet before a court martial. That is
all, sir. You may go."

" Very good, sir," replied the younger officer, bowing, and retiring with a pale face, and a mind filled
with bitter thoughts.

That night the island seemed a very abode of ma-
licious spirits. Low-hanging clouds covered it with
a veil of darkness so intense as to be oppressive. A
strong wind moaned among the forest trees, and
borne on it from the surrounding swamp came blood-
chilling shrieks and yells, weird and foreboding, but
whether produced by wild beasts or wild men, the
shuddering listeners, gathered closely about flaring
camp-fires, could not determine. So terrible were
some of these wind-borne cries, that certain among
those who listened declared them to be the despairing accents of lost souls; for which sentiment they
were derided by the bolder of their comrades. But
when the midnight relief went its round of the
outposts, and found four of them guarded only by
corpses, even the scoffers were willing to admit that
in the rush of the night wind they had heard the
wings of the angel of death.

As, one after another, the dead sentinels were
brought in to the firelight, they were found to
be without wounds, unless a scratch of five fine
lines on each pallid forehead could be called such.
In each case the cause of death was a broken
neck. From this and the scratches, that looked
as though they might have been made by the brush-
ing of a mighty paw, it was at first thought that

the unfortunate soldiers might have been done to
death by one of the more powerful beasts of the
forest.

This belief was, however, quickly upset by an old
frontiersman who accompanied the troops as a
scout. Pointing out that all the scratches were
located in the same place, and all had been made
with equal lightness of touch, he declared them to
be the mark of Coacoochee the Wildcat.

Already the terror of this name had spread so far,
that when Ralph Boyd asserted that Coacoochee was
indeed leader of the band just driven from that
stronghold, a great fear fell upon the soldiers, and
to a man they refused to perform outpost duty beyond the limit of firelight.

To enlarge this lighted circle, one hut after
another was set on fire, until the whole village,
including the great storehouses full of provisions
and the granaries of corn, was one roaring, leaping mass of flame. The leafy crowns of the giant
oaks that had shaded it, shrivelled, crackled, and
burst into a myriad tongues of fire; while to render
the destruction of the forest monarchs more certain,
some of the soldiers seized axes and girdled their
trunks.

So bright was the circle of light in which the troops
foolishly sought for safety, that had Coacoochee been
leader of one hundred warriors at that moment, he
could have wiped out the entire force of invaders;

Q

but he was alone, and from the black recesses of a thicket he gazed upon the scene of destruction in impotent wrath.

Having seen the band intrusted to his care safely across the great swamp, and well on their way to another place of refuge, he had returned alone to watch the invasion of Osceola's stronghold. With the noiseless movements of a gliding shadow he had skirted the camp of the soldiers, and four times had he left silent but terrible witnesses of his presence. With a heavy heart he now watched the burning of the great stores of food that he had gathered for the support of his people during months of fighting; for he knew that with this destruction a heavy blow had been dealt against the Seminole cause.

With the earliest coming of daylight, the troops, impatient to finish their task and leave that place of terror, began to destroy the growing crops beyond the village. Safe hidden among the spreading branches of a live-oak, where he was screened by great clusters of pale-green mistletoe, Coacoochee watched them tear up acres of tasselled corn, and laden vines, cut down scores of trees heavy with ripening fruit, and burn broad areas of waving cane.

At length, the work of destruction was completed, all stragglers were called in by a blast of bugles, a parting volley was fired over the single long grave, in which a dozen dead soldiers lay buried; and, taking their wounded with them, the blue-coated col-

umn marched gladly away from the place they had
so little reason to love.

Descending from his post of observation, the young
Indian followed them, until he had seen the last
trooper disappear along the narrow causeway, amid
the sombre cypresses of the Great Swamp. Then
slowly and thoughtfully he retraced his steps, walking now in the full glare of sunlight, until he stood
again beneath the clump of dying trees that, but a
few hours before, had shaded the peaceful village.
As he gazed about him on charred embers, and smoking ruins, deserted fields, and prostrate orchards, the
bold heart of the young war-chief sank like a leaden
weight within him.

"Thus must it be to the end," he said half aloud,
as though his brimming thoughts were struggling
for expression. "Ruin and destruction follow ever
the tread of the Iste-hatke. He is strong, and we
are weak. He is many, and we are few. We
may kill his hundreds, and he brings thousands to
devour us. We may plant, but he will gather the
fruit. The Seminole may starve, and at the cry of
his children for food the white man will make
merry. My father was right when he said that to
fight the white man was like fighting the waves of
the great salt waters. What now shall be done?
Shall we continue to fight, and die fighting in our
own land, or shall we again trust to the lying tongue
of the Iste-hatke, and go to the place in which he

says we may dwell at peace with him? Oh, Allala! my sister, hear me, and come to me with thy words of wisdom."

At that moment, as though in answer to his prayer, Coacoochee caught sight of a figure advancing hesitatingly towards where he stood. It was that of a warrior, whom he recognized even at a distance as belonging to his own band. The newcomer cast troubled glances over the pitiful scene of ruin outspread on all sides. Until now he had not noted the presence of his chief; but, when the latter uttered the cry of a hawk, which was the familiar signal of his band, the warrior quickened his steps, and came to where the young man stood.

He proved to be a runner, sent out by Louis Pacheco, to notify Coacoochee that Philip Emathla with all the people of his village had been captured and conveyed to St. Augustine, whence it was proposed to remove them to the unknown land of the far west. The old chief had begged so earnestly for an interview with his eldest son, that the general in command had sent out a written safe-conduct for the latter to come and go again in safety. This the runner now delivered to Coacoochee, assuring him at the same time that Louis Pacheco had looked at it and pronounced it good.

The young chief took the paper, regarded it curiously, and thrust it into his girdle, then without delay, he set forth on his long journey to the eastern coast. The runner was able to inform him of the present location of Osceola, and accordingly he first directed his steps to the camp of that fiery young chieftain to apprise him of the destruction of his swamp stronghold.

Here he found a delegation of Cherokees, bearing an address from John Ross, their head chief, to Coacoochee and Osceola, who were regarded as the most important leaders of the Florida Indians. This address prayed the Seminoles to end their fruitless struggle against the all-powerful whites. It assured them that should they consent to removal, the promises made by the latter would be kept, and that the Cherokees, as their nearest neighbors in the western land, would ever be their firm allies in resistance to further oppression.

The conference was long and earnest. Osceola, discouraged by the loss of his stronghold, and by the destruction of its great store of provisions, which he foresaw would entail much suffering among his people during the coming winter, was inclined to make peace, though still resolutely opposed to removal.

Coacoochee, filled with thoughts of his aged father and Nita Pacheco held captives by the whites, was even more anxious to make an honorable peace than was his brother chieftain. So it was finally decided that he should take advantage of his safe-conduct, to visit St. Augustine, advise with Philip Emathla, talk with the general in command, so as to ascertain the exact views of the whites, and return to Osceola with his report.

Thus, three days later the young war-chief, clad as befitted his rank, and bearing a superb calumet as a present from Osceola, presented himself boldly before the gates of St. Augustine, exhibited his safe-conduct, and demanded to be taken to the general.

The manly beauty of his features, his haughty bearing, and gorgeous costume attracted universal admiration, as he strode proudly through the narrow streets of the quaint old city. Before he reached the house in which the commandant was lodged, he was surrounded by a curious throng of citizens, through which the corporal's guard escorting him found some difficulty in clearing a passage.

The general greeted the son of Philip Emathla with honeyed words, and caused him to be treated with the consideration due his rank and importance. His father was brought to welcome him, and the two were allowed to depart together to the encampment of the captives, which was in the plaza, or central square of the city, where it was surrounded by a cordon of soldiers. Here, after a separation of many months, the young chief met her to whom he had plighted his troth by the blue Ahpopka Lake. In his eyes she appeared more lovely than ever, and he longed ardently for the time of peace that should enable him to make for her a home in which they might dwell together in safety.

So much was there to tell and to hear, and so many grave questions to be discussed, that the night was spent in talking, and the dawn of another day found them still seated about the cold embers of a small fire in front of King Philip's lodge.

The old man advised earnestly for peace, even at the cost of removal, though at the same time declaring that with leaving his own land his heart would break, so that he should never live to reach the strange place set apart for his people.

Nita, happily content to sit close beside her lover, only leaving him now and then to replenish the fire, refill the pipes, or to bring from the lodge some dainty morsel of food, had little to say; but such words as she uttered were in favor of peace.

Thus was the mind of Coacoochee the Wildcat turned from thoughts of fighting and vengeance, to those of peace and happiness for his loved ones, his oppressed people, and himself. So convinced was he that the war must be ended, that he readily consented to go again to Osceola, and persuade him to come in, with such other chiefs as could be gathered, to attend a solemn council, with a view to the speedy settlement of all existing troubles. On leaving the city, he was laden with presents, both for himself and Osceola, and promising to return in ten days, he set forth with a lighter heart than he had known for more than a year.

Alas for human nature, that they who trust most

should be most often deceived! By the swift turning of affairs that gave the army in Florida a new
commanding general every few months during the
Seminole War, General Scott had been succeeded by
General Jesup. From him the commandant at St.
Augustine had recently received a despatch which,
could Coacoochee have known its contents, would
have filled the young chief's heart with renewed
bitterness, and turned his peaceful longings into a
fierce resolve for a fight to the death.

CHAPTER XXIX

TREACHEROUS CAPTURE OF COACOOCHEE AND OSCEOLA

To the great satisfaction of the general of militia commanding at St. Augustine, Coacoochee, unsuspicious of evil, and intent only upon carrying out his avowed purpose of arranging for a new treaty of peace, returned to the city on the exact date he had named. With an honest pride at the success of his negotiations he announced that Osceola, Coa Hadjo, Talmus Hadjo, and others would come in on the following day, and, camping a short distance outside the city, would there await the white commissioners. He also brought information that the Cherokee peace delegation had gone to the westward for a conference with Micanopy and other chiefs.

The general, still treating the young chief with a lofty consideration, thanked him profusely for his services, and asked as a favor that he would guide a wagon-load of provisions, intended as a present for Osceola and his people, to the place selected for their encampment. This, he said, was a small portion of the supply he was collecting for his Indian friends; and, when he went to meet them on the morrow, he

233

should take with him several other wagons laden with provisions, that they might have plenty to eat in case the negotiations were extended over a number of days.

Much pleased by this proof of the white man's thoughtful kindness, Coacoochee willingly consented to act as guide to the first wagon, and then asked that he might visit Philip Emathla's camp while it was being got ready, — a request that was granted, though with evident reluctance.

As the young Indian turned away from the general's quarters, he almost ran into the arms of Ralph Boyd, who had come to St. Augustine with his sister but two days before, intending to remain there until the end of the war should render it safe for them to return to their plantation. While Coacoochee was delighted to thus encounter the only white man whom he could call friend, the young Englishman was more than amazed to meet him amid such surroundings.

"Coacoochee!" he exclaimed. "How is this? why are you here? Is it as a prisoner? Or have you decided to join the winning side, and become an ally of the Americans?"

"I am here neither as a prisoner or a traitor," answered the other, proudly, "but to help in making a peace for my people while they are yet strong enough to insist upon honorable terms."

"And do you trust the man whom you have just

left?" asked Boyd, indicating by a gesture the quarters of the general.

"Yes," replied Coacoochee, slowly. "I trust him, for I must trust him. Without trust on both sides there could be no treaty. Without a treaty the Seminole must be wiped out. My father and others of my people are even now held here as captives, and only through a treaty can their liberty be restored. I go now to see them. Will my white brother go with me?"

"With pleasure. I knew there were Indian prisoners here, but had no idea that your father was among them, or I would have visited him ere this, to congratulate him on having so fine a son. Ah! here is their camp now; but I say, Coacoochee, who is that white girl sitting among the Indian women? By Jove! she is the most beautiful creature I ever saw."

"Her name is Nita Pacheco," answered the young chief, gazing fondly at the girl, who, intent on a bit of sewing, was as yet unaware of his presence.

"Not your Nita! Not the one that you — Why, confound it, man! You never told me she was white. You said she was a —"

"So she is," admitted Coacoochee, very quietly. "She is one of the Iste-lustee, as you were about to say. Her mother was an octoroon, and of every sixteen drops in Nita's veins, one is black. Although she was born free as you or I, she has been claimed as a slave; and Philip Emathla was obliged to pay a large sum of money to establish her freedom. With the ending of this war she will become my chee-hi-wah, or what you would call wife."

"In which case I don't wonder that you are so keen for peace. If I were in your place, I would have it at any price, and I only hope I may speedily have the pleasure of dancing at your wedding. Won't Anstice be pleased, though? Ever since she discovered that you had a sweetheart, she has wished to meet her."

"Would the white maiden take the hand of her who is of the Iste-lustee?" asked Coacoochee, abruptly.

"Oh bother your Iste-lustees! of course she would," cried Boyd. "Not only that, but she would love her dearly. Why, the girl is as white as Anstice herself, and even if she were not, do you suppose that would make any difference? Don't you know that any one precious to you must also be dear to us, who owe you everything, including our lives. Don't you know the meaning of the word 'gratitude'? And don't you suppose we know it, too, you confoundedly proud Seminole, you?"

Ere he finished this speech the Englishman was left alone; for, at the sound of his raised voice, Nita looked up, and flushed so rosily at sight of her lover, that he was drawn to her side as irresistibly as needle to magnet. Then, forgetful of all save each other, they strolled among the lodges of the little encampment.

Suddenly while they walked, Coacoochee started as though he had been shot. In a whisper he bade the girl at his side return to her companions, and as without comment she obeyed him, he stood motionless, his face black with rage, and his whole frame quivering with excitement. The cause of this emotion was a voice coming from the opposite side of a tent that had been appropriated to the especial use of Philip Emathla. The voice was saying :

" They tell me, old man, that you don't savey American ; but I reckin you can understand enough to know what I mean when I say that if you've got any niggers to sell, I'm the man that'll buy them of you, of co'se at a reasonable figger. As things stand now, your travelling expenses are likely to be heavy, and there's two or three wenches in your camp that I'd be willing to stake you something handsome for. There ain't no drop of Injun blood in ary one of them, and they are certain to be took from you, anyway. So you, might as well make something out of 'em while you've got the chance. One of 'em, that Pacheco gal, is mine by rights, anyhow ; but if — "

At this point the speaker uttered a yell of terror, and instinctively reached for his pistol, as with a bound like that of a panther and blazing eyes, Coacoochee leaped upon him. Mr. Troup Jeffers was hurled to the ground with such force that for a moment he lay stunned and motionless. As the Wildcat glared about him for some weapon with which to complete his task, two of the guards rushed in and dragged the slave-trader beyond the lines of the camp. At the same time, Boyd, who had witnessed the scene from a distance, came hurrying up from an opposite direction.

"For Heaven's sake Coacoochee! What does this mean?" he cried; "you'll have a war on your hands right here if you don't look out."

Without answering him, the young Indian turned to Philip Emathla, who was sitting before the tent, and uttered a few hurried words in his own tongue, the purport of which was, "Look well on this man, my father; for he is my friend, whom you can trust as you would me. If he comes to thee for Nita, let her go with him."

Then he and Ralph Boyd hurried away in the direction from which they had come. As they passed the group of women, Coacoochee stopped to whisper in the ear of Nita Pacheco, who was also bidden to trust the white man now before her, and then they passed on.

"That dog, whom I would I had killed," said the young Indian, when they were safely beyond the camp, "is a catcher of slaves, who seeks to steal my promised wife. For this night, I cannot protect her, for I must meet Ah-ha-se-ho-la. If I do not,

he will not stay, and there will be no peace. Before
the setting of to-morrow's sun Coacoochee will be
free to protect his own. For this night, then, I
would have you and the white maiden, thy sister,
give to Nita the shelter of thy lodge; or, if that be
not possible, watch over her and see that she is not
stolen away."

"Certainly, my dear fellow! Of course we will
look out for her as long as you like, and glad of the
chance to thus repay some portion of our indebted-
ness," interrupted Ralph Boyd, heartily. "But who
is the rascally beggar?"

"His name I know not," replied the other; "but
certain things concerning him I do know. He, more
than any other, caused this war between the Iste-
chatte and the white man. He broke up the home
of the Pachecos and sold the mother and brother of
Nita into slavery, as he would now sell her. He
stole and sold into slavery the wife of Osceola."

"The scoundrel!" exclaimed Boyd.

"When my white brother was shot down at the
battle of the Withlacoochee, the bullet came from
behind, and from the rifle of this man."

"What!"

"When the home of my white brother was attacked
by white men, painted to look like the Iste-chatte,
this man was leader of the band. He it was who
took the white maiden, thy sister, captive and left
her to perish in the forest."

" Good Heavens, man ! Do you know what you are talking about ? Can all this be true ? "

" The tongue of Coacoochee is straight. He would not lie to his white brother."

" Yes, but may you not be mistaken ? I did not know I had an enemy in the world, who would thus injure me. Who can it be ? "

" What I have said is true. Does my brother remember talking with a man under a tree the day before the white soldiers reached the ferry of the Withlacoochee, _and speaking scornful words to him ? "

" Yes, though I don't see how you could know of that. I inquired about him and found out his name, which proved to be the same as that of the last overseer on my plantation. I had heard bad accounts of the man, and had him discharged before taking possession."

" This man is the same who talked with my brother under the tree."

" Well, whoever he is, you may be very certain that I shall look into this thing thoroughly, and if I find him to be guilty of half of these things, I will make him suffer sweetly. Meantime, my lad, do you rest easy about your sweetheart. Anstice shall go to her, and for your sake, if not for her own, her safety shall be guarded with our lives."

By this time they had reached again the general's quarters, and the wagon that Coacoochee was to

guide stood in readiness. So, with a warm hand-
clasp, the friends parted, one to go on a mission that
he fondly hoped would bring a lasting peace to his
people, and the other to take measures for the safety
of Nita Pacheco.

According to promise Osceola, escorted by some
seventy warriors, all mounted, and preceded by a
white flag, in token of the peaceful nature of their
mission, arrived promptly at the appointed place of
encampment. There they were met by Coacoochee
with a welcome supply of provisions.

Long and earnestly did the two young chieftains
talk together that night, in planning for the morrow,
on which they believed the fate of their nation would
be decided. On one point they were fully agreed.
The negro allies, who had fought so bravely with
them, and who were as free as themselves, must be
considered as equal with them, and must, in any
negotiations, be granted the same terms as themselves. If this should not be allowed, they would
refuse to make peace, and would return under protection of their white flag, whence they came.

At ten o'clock on the following morning a blare
of trumpets announced the coming of the general.
He was accompanied by a staff of uncommon gor-
geousness, and escorted by one hundred mounted
militiamen, all armed to the teeth. Behind these
rumbled several large, covered wagons similar in
appearance to the one that had brought provisions

R

the evening before. These were halted a short distance away, where they were partially hidden in the palmetto scrub.

Coacoochee, Osceola, Coa Hadjo, and Talmus, arrayed in such finery as befitted the occasion, stood forth to meet the newcomers, while their handful of warriors clustered close behind them. Above their heads fluttered the white flag of truce.

Approaching to within a few yards of them, and utterly ignoring the formalities usual at such a time, and so dear to the heart of an Indian, the general began abruptly to read a list of questions from a paper that he held in his hand. The first of these struck like a blow:

"Are you prepared to deliver up at once all negroes taken from citizens?

" Why have you not done this already?

" Where are the other chiefs, and why have they not surrendered? "

There were other questions of a similar nature, and realizing from these, as well as from the tone of the speaker's voice, that the whites had not come there with any thought of discussing a treaty, Osceola, with a quick glance about him, like a stag brought to bay, attempted to speak, but his voice choked and failed him. He looked appealingly at Coacoochee, as though requesting him to frame an answer; but the son of Philip Emathla stood like one who is stunned.

" You, Powell," continued the general, harshly, " having signed the treaty of Fort King, shall be made to abide by it.

" As for you, Wildcat, I have learned of your recent outrages in the Withlacoochee Swamp. Never again shall you have a chance to murder white men, like the cowardly beast whose name you bear."

Thus saying, the speaker waved his arm, a loud command rang out, there came a rush through the palmettoes, a clash of weapons, and the too trusting Seminoles found themselves hemmed in on all sides by a hedge of glittering bayonets.

A strong body of infantry, brought in the supposed provision wagons, had gathered in a circle about the unsuspecting Indians. Thus, within ten minutes after the arrival of the troops, under the very shadow of a truce flag, was this most shameful deed of treachery accomplished.

Disarmed and bound like so many slaves, and guarded by double ranks of soldiers, the forest warriors were driven, like sheep, to the city and through the massive gateway of its frowning fortress. Here Coacoochee was separated forever from Osceola, who was soon afterwards taken to Fort Moultrie in Charleston harbor. There, a few weeks later, he died of a broken heart, far away from his friends and from the dear land for which he had fought so bravely.

With only Talmus Hadjo for a companion, the Wildcat was roughly thrust into one of those narrow dungeons from the deadly gloom of which he had shrunk with such horror on the occasion of his long-ago visit to the fort in company with Louis Pacheco.

CHAPTER XXX

IN THE DUNGEONS OF THE ANCIENT FORTRESS

THE capture of Coacoochee and Osceola created an extraordinary degree of excitement in St. Augustine, where the news of this most important event was hailed with extravagant joy and openly expressed sorrow. Those who rejoiced were of that class who wanted the war ended, and the Seminoles removed by any means, fair or foul, they cared not which. To such persons an Indian was only a species of noxious animal, for the trapping of which any deception was justifiable. On the other hand were many honorable men and women whose indignation, at the deed of treachery by which the fair name of the Government had been smirched, knew no bounds. Of all these, none was so filled with righteous wrath as were Ralph and Anstice Boyd.

"I was not wholly unprepared for some such rascality," said the former, "and I tried to convey my suspicions to Coacoochee yesterday; though, knowing nothing definite, I dared not speak plainly. He, poor fellow, is so entirely honest and incapable of such a cowardly act himself, that he failed to comprehend what I was driving at. To his simple mind,

a great chief must be an honorable man ; otherwise
he would not be a great chief, or, indeed, a chief of
any degree.   Rather different from the idea prevail-
ing in most white communities, is it not ? "

"I should say so, judging from what we have seen
lately,". cried Anstice.   "But I am too furious to
talk about it.   I am almost ashamed of being white.
I only wish I were a man ! "

"What would you do in that case?" inquired her
brother curiously.

"Do?   I would fight, and devote my life to fighting just such outrageous wrongs as this.   That's
what I would do."

"I don't doubt you would, you precious little spit-
fire, and a mighty plucky fight you'd put up.   You'd
lose, though, every time; for, besides pluck and pug-
nacity, it takes coolness and infinite patience to fight
the battle of right against might.   But, to return to
practical matters, what is to become of our guest,
now that Coacoochee is no longer in a position to
elope with her, or afford her other protection than
that of his prayers ? "

"She is to stay with us, of course, for just as long
as we can keep her.   In the meantime, we must
manage in some way to get him out of that terrible
prison.   Poor fellow !   How he must be suffering at
this minute.   I only hope he remembers that he still
has some friends, and that there are still a few faint
sparks of honor and gratitude glowing in the bosoms

of the 'Iste-hatke,' as he calls us.   We must get Irwin Douglass to help us, and I only hope he will call to-day, so that we can begin to plan at once."

" Hold hard, sister ! Remember that the awkward situation Douglass is already in is largely owing to us.   If you take my advice, you will not mention to him our desire that Coacoochee should escape, or disclose to him the identity of our guest.   I agree with you, that we are bound to do whatever we can to aid our Indian friend, and that the forest maiden shall make her home with us so long as she chooses to do so ; but, for the present, I beg that no one else, not even Irwin Douglass, be admitted to our secret."

" Very well, Mr. wise man, I will let you have your own way for a time ; but don't try my patience too far, lest I do something desperate.   Red-headed girls aren't expected to be cool-headed as well, you know, and so when I have once set my heart on having a thing done, I want it done without delay."

Thus it happened that, when Lieutenant Douglass called on the Boyds that evening, and was formally presented to a Miss Annette Felipe, he did not, for a moment, doubt that she belonged to one of the old Spanish-American families of the Territory.   She had a darkly beautiful face, was quietly but stylishly dressed, and was demurely silent.   That she spoke so little was explained by Anstice on the ground that Spanish was her native tongue, and that she was visiting her in order to improve her English.

As the lieutenant did not speak nor understand Spanish, he was more than content to devote himself to Miss Anstice, leaving the stranger to be entertained by Ralph Boyd. Douglass and the English girl discussed his present prospects, and wondered how long he would be obliged to wait in idleness before a court-martial could be convened to hear his case, and of course dismiss the absurd charges preferred against him. They talked of their recent exciting experiences, and finally Anstice said :

"By the way, Mr. Douglass, I wish you would take us to visit the prisoners in the old fort. I am so anxious to see that splendid Osceola. Besides, we want to do everything we can to make Annette's visit pleasant, and there is so little to amuse one in this stupid place. I am sure she would be so interested in those Indians. Won't you please arrange it, like a dear man ?"

"Certainly, I will if I can," replied the young officer. "At the same time, I am not at all sure that the general will regard with favor an application for a permit from one in my peculiar position."

"Oh, I fancy he will. At any rate, you manage it for us somehow, and make as early a date as possible ; for Annette may be compelled to leave us at any time, and I wouldn't have her miss seeing the interior of the fort. She has never seen anything like it, you know. We are going to take a walk to-morrow morning just to show her the outside of it, and you may come with us if you choose."

So Douglass promised to do what he could, and when he joined the walking party on the morrow, he announced that he had thought of a plan which he believed would work. "You see," he said, "Mrs. Canby, wife of Canby of the Rifles, has just arrived from the North, and as she has never seen any Indians, of course she will be anxious to visit the fort. So I will get Canby to secure the permit, and invite us all to join his party."

While discussing this plan and deciding that it would be the very thing, they reached the ancient fortress, and as they skirted its frowning walls, Miss Felipe, who had hardly spoken since starting, and then only to Anstice, became so visibly affected, that the English girl threw an arm protectingly about her, exclaiming, "Annette is so tender-hearted that she can't bear the thought of captives being shut up in that gloomy place."

"It is tough luck," agreed the young officer. "And there is not the slightest chance of their escaping either, for the only openings into the cells are those small embrasures through which even a boy would find it difficult to squeeze. They are some eighteen feet above the floor, too, so that it would be impossible to reach them without a ladder."

A few days later, a permit for a party of six to visit the fort having been secured, Mrs. Canby, the

Boyds, their guest, and Douglass set forth, Mr. Canby being detained by urgent duty, and excusing himself at the last moment. After passing the strong guard stationed at the gateway, the sight-seers found themselves in a large, open space, where many of the captives were lounging or walking about. In these, the Spanish girl showed not the slightest interest, but seemed inclined to hasten on. She carried a light shawl thrown over her arm, of which slight burden Douglass had politely but in vain attempted to relieve her.

"Your friend seems very odd, and not at all like other girls," he confided to Anstice Boyd.

"Yes. Isn't she?" replied the English girl, readily. "But then you must remember her bringing up. I wonder if Osceola is among these Indians?"

"Oh no, miss," answered the sergeant who had been detailed to act as guide. "The chiefs are only allowed out, one at a time, under guard, after the others have gone in. They are in their cells now."

"Well, take us to them, then," said Anstice, for they are the ones we care most to see. Don't you think so, Mrs. Canby?"

"Yes, indeed," agreed that lady; "only I hope they will prove better looking and more interesting than these creatures out here."

So the party was guided to the cell occupied by Osceola, in front of which paced a sentry, and its massive door was swung back on creaking hinges.

The haughty chieftain, still clad in his most splendid costume, was seated on a stool, gazing blankly at the opposite wall. He roused slightly as the sergeant said :

"Here's some ladies come to visit you, Powell," and when Mrs. Canby and Anstice expressed a wish to shake hands with him, he extended his hand to them mechanically. When, however, the lieutenant also offered to shake hands, a fierce flash of anger leaped into the eyes of the forest warrior, and he drew back haughtily, exclaiming as he did so :

"No, sir! Never again shall the hand of Ah-ha-se-ho-la meet in friendship that of one wearing the disgraced livery of a United States officer."

"Horrid thing!" cried Mrs. Canby, as the party hurriedly withdrew from the cell. "The idea of a mere savage daring to speak so to an army officer! You did well, Miss Felipe, not to go near the wretch, and I only wish I hadn't. I certainly don't want to see any more of them."

As the speaker absolutely refused to visit the remaining prisoners, which the others were still desirous of doing, Douglass remained with her, leaving but three of the party to inspect the cell occupied by Coacoochee and Talmus Hadjo. It, like the other, was guarded by a sentry, with whom the guide, after throwing open the door, stepped aside to speak.

Although the Spanish girl had remained outside the other cell, she pushed eagerly forward into this one, while Anstice and her brother stood in the doorway. Talmus Hadjo lay on a pile of forage-bags that served as a bed, while Coacoochee, the very picture of despair, stood leaning, with folded arms, against one of the walls. He hardly noticed his visitor, until in a low, thrilling tone she pronounced his name. Then, as though moved by an electric shock, he sprang forward, gasped the single word " Nita ! " and clasped the girl to his breast.

A few murmured words passed between the two; then he released her, and, stooping, she slipped something from her shawl beneath one of the forage-bags lying on the floor.

When the sergeant reappeared at the doorway a second later, the Spanish girl, looking perfectly composed, was standing quietly at one side, Talmus Hadjo was regarding her with undisguised amazement, while Coacoochee, with a new light shining in his face, was silently exchanging hand-clasps with Ralph and Anstice Boyd.

" Rather a more decent and civil sort of a chap than the other," remarked the sergeant as he again locked the door, and the visitors turned away. " Now there's only one more cell, and — "

" I don't think we care to inspect any more cells to-day," interposed Anstice, hastily ; and so a few minutes later the reunited party were breathing once more the outer air of freedom, while Mrs.

Canby expressed very freely her opinion of Indians in general and of those whom they had just seen in particular.

While the transformation of Philip Emathla's adopted daughter into Miss Annette Felipe, clad in the costume of civilization, and guest of Anstice Boyd, may appear as surprising to the reader as it did to the captive war-chief whom she had just left filled with a new hope, it was all brought about very simply. On the evening that Coacoochee confided her to the protection of Ralph Boyd, that gentleman, accompanied by his sister, strolled down to the Indian encampment. First they received permission to speak with the aged chieftain, who was summoned to the lines for that purpose. A few minutes later their strolling carried them past the darkest corner of the camp, where they were joined by a slender figure that had slipped through the lines without attracting the attention of a guard. Over this figure Anstice threw a long cloak that she had carried on her arm, and thus disguised, Nita Pacheco accompanied her new friends to their home. Her absence from the Indian camp was not discovered until two days later, when Mr. Troup Jeffers, claiming her as his escaped slave, and armed with an authority from the general for her recapture, visited the Indian camp in search of her.

The slave-catcher made a great outcry when he found that his prey had again eluded him, but he was speedily silenced by a very unexpected meeting with Ralph Boyd, who had been watching for the man who should make that very claim.

At sight of him whom he had every reason to believe was long since dead, the scoundrel's face turned livid, and he staggered back like one who has received a knife-thrust.

"Drop this business, and leave town inside of an hour if you value your wretched life!" hissed Boyd in his ear, and an hour later St. Augustine was well rid of Mr. Troup Jeffers.

CHAPTER XXXI

A DARING ESCAPE

NOT until his prison door was again closed, and the footsteps of his visitors had died away in the distance, did Coacoochee turn from listening, and stoop to see what it was that Nita had brought him. From under the forage-bag he first drew a Spanish hunting-knife, beautifully balanced, and with the keen edge of a razor. It was of dull blue Toledo steel, and its shapely haft was exquisitely silver-mounted. At sight of it the young Indian uttered an exclamation of joy, for it was his own well-tried weapon, endeared by long association, and his unfailing friend in many a combat with man and beast. It had been his father's before him, and with it Anstice Boyd had severed the bonds confining Irwin Douglass, when his life hung by a thread, in the swamp stronghold of Osceola. She had kept it ever since, awaiting an opportunity to restore it to its owner, and had now done so, by the hand of Nita Pacheco.

While Coacoochee gloated over this treasure, his comrade in captivity pulled aside the bag beneath which it had been concealed, and disclosed another

255

object of equal value with the precious knife. It was a coil of rope, slender and finely twisted, but of a proved strength, capable of supporting the weight of two men.

"Now, Talmeco," cried Coacoochee, in the Indian tongue, "we have something to live for. Already do I breathe again the free air of the forest, for want of which I had died ere many days. Now will we show these dogs of the Iste-hatke that their cunning is no match for that of the Wildcat. Again shall the war-cry of Coacoochee ring through hammock and swamp, glade and savanna, and the Iste-hatke shall tremble at its sound."

"But," said Talmus, "was it not one of the Iste-hatke who brought us these things? Has my brother won the heart of a pale-faced maiden?"

"Ho, ho!" laughed the young chief. "Are the eyes of Talmeco grown so dim from long gazing at stone walls that he did not see, through the dress of the white squaw, the form of Nita Pacheco, daughter of Philip Emathla, and the beloved of Coacoochee? She it was, and no other, who found a way to this hole of rats, and brought the means of escape. Let us hasten, then, to make use of them, that she may not be disappointed."

"How can we?" queried Talmus. "There is but one opening, and it is too small for the passage of a warrior. A boy could hardly make his way through it. Besides, it is too high for us to reach, and, even if we got outside, would we not fall again into the hands of the soldiers?"

"Ho-le-wau-gus, Talmeco!" exclaimed the other. "Is thy man's heart turned by thy captivity into that of Cho-fee [the rabbit], and art thou become one who trembles at the sight of his own shadow? Listen, that thy heart may again become strong. The Wildcat will climb to yonder opening, and show his brother the way. It is small, but we will make ourselves smaller. We will go when the Great Spirit has drawn his blanket over the face of the sky, so that no light may shine from it, and no man can see us. Is it well?"

"It is well, my brother. Let Coacoochee lead, and Talmus Hadjo will follow in his steps."

For long hours during the weary days of captivity, had the young chief lain on his bed of bags, and gazed hopelessly at the single narrow opening in the wall far above him. He had believed that, if he could only reach it, he could so reduce his body as to pass through the aperture. Now he saw a way to reach it. Standing on his comrade's shoulders, and using his knife, he soon worked its point into a little crevice between the stones, just above his head. As Talmus could not support his weight very long at a time, and as there came days of such frequent interruptions that they dared not work, it was several weeks before the crevice was so enlarged that it would receive the knife up to its hilt. Then, by

s

drawing himself up on it, Coacoochee found to his delight that he could gain the narrow slit piercing the thick wall. To his dismay, it was barely wide enough to permit his head to pass through, but not his body.

The prisoners at once decided to starve themselves, and reduce their flesh by taking medicine. This they did, until they became mere skeletons, and their keeper began to fear that they would die on his hands.

In the meantime they cut up many of the bags on which they slept, into short lengths, which they bound closely, at intervals, about their slender rope, so as to afford a grasp for their hands. When all was in readiness, they were obliged to wait many days longer for a cloudless and moonless night.

At length it came as dark as Erebus, with squalls of rain, and a fierce wind that howled mournfully about the bastions and through the embrasures of the old fort. Much to the disgust of the captives, one of the prison keepers was in an unusually sociable mood that night, and made repeated visits to their cell, talking and singing, until they feared they would be compelled to kill him, in order to get rid of his presence. Finally they pretended to be asleep when he entered, and upon this he left them for good.

The time for action had arrived ; and, taking one end of the rope with him, Coacoochee, stripped to the skin, save for a breech-cloth, mounted on his comrade's shoulders, felt for the deeply cut crevice, thrust his knife into it, and, in another minute, had gained the embrasure. Here, after first regaining and securing his precious knife, he made the rope fast, by passing a loop about a projecting ledge, and leaving only enough inside for his comrade to climb up by, he passed the remainder through the opening, and let it drop, hoping that it might be long enough to reach ground at the bottom of the moat.

With great difficulty, the young Indian thrust his head through the narrow slit. Then, with the sharp stones tearing the skin from his breast and back, he slowly and painfully forced his body through, being obliged to go down the rope head foremost, until his feet were clear of the opening. With each minute of this desperate struggle, it seemed as though his weakened powers of endurance must yield to the terrible strain, and that his grasp on the slender rope must relax; in which case he would have pitched headlong into the yawning depths below. But the indomitable will that had already aided him so often finally triumphed over physical weakness, and after a half-hour of struggle, the young war-chief slid in safety down the line that led to freedom, and lay panting on the ground, twenty-five feet below the aperture that had so nearly proved fatal.

Fortunately he lay in the deep angle of a bastion,

where the shadows were blackest, for just then two men, evidently officers, passed close to him engaged in earnest conversation. He overheard one of them say that arrangements were perfected for removing all the prisoners on the morrow to Charleston, South Carolina, where they would be beyond a possibility of rescue or escape.

So overjoyed was Coacoochee at thus learning of the timeliness of his venture for liberty that he became filled with fresh vigor, and feeling a movement of the rope, that he still held in one hand, he instantly gave the signal that all was well, and the way clear for his comrade to descend. As he waited in breathless anxiety, he could plainly hear the struggle that was taking place far above him. At length it ceased, and in a low, despairing voice Talmus informed him that having forced his head through the embrasure, he could get no further, nor could he even draw it back.

"Throw out thy breath, Talmeco, and try again! Throw out thy heart and soul, if needs be, and tear the flesh from thy body," urged the young chief, in a voice little above a whisper, but thrilling in its intensity.

Thus adjured, Talmus Hadjo made one last desperate effort, with such success that he not only forced his bleeding body through the aperture, but lost his hold of the rope and came tumbling down the whole distance.

HADJO LOST HIS HOLD OF THE ROPE AND CAME TUMBLING DOWN THE
WHOLE DISTANCE.

With a smothered cry of horror, Coacoochee sprang to his side, and, feeling a faint heart-beat in the stunned and motionless form, dragged it to a near-by pool of water. This he dashed over the injured man with such effect that, in a few minutes, his consciousness returned. He was, however, so injured by his fall as to be unable to walk, and feebly begged Coacoochee to save himself and leave him to his fate. For answer the young chief, with an astonishing display of strength, considering his condition, picked up his helpless friend, slung him across his back, and thus bore him nearly half a mile, to where the palmetto scrub afforded temporary concealment.

Daylight was now breaking, and some means must be devised for moving rapidly. So, depositing his burden on the ground, Coacoochee turned back to an open field in which he had seen several mules. Hastily twisting some shredded palmetto leaves into a rude bridle, he had the good fortune to capture one of the animals, on which he mounted both himself and his comrade.

For several hours they rode through the trackless pine forest, and at length reached a travelled road, which it was necessary they should cross. Before doing so Coacoochee slipped from the mule to assure himself that no enemy was in sight. He had gone but a few paces, when the animal, with a loud bray, dashed into the open, and galloped madly towards a small party of mounted volunteers, who happened to be making their way towards the city.

The sight of a single naked Indian dashing toward them was too great a temptation to be resisted. A dozen rifles poured forth their deadly contents, both the mule and his helpless rider pitched headlong, and in the death struggle of the animal, the dead face of Talmus Hadjo was crushed beyond recognition. One of the white men, coolly and as neatly as though well accustomed to the operation, took the scalp of the fallen warrior. Then the party rode merrily forward, exchanging coarse jests concerning the handsome manner in which the redskin had been potted.

Filled with rage and grief at this loss of his companion, Coacoochee also hastened from the scene, plunging deep into the recesses of a near-by hammock and vowing a future but terrible vengeance upon the cowardly perpetrators of this cold-blooded murder. Living on berries, roots, and the succulent buds of cabbage palmettoes, sleeping naked on the bare ground, and slinking from hammock to hammock like a wild beast who is hunted, the fugitive worked his way southward for three days.

On the evening of the third day he walked into the camp of his own band on the headwaters of the Tomoka River. By Louis Pacheco and his warriors the young chief was greeted as one raised from the dead. When, after they had fed and clothed him, they listened to his wonderful tale of treacherous capture, long imprisonment, timely escape, and the cruel death of Talmus Hadjo, they vowed themselves to a fiercer resistance than ever of the white oppressors.

Within an hour runners were despatched to several bands who were known to be contemplating surrender, urging them to abandon their intention and continue the fight to its bitter end. Thus was the conflict which General Jesup had just declared ended, renewed with a greater fury than ever, and Coacoochee the Wildcat became the acknowledged leader of his people.

CHAPTER XXXII

NITA HEARS THAT COACOOCHEE IS DEAD

LONG and anxiously had the friends of Coacoochee in St. Augustine awaited the result of their effort to aid him in regaining his freedom. They dared not attempt to visit him again, lest by so doing they should arouse suspicion and injure his cause; for the two principal chiefs were so closely guarded that visitors were only admitted to them at long intervals and as a great favor. So Nita was forced to endure a weary period of suspense and feverish anxiety, that caused her to droop like a transplanted forest lily.

Although Ralph Boyd sought daily for information concerning the prisoners, he could gain little, save that of a depressing nature, much of which he and Anstice dared not share with their guest. He heard that Coacoochee's strength was so weakened on confinement that it was believed he could not live much longer, and there was a rumor that he and Osceola were to be hanged for their perversity in continuing the war.

In the meantime, the number of Indians held captive in St. Augustine had been greatly increased by

the bands of Micanopy, Cloud, Tuskogee, and No-
coosee, all of whom, urged to do so by the Cherokee
delegation, had accepted General Jesup's invitation
to meet him for a peace talk.   Again was the flag
of truce violated, again was treachery substituted for
honest fighting, and again were the too trusting savages seized, disarmed, and sent to St. Augustine as
prisoners of war.

So many captives were now crowded into the ancient city, that, in order to secure them beyond all
hope of escape, as well as to make room for others
who, it was hoped, might be enticed to *make peace* in
a similar manner, it was deemed advisable to transfer
them to Charleston.   There they could be detained
in safety until the time came for their final removal
to the west.   Preparations for this movement were
made with great secrecy, that the Indians might not
learn of it until the last moment.   Transports were
secured, and finally it was made known to the officers of the post only that an embarkation would be
effected on the following day.

Rumors of the contemplated removal had reached
the Boyds, and had, of course, been communicated to
Nita.   She declared that, if Coacoochee did not succeed in escaping before it took place, she should re-
sume her position as the adopted daughter of Philip
Emathla, and so follow her lover into exile.   In this
determination, Anstice warmly upheld her friend,
but begged her to wait until the latest possible mo-

ment, before exchanging her present security for the uncertain fate of a captive.

One evening, Lieutenant Douglass, who, having safely passed the ordeal of a court-martial, and, honorably acquitted, had been restored to duty, called on the Boyds. In course of conversation with Anstice he casually remarked, that the morrow would probably offer the last chance they would ever have of seeing their friend Coacoochee.

"What do you mean?" asked the startled girl.

"I mean that the Indians in St. Augustine are to be embarked for Charleston to-morrow morning; and Coacoochee, poor fellow, is reported to be in such wretched health that it is not probable he can live long, especially in a climate so much colder than this."

Nita, who sat in another part of the room, listlessly engaged in a bit of fancy-work, glanced up quickly as she caught the name of her captive lover. She did not hear what else the young officer said, and waited eagerly for his going, that she might question her friend. Anstice, on her part, was so impatient to communicate to Nita the news she had just learned, and became so absent-minded in her conversation with Douglass, that he suspected something had gone wrong, and so took his departure earlier than usual.

Long and earnestly did the two girls, who had grown to love each other like sisters, talk together

that night. Very early the next morning, escorted
by Ralph Boyd, they left the house and turned in
the direction of Philip Emathla's encampment. Nita
had resumed her Indian dress, but over it she wore
the same long cloak that had served to disguise her
on a former occasion. Its hood was drawn over
her head and about her face, so that but little of
her features could be distinguished.

As they hastened through the narrow streets of the
quaintly built city, their attention was attracted by
a clatter of iron-shod hoofs, and a mounted officer in
service uniform came dashing toward them. It was
Irwin Douglass, and he reined up sharply at sight of
his friends. As he lifted his cap to the ladies, he
exclaimed:

" Well, you are early birds this morning ! I suppose you have heard the great news and are come
out to verify it ? "

"No, we haven't heard any news; what is it?"
asked Boyd.

" Coacoochee has escaped from the fort! got out
somehow during the storm last night, and made off.
The general is in a terrible temper over it. I am
ordered out with a scouting party to see if we can
pick up the trail. So I must hurry on. Good-bye."

In another minute the bearer of this startling bit
of news was clattering away down the street, while
the three who were left stood staring blankly at one
another.

Nita was saying over and over to herself, "Coacoochee has escaped, has escaped, and is free. Oh! how happy I am! And that soldier is going to try and recapture him. Oh, how I hate him! But he cannot. Coacoochee is free, and will never let them take him again. Oh, how happy I am!"

As Anstice Boyd reflected upon the full meaning of what she had just heard, her heart was crying out: "Coacoochee has escaped, and I aided him. Now Irwin has gone to find him. They will meet and kill each other. I know they will! Oh! why did I do it? Why did I do it?"

Ralph Boyd expressed his feelings aloud by exclaiming: "That is one of the best bits of news I have heard in many a day. It will continue the war, no doubt, but I don't care if it does. Serve the sneaks right who thought to end it by treachery. They will get some greatly needed lessons in honest fighting now."

"You don't mean Mr. Douglass, brother?"

"Douglass? No! Bless his honest soul! He's no sneak, but only an unfortunate victim of circumstances. But never you fear, sister. Douglass won't catch Coacoochee, even if he has to ride half around the territory to avoid him. He is too honorable a fellow to do a mean thing, or forget a debt of gratitude. If Douglass is the only one sent after him, Coacoochee is all right. I am afraid, though, there are others. I'll find out as soon as I get you two back to the house.   What!   Not going back ? "

" Not just yet, brother.   Nita wants to be the first to tell the great news to Coacoochee's father, so as to give the old man courage to bear his exile and his sad journey.   She wants to bid him good-bye too, for of course she will not go with him now."

" Of course not, and I suppose we must let her do as she wishes," agreed Boyd, reluctantly.   " I hope, though, she will be very careful not to be recognized."

" I will see that she is careful, brother."

So the three continued their way to the Indian camp, which they found in a state of dire confusion on account of the order for removal just received. There were already many white persons in the camp ; soldiers who were hastening the preparations, and mere curiosity-seekers who were retarding them by their useless presence.   All of these, as well as the Indians themselves, gazed curiously at the two ladies and the stalwart young Englishman, who walked directly to the tent of Philip Emathla.   The old man, who was sitting in a sort of a daze just outside, recognized Ralph Boyd at once, and when Nita stooped and whispered in his ear, he immediately rose and followed her inside the canvas shelter.   Anstice also went inside, and the flap curtaining the entrance was dropped, leaving Boyd outside on guard.

As he gazed curiously on the novel scene about him, and even walked a few steps to one side the better to observe it, a white man of sinister aspect passed him twice, each time regarding him furtively but keenly. Suddenly he darted to the tent, pulled aside the flap, and thrust his head inside.

A startled cry from the interior attracted Boyd's attention, and, ere the man had time for more than a glimpse, he was seized by the collar, and jerked violently backward.

"What do you mean, scoundrel! by your rascally intrusion into other folk's privacy?" demanded the young Englishman, hotly. "I've a mind to give you the kicking you deserve."

"I didn't mean nothin', cap'n," whined the man, squirming in the other's fierce clutch. "I didn't know thar was any privacy in thar. I'm thought 'twas only Injuns; and I'm got orders to take that tent down immejiate."

"Well, you won't take it down, not yet awhile; and you'll vanish from here as quick as possible. So get!"

With the utterance of this expressive Americanism the speaker released the man, and at the same time administered a hearty kick that caused its recipient to howl with anguish. Ere he disappeared he turned a look of venomous hate at his assailant and muttered:

"I'll git even with you for this, curse you! Anyway, I saw what I wanted to see, and I know whar the gal's to be found."

He was Ross Ruffin, Mr. Troup Jeffers' human jackal, who, at the bidding of his master, had been hanging about the Indian camp for weeks, watching for the reappearance of Nita Pacheco. His suspicions had just been aroused by the disappearance, into Philip Emathla's tent, of two ladies, and in the single glimpse caught by his bold manœuvre they had been confirmed. He had seen Nita, whose cloak having fallen to the ground, was fully revealed in her Indian costume, standing with her hands on the old chieftain's shoulders and imparting to him the glorious news of Coacoochee's escape from captivity. Now all that he had to do was to discover whether the girl accompanied the Indians to Charleston or remained behind, and this information he had acquired ere nightfall.

Nita had not seen him, and it was Anstice who uttered the cry that attracted her brother's attention. Of course neither of them recognized the man, nor when, a little later, they returned to the house that Nita had believed on leaving she should never see again, did they notice that he was stealthily following them at a distance. After that he watched the embarkation of the captives, to assure himself that Nita Pacheco did not accompany them. As the transports sailed, Ross Ruffin also left the city, and that night he held a conference with Mr. Troup Jeffers.

The inmates of the Boyd house experienced mingled feelings of satisfaction at Coacoochee's escape, apprehension lest he should be recaptured, and anxiety in behalf of their friend Douglass. Only Nita was confident and light hearted.

"He will not be caught," she said, "nor will he harm your friend; we shall hear from him very soon by some means."

She was right; they did hear very soon, and when the news came, it was of such a terrible nature that the others would gladly have kept it from her. Lieutenant Douglass, returning at nightfall from his scout, went directly to the Boyds' house; and, in answer to the eager queries that greeted his entrance, said:

"Yes; I found him, poor fellow! About a dozen miles from the city we met a squad of volunteer cavalry. In reply to my question if they had seen any sign of Coacoochee, who had just escaped from the fort, one of them said: 'You bet we have, cap'n, and here's his scalp.' With that—"

Here the speaker was interrupted by a stifled cry and a heavy fall. Nita Pacheco lay unconscious on the floor. The two men bore her to a bed in an adjoining room, where they left her to the gentle care of Anstice. When they returned to the outer room, Douglass asked curiously:

"What does it mean, Boyd? What possible interest can your guest have in Coacoochee?"

"My dear fellow, I see now that we ought to have told you sooner, and so saved her this cruel blow. She is Nita Pacheco, Spanish by descent, but Indian by association and bringing up. She is the adopted daughter of Philip Emathla, and the betrothed of Coacoochee."

"Good Heavens!" cried Douglass. "No wonder she fell when struck such a blow. What a brute she must think me."

"Don't blame yourself, old man," said Boyd, soothingly; "the fault lies entirely with us. But are you certain that Coacoochee is dead?"

"The man who scalped him said he knew him well, and could swear to his identity. We went on to examine and bury the body, and it answered fully the description of Coacoochee. Oh yes, there is no doubt that he is dead, though his companion has thus far eluded all search. In one way, I suppose his death will be a good thing for the country; but I must confess, that for the sake of that poor girl, I would gladly restore him to life if I could, and take the consequences. Well, good night. Make the best apologies you can for me to Miss Anstice."

T

CHAPTER XXXIII

TOLD BY THE MAGNOLIA SPRING

The reported death of Coacoochee, which was generally believed, gave great satisfaction to the people of Florida, and to the troops who had been for so long engaged in the thankless task of trying to subdue the Seminoles. With many of their leading chiefs removed beyond hope of return, and with their most daring spirit dead, the Indians must, of course, relinquish all hopes of successfully continuing the struggle. So the war was supposed to be ended, and many families of refugees now returned to their abandoned homes.

Among these were the Boyds, who had no longer any reason for remaining in St. Augustine, and who were particularly anxious to remove Nita from the sorrowful associations surrounding her there. She was slow to recover from the shock caused by the news of her lover's death, but as soon as she was able to bear the journey, they took her with them to the plantation, which they begged her to consider her own home.

Ralph Boyd began at once the energetic restoration of his property. A few of the old servants had

already found their way back, and others, tired of
dwelling amid the constant alarms of Indian camps,
began to arrive in small bands, as soon as they heard
that the proprietor had returned, until nearly the
whole of the original force of the plantation was restored to it.   Aided by these free and willing work-
men, the young planter repaired the great house and
numerous outbuildings, cleared and replanted the
weed-grown fields, trimmed the luxuriant growth
of climbing vines and shrubbery, and, within a few
months, could gaze with honest pride over an estate
unexcelled for beauty by any in Florida.

In these undertakings Nita tried, for the sake
of her friends, to exhibit an interest, and in their
presence to appear cheerfully content.   With all
her efforts, however, she could not conceal the fact
that she was pining for her old forest life, and
would gladly exchange the luxuries of civilization
for the rude camp of her warrior lover, could he
but be restored to her.   She spent much time, clad
in her Indian costume, and roaming the wilder portions of the plantation, mounted on one of those
fleet-footed ponies for which Florida was famous,
and which were descendants of the old Andalusian
stock brought over by De Soto.   One of the girl's
favorite haunts was the bank of a spring that boiled
from a bed of snow-white sand, amid a clump of
stately magnolias, about a mile from the great
house.   Here she would sit for hours, plaiting

sweet-scented grasses into graceful shapes, as she
had learned to do among the maidens of King
Philip's village ; but always thinking such sad
thoughts that her work was often wet with scald-
ing tears. At such times Ko-ee, as she called her
pony, circled about her in unrestrained liberty,
nibbling at grasses or leaves, here and there, but
always quick to come at her call, and behaving
much like a well-trained watch-dog, fully aware of
the responsibility of his position.

One mild and hazy afternoon early in the new
year, when the weather was of that degree of per-
fection that it so often attains just before the coming of a "Norther," Nita sat by her favorite spring,
and Ko-ee browsed near at hand. All at once the
pony uttered a snort, pricked up his delicate ears,
and began to move uneasily toward his mistress.
As she glanced up from her work, she was filled
with terror at the sight of a man standing but a
few paces away, and regarding her earnestly. Her
first impulse was to fly, and her next was to fling
herself into his arms ; for in that instant she recognized the brother whom she had not seen since that
night of cruel separation nearly four years before.

"Louis!" she cried. "Louis, my brother! Is it
you? Are you really alive? I thought you were
dead, together with all whom I have ever loved.
I knew you had escaped and joined our friends in
fighting for their rights and our rights ; but they

NITA SAT BY HER FAVORITE SPRING.

told me you were killed, and I thought I was alone in the world."

" Even if I had been killed, dear, you would not be alone, so long as Coacoochee is left; for he — "

"Louis! How dare you? He is dead!"

" Dead, sister! Coacoochee dead, when he but now sent me here to find you ; when but four days ago I fought by his side in the fiercest and most splendid battle of this war? He was wounded, to be sure, though not seriously; but as for his being dead, he is no more dead than you or I. What could have put such a belief into your mind?"

For a moment the girl stared at her brother with unbelieving eyes and colorless face. "Is it true?" she whispered at length. " Can it be true? Tell me, Louis, that you are not saying this thing to tease me, as you used when we were children. Tell me quick, brother, for I can bear the suspense no longer."

As Louis assured her that he had spoken only the truth, and that her lover still lived, the girl's over-strained feelings gave way, and she sank to the ground, sobbing, and panting for breath.

Louis Pacheco, clad in the costume of a Seminole warrior, battle worn, and travel stained, sat by his sister's side and soothed her into quietness. Then he told her the story of the great fight on the shore of Lake Okeechobee. He told how Coacoochee and three other chiefs, with less than five hundred warriors, fought for three hours in the saw-grass and tangled hammock growth, against eleven hundred white troops under General Zachary Taylor, and finally retired for want of ammunition, taking with them their thirteen dead and nineteen wounded. "The white soldiers were killed until they lay on the ground in heaps, and their wounded could not be counted. If we had only had plenty of powder, and as good guns as they, we would not have left one of them alive," concluded the narrator, fiercely.

"Oh, Louis, it is awful!" cried the girl, with a shudder.

"What is awful? That we left so many of them alive? Yes; so it is, but —"

"I do not mean that. I mean this terrible fighting."

"Yes, sister, the fighting is terrible, and so is the suffering; but neither is so terrible as tamely submitting to slavery, and injustice, and oppression, and the loss of everything you hold most dear on earth. Those are the terrible things that the whites are trying to force upon us. But we will never submit. We will fight, and cheerfully die, if needs be, as free men, rather than live as slaves. As for the white man's word, I will never trust it. Coacoochee trusted it, and it led him to a prison. Osceola trusted it, and it led him to death. Micanopy trusted it, and it led him into exile."

" But, Louis, some of the whites are honorable. The Boyds have treated me like an own sister, and, but for them, Coacoochee would not now be free."

" Yes," admitted Louis, with softened voice. " Coacoochee has told me of them, and with my life would I repay their kindness to you and to him. With them you are safe, and with them will I gladly leave my sister until such time as I can make a free home for her."

" Oh, Louis! Haven't you come for me? Can't I go with you?"

" Not now, Ista-chee [little one]. Here is greatest safety for you; for to all the Iste-chatte has word been sent that none may harm this place, nor come near it. The suffering of the women and children with us is very great, and I would not have you share it. Now I must go; for I am sent to notify the northern bands of our victory, and bid them follow it up with fierce blows from all sides. In two days will I come to this place again, when, if you have any token or message for Coacoochee, I will take it to him. Soon he hopes to come for you himself, and until that time you must wait patiently."

So saying, and after one more fond embrace of his sister, Louis disappeared in the undergrowth, leaving Nita radiant and filled with a new life. Her brother had bound her to secrecy concerning his visit, at least until he had come and gone again, but she could not restrain the unwonted ring of happiness in her voice, nor banish the light from her face. Both of these things were noted by Anstice, as she met the girl on her return to the house.

" Why, Nita! What has happened? " she exclaimed. " Never have I seen you look so happy. One would think you had heard some glorious news. What is it, dear? "

" Please, Anstice, don't ask me; for, much as I am longing to tell you, I can't; that is, not for a few days. Then I will tell you everything. But I am happy. Oh, I am so happy! "

With this, the girl darted away to her own room, leaving Anstice in a state of bewilderment not unmixed with vexation.

" I'm sure she might have told me," she said to herself. " It can't be anything so very important, for there is no possible way of receiving news at this out-of-the-world place, unless it is brought by special messenger, and none could arrive without my knowledge. I do believe, though, that one is coming now."

Anstice was standing on the broad front verandah, over which was trained a superb Lamarque rose, so as to form a complete screen from the evening sun. Her ear had caught the sound of hoof-beats, and, as she parted the vines before her, she saw two horsemen coming up the long oleander avenue. Both were in uniform, and it needed but a glance for the blushing girl to discover the identity of the foremost rider. It was Irwin Douglass, hot, dusty, and weary with long travel. He dismounted, tossed his bridle to the orderly, who rode back toward the stables with both horses, and slowly ascended the steps.

As he gained the verandah, his bronzed face flushed with pleasure at sight of the daintily clad girl who was stepping forward with outstretched hand to greet him.

"Oh, Miss Anstice! If you could only realize how like a bit of heaven this seems!" he exclaimed.

"You must indeed have undergone hardships to find your ideal of heaven in this stupid place," laughed the girl, at the same time gently disengaging her hand, which the young man seemed inclined to hold. "Now sit down, and don't speak another word until I have ordered some refreshments, for you look too utterly weary to talk."

"But I have so much to tell, and so short a time to tell it in," remonstrated the lieutenant. "I must be off again in an hour."

"Never mind; I won't listen to such a woe-begone individual. Besides, Ralph will want to hear your news as well."

With this, Anstice disappeared in the house, and Douglass sank wearily into a great easy-chair.

Directly afterward Ralph Boyd appeared with a

hearty greeting, and a demand to hear all the news at once. Before his desire could be gratified, his sister returned with a basket of oranges, and followed by a maid bearing a tray of decanters, glasses, and a jug of cool spring water.

"These will save you from immediate collapse," said the fair hostess, "and something more substantial will follow very shortly. Now, sir, unfold your budget of news, for I am dying to hear it."

"Well," began Douglass, "there has been the biggest fight of the war, away down south on the shore of Lake Okeechobee, and I was in it."

"Oh!" exclaimed Anstice.

"That, of course, is nothing wonderful," continued the young soldier, "but it is surprising that I came out of it without a scratch, for there were plenty who did not. On our side we left twenty-six dead on the field, and brought away one hundred and twenty severely wounded, besides a few score more suffering from minor injuries."

"Whew!" ejaculated Ralph Boyd. "Who was in command?"

"General Taylor, on our side. And now for my most surprising bit of news." Here the speaker hesitated and looked carefully about him. "I want to be cautious this time," he said. "But it was confidently asserted by scouts and prisoners that the Indian commander was no other than our late lamented friend, the Wildcat."

"Coacoochee! So that was Nita's secret!" cried Anstice. "I might have known that nothing else would make her look so radiant. Oh! I am so glad!"

"What do you mean?" demanded the astonished lieutenant. "How could she have heard anything about the battle, when I have just come from the field with despatches for St. Augustine, and have ridden almost without stopping?"

"I don't know, for she wouldn't tell me; but I am certain she did hear some time this afternoon. But oh! Mr. Douglass, we are so thankful that you escaped so splendidly. It must have been awful. Of course you gained the victory, though?"

"I don't quite know about that," replied the lieutenant, doubtfully. "We silenced their fire, and drove them from the field after a three-hours fight; but it is said that they had less than half our number of men, and we are in full retreat. Officially, of course, we have won a victory; but it wouldn't take more than two or three such victories to use up the whole Florida army."

They discussed the exciting event for an hour longer, and then Douglass was reluctantly forced to continue his journey. When he left, he promised to be back in three days' time, as his orders were to proceed from St. Augustine to Tampa.

This promise was fulfilled; but when the lieutenant again drew rein before the hospitable plantation house, that seemed so much like a home to him, he found its inmates filled with anxiety and alarm. Nita Pacheco had disappeared under very mysterious circumstances the evening before, and no trace of her whereabouts or fate could be discovered.

CHAPTER XXXIV

FOLLOWING A MYSTERIOUS TRAIL

NITA had not appeared during the lieutenant's former brief visit to the plantation, and when, on his departure, Anstice sought her to charge her with having already learned that Coacoochee still lived, the happy girl made no denial of her knowledge. At the same time she would not reveal the source of her information, though when Anstice declared her belief that Nita had seen the young chief himself, the latter denied that such was the case. "He is wounded," she added, "and could not come. Besides," she continued proudly, "he is now head chief of the Seminole nation, and has much to think of. But he remembered me, and sent me a message."

"Remembered you, indeed!" cried Anstice. "I should think he ought to; but I am sorry to hear that he is wounded, for he is a splendid fellow. Isn't it wonderful, though, that Lieutenant Douglass went through that same awful battle, and came out without injury. I can't understand it."

"In a battle where Coacoochee commands, no friend of Ralph Boyd can be struck, save by accident," replied Nita, simply.

" Do you believe that ? If I thought it were true, I should love your Indian hero almost as much as you do, dear. I wonder, though, if that can be the secret of Irwin's escape ? "

So the two girls talked and became drawn more closely to each other with their exchange of innocent confidences.

On the following day, Nita rode Ko-ee as usual, though not in the direction of the magnolia spring ; but on the one after, she haunted its banks for hours. She went to it in the morning, reluctantly returning to the house for lunch and to have Ko-ee fed at noon, and made her way back to the place appointed for meeting her brother, as soon afterwards as she could frame a decent excuse for so doing.

She was in the gayest of spirits as she rode away, and she laughingly called back to Anstice, " To-morrow, dear, I am going to spend the whole day with you."

" Isn't it a pleasure to see her so happy ? " asked Anstice of her brother, as they watched the girl ride away. " And did you ever see such a change in so short a time? A few days ago she was listless and apparently indifferent whether she lived or not. Now she is full of life, and interested in everything. Then, I did not consider her even good-looking ; while at this minute, she seems to me one of the most beautiful girls I ever saw."

" Yes," replied Boyd, " I have noticed the change ;

but I wish, Anstice, you would persuade her to give up these lonely rambles; though she has promised me not to go beyond the limits of the plantation, I can't help feeling uneasy.   If I weren't so awfully busy, I would ride with her myself, since she insists on riding."

"No you wouldn't, brother," laughed Anstice.   "I couldn't afford to have the jealousy of the savage lover aroused in that way.   Besides, it is absurd to regard Nita as though she were a daughter of civilization, needing to have every step carefully guarded. In spite of her sweetness, and the readiness with which she has fallen into our ways, she is still so much of an Indian as to be more at home in the trackless forest, than in the *chaco* of the *Iste-hatke*, as she is pleased to term the house of the white man. So let her alone, brother; for, if she is to be the wife of an Indian, the more she retains of her Indian habits, the better it will be for her."

Thus Nita was allowed to go her own way.   And when, at sunset, she had not returned, but little uneasiness was felt in the great house on her account, though Anstice did sit with her gaze fixed on the long avenue up which she expected each moment to see the truant appear.

A few minutes later her uneasiness was exchanged for alarm, as one of the stable boys came running to the house to report that Ko-ee, the pony, had shortly before appeared at the stables, riderless and alone, though still saddled and bridled, and that Miss Nita was nowhere to be seen.

Filled with dismay at this report, Ralph Boyd and his sister hastened to the stables, and there were greeted by the further news that four of the best horses belonging to the plantation were missing. This had only been discovered when one of the stable boys went to the field into which all the horses not in use were turned during the daytime, to drive them up for the night.

By this time a group of excited negroes was collected, and it seemed as though it had only needed the starting of disquieting reports to cause others to come pouring in. It now appeared that saddles and bridles had been stolen, that provisions had disappeared, that a boat was missing from the river bank, that unaccountable noises had been heard, and mysterious forms had been seen at night, in various parts of the plantation.

When Boyd sternly demanded why he had not been informed of these things before, the negroes replied that they had not dared offend their Indian friends, whom they believed to be at the bottom of all the trouble.

"If Indians are prowling about here, the sooner we locate them and discover their intentions, the better," announced the proprietor, "and if Miss Nita has come to any grief from which we can extricate her, the sooner we do that, the better also."

With this, he armed himself and a dozen or so of the more trusted negroes, provided a dozen more with torches, for the night had not grown very dark, let loose all the dogs of the place, wondering at the time why they had not given an alarm long before, and thus accompanied made a thorough examination of all Nita's known haunts within the limits of the plantation. Midnight had passed ere the fruitless search was ended, and the young man returned wearily to the great house.

"It is my honest conviction," he declared to Anstice, as she hovered about him with things to eat and to drink, "that Nita has met some band of Indians and gone off with them. I shouldn't be surprised to learn that Coacoochee had sent for her, or even come for her himself."

"I don't believe any such thing," said Anstice, decidedly. "She would never have gone off without bidding us good-bye. Nor do I believe that Coacoochee would take, or allow to be taken, one pin's worth of property belonging to you. Whatever has happened to Nita, and I am afraid it is something dreadful, she has not left us in this state of suspense of her own free will."

"Well," replied the other, "I am too tired to discuss the question further to-night, and perhaps daylight will aid us in solving it."

Soon after sunrise the next morning, according to his promise of returning on the third day, Lieutenant

u

Douglass, heading an escort of troopers, and accompanied by one of the most experienced scouts in Florida, reached the plantation. While at breakfast he gathered all the known details of what had happened on the previous evening. Then he asked which of Nita's usual haunts she would have been most likely to visit the afternoon before.

"The magnolia spring," replied Anstice, without hesitation. "She was going in that direction when last seen."

"Let us take a look at the magnolia spring, then, and see if Redmond, my scout, can discover any signs of her having been there."

So they four, the Boyds, Douglass, and the scout, visited the bubbling spring beside which Nita was known to have passed so much of her time. Within two minutes the scout pointed out a place in a thicket but a short distance from the spring, where a struggle had taken place, and from which a plainly marked trail led through the undergrowth toward the river.

"There were only two men," he said, "and they warn't Injuns, for no redskin ever left such a trail as that. Besides, Injuns don't wear boots, which them as was here yesterday did. It's my belief that them men has made off with the girl. Leastways, one of 'em carried something heavy; but they've been mighty careful not to let her make any footprints."

The trail was followed to a place on the river-
bank where a boat had been concealed, and from
signs undistinguishable to untrained eyes, the scout
described the craft so minutely, that Ralph Boyd
knew it to be the one missing from his own little
fleet.

"But what have white men got to do with this
business?" the latter asked, in perplexity, and un-
willing to drop his Indian theory.

"Dunno, cap'n," replied the scout; "but you can
take my word for it, that white men have been, and
Injuns hasn't. Yes, they have too!" he cried, as
at that instant his eye lighted on another, almost
illegible print, near where the boat had grounded.
"Here's a moccasin track, and it ain't that of any
woman either. What I want now is to have a look
on the other side."

In compliance with this desire, a boat was procured,
and the whole party crossed the river. Then a short
search located the point where the other boat had
landed. It also disclosed a most puzzling trail, for
here were the prints of *four* pairs of booted feet
instead of two, while no trace of moccasins was to
be found. The trail led from the water's edge to
a grove in which four horses had been tied to trees,
and from there it bore away to the southwest.

"They're headed for the Tampa road," remarked
the scout; "and I reckon Tampa's where they're
bound for."

" Then we'll have a chance to find out something more about them," said Douglass; "for I must be a long way toward Tampa before another nightfall."

" By Jove, old man! I'm going with you," declared Ralph Boyd; " I want to know something more of this affair myself."

" If you go, Ralph, I shall go too," announced Anstice, firmly. " I'm not going to be left here alone again. Besides, I am as anxious to find out what has become of poor Nita as you are, and I have always wanted to visit Tampa."

As Douglass assured his friends that nothing would afford him greater pleasure than to have them accompany him, and joined with Anstice in her plea, Ralph Boyd reluctantly gave consent for his sister to form one of the party. Thus, before they regained their own side of the river, all details of the proposed trip were arranged.

While Anstice was making her preparations for departure, her brother summoned the entire working force of the plantation, and telling them that he had reason to believe the recent thefts to have been committed by white men, asked if any of them could remember having seen any strange white man about the place within a week.

All denied having done so, save one of the old field hands, who hesitatingly admitted that he had seen the ghost of a white man, on the night of the " Norther."

" Where did you see it ? " demanded Boyd.

" At de do' ob de chickun house."

" What were you doing there ? "

" Jes' projeckin' roun'."

" How do you know it was a ghost, and not a live man ? "

" Kase I seen him by de light ob de moon, an kase I uster know him when he war alive."

" Whose ghost do you think it was ? "

" Marse Troup Jeffers, de ole oberseer."

" The very man I ought to have thought of at first ! " exclaimed the proprietor, turning to Douglass. " He is not only so familiar with the place that he knows where to lay his hands on such things as he needs, and is friendly with the dogs, but he is so bitter against me for turning him off, that he has already attempted to take my life, as well as that of Anstice. He is now a slave-trader, and, in company with other ruffians like himself, disguised as Indians, he very nearly succeeded in running off all the hands on the plantation. He has already made several attempts to capture Nita, for the purpose of selling her into slavery, and now I fear he has succeeded. I swear, Douglass, if I ever get within striking distance of that scoundrel again, his death or mine will follow inside of two seconds. Now, let us hasten to pick up the trail, and may God help Nita Pacheco, if she has fallen into the clutches of that human devil."

The plantation being left in charge of old Primus, the travellers set forth, and, a number of boats having been provided, they were speedily ferried across the river, towing their swimming horses behind them. On the farther side they resaddled and mounted, Anstice riding Nita's fleet-footed Ko-ee.

By hard riding they struck the Tampa road before noon, and Redmond immediately pointed out the trail of four shod horses, which he affirmed had been ridden at full speed, late the evening before. Soon afterward, the scout discovered the place where the outlaws had camped. He declared that they had reached it long after dark, and had left it before sunrise that morning.

"Mighty little hope of our overtaking them this side of Tampa, then," growled Douglass.

For two days longer did the pursuing party follow that trail. They found two other camping-places; but study the signs as they would, they could discover nothing to indicate the presence of a woman, nor of any save booted white men. "Which is what beats me more than anything ever I run up against," remarked the puzzled scout.

On the third day, by nightfall of which they expected to reach Fort Brooke on Tampa Bay, the plainly marked trail came to a sudden ending, amid a confusion of signs that Redmond quickly interpreted.

"They were jumped here by a war-party of Reds,"

he said, " were captured without making a show of
fight, and have been toted off to the northward.
Would you mind, sir, if I followed this new trail a
few miles, not to exceed five?   I might learn something of importance from it."

" No," replied Douglass.   " We can afford to rest
the horses here for an hour or two, and I will go with
you."

"So will I, if you have no objection," said Boyd.

The three went on foot swiftly and in silence for
about three miles, then the guide suddenly stopped
and held up his hand for caution.   Creeping noiselessly to his side, the others peered in the direction
he was pointing, and there beheld a scene of horror
that neither of them forgot so long as he lived.

CHAPTER XXXV

FATE OF THE SLAVE-CATCHERS

FOR some time, Boyd, Douglass, and the scout had been aware of an odor, pungent and sickening; but neither of the two former had been able to determine its character. Now, as they gazed into an opening in the pine forest, beside a small pond, its hideous cause was instantly apparent. Although there was no sign of human life, there was ample evidence that human beings, engaged in the perpetration of an awful tragedy, had occupied the place but a few hours before. Chiefest of this evidence were the charred remains of two human bodies, fastened and supported by chains to the blackened trunks of two young pine trees. At the foot of each tree a heap of ashes, and a few embers that still smouldered, told their story in language so plain that even the civilian and the soldier had no need of the scout's interpretation to enable them to comprehend instantly what had taken place.

For a few minutes they remained in hiding while he cautiously circled about the recent encampment to discover if any of the Indians still lurked in its vicinity. At length he reappeared on the opposite side of the opening, and entering it disturbed a number of buzzards that were only awaiting the cooling of the embers to begin their horrid feast. These rose on heavy wings, and lighting on neighboring branches, watched the intruders with dull eyes.

" The Injuns have gone," said the scout as he met his companions in the middle of the opening, " and taken the four horses with them. It was a small war-party, all on foot and without women or children ; but what beats me is that there ain't no tracks of white men along with theirs. Here are two accounted for, but what has become of the other two ? They might have rid horseback, it's true ; but then, it ain't Injun way to let prisoners ride when they are afoot themselves."

" Is there any way of finding out who these poor devils were ? " asked Douglass, indicating the pitiful remnants of humanity before them.

"No, sir, I can't say as there is," replied the scout, doubtfully. " All I know for certain is that they was human, most likely men, and more than likely white men. They must have done something to make the Reds uncommon mad, too ; for even Injuns don't burn prisoners without some special reason, and never, in my experience of 'em, have I run across a case where they did it in such a hurry. Generally when they've laid out to have a burning, they save it till they get back to their village, so as to let all hands share in the festivities. No, sir; this case is peculiar, and you can bet there was some mighty good reason for it."

As it would have been useless to follow the Indian trail any further, the scouting party turned back from this point.

" If I could only be sure that one of those wretches was Jeffers," said Boyd to Douglass as they made their way among the solemn pines, " I should feel that he had met with his just deserts. Certainly no man ever earned a punishment of that kind more thoroughly than he. As the matter stands, I fear it will be long before this mystery is cleared, if, indeed, it ever is. Under the circumstances, don't you think it will be just as well not to tell Anstice what we have seen ? "

" Certainly," replied Douglass, "and I will instruct Redmond not to mention our discovery to any one. Of course, I shall be obliged to report it to the general, but beyond that it need not be known."

So Anstice was only told that the scouts had followed the Indian trail as far as they deemed advisable, without discovering a living being, and she rode on toward Tampa, happily unconscious of the hideous forest tragedy that had been enacted so near her. Although she was still anxious concerning Nita, she was not without hope that the girl had fallen into friendly hands, who would ultimately restore her to Coacoochee.

At Tampa, which presented at that time a scene of the most interesting activity, the Boyds formed many friends. A large military force was stationed here in Fort Brooke, a post charmingly located on a point of land projecting into the bay, and shaded by rows of live-oaks, vast in size, and draped in the cool green-gray of Spanish moss. Beneath these were the officers' quarters, and long lines of snowy tents. One of the married officers, whose wife had gone North, tendered the Boyds the use of his rudely but comfortably furnished cottage until they should find an opportunity for returning safely to their own home. They gladly accepted this offer, and their cottage quickly became a centre of all the gayety and fun of the fort.

Just back of the post was a large encampment of Indians, who had surrendered or been made prisoners at different points, and were now collected for shipment to New Orleans, on their way to the distant west.

Although Anstice, in her pity for these unfortunates about to be torn from the land of their birth, often visited them, and made friends with the mothers through the children, she did not realize their sorrow so keenly as she would had any of her own friends or acquaintances been among them.

On the day before that fixed for their embarkation, Colonel Worth, of the 8th Infantry, came in from a long and finally successful scout after Halec Tuste-

nugge's band of Indians. Although the leader of
this band, together with a few of his warriors, succeeded in eluding capture, a large number, including many women and children, had been brought in.
These it was decided to start for New Orleans in
the morning with the captives already on hand.

The colonel who had just concluded this arduous
campaign was a fine specimen of the American
soldier, as honest as he was brave ; and a cordial
friendship already existed between him and the
Boyds. As was natural, therefore, the morning
following his arrival at Fort Brooke saw him seated
at their cheerful breakfast table, where, of course,
the conversation turned upon the existing war.

" There is just one man in Florida to-day, with
whom I wish I had a personal acquaintance," remarked the colonel.   " He alone could put a stop
to this infernal business of hiding and sneaking and
destroying cornfields, and running down women and
children, if he only would.   His name is Coacoochee."

" Yes, I know him well, and believe what you say
of him is true," responded Boyd.

" You know him !   Then you are just the man
to aid me in meeting him.   I am to be sent into his
country in a few days, and am extremely anxious to
have a talk with him.   Will you go with me, and
exert your influence to induce him to come in ? "

" I am afraid my influence would prove of small
avail, colonel.   You see, Coacoochee has been already

caught by chaff and made to suffer dearly for his credulity."

"Yes, I know, and it was one of the most outrageous — But I have no business criticising my superior officers, so I can only say that — "

Just here came an interruption in shape of a lieutenant, who wished the colonel's instructions concerning an awkward situation. "You see, sir," he began, "we had just got the prisoners, whom you brought in yesterday, nicely started for the boats, when one of them, and a mighty good-looking one for a squaw, darted out from among the rest and ran like a deer towards the woods. Two of the guards started after her, and several men ran so as to head her off. At this, and seeing no other chance of escape, she sprang to a small tree and climbed it like a kitten. Once up, she drew a knife from some part of her clothing and declared in excellent English that she would kill any man who dared come after her and then kill herself. I have been talking to her and trying to persuade her of her foolishness. She only answers that she will never be taken from Florida, and will do exactly what she threatens, in case we attempt her capture. She is terribly in earnest about it, and I am afraid means just what she says. Now all the boats have left, save one that is only waiting for her, and I am in a quandary. I dare not order any man to go up after her. I can't have her shot. I can't shake her down, nor can I persuade her to come down, and the transports will have sailed long before she is weary or starved into submission."

"It certainly is a most embarrassing situation," laughed the colonel, rising from the table as he spoke, "and one that would seem to demand my official presence. Will you come with us, Boyd?"

"Can't I go too, colonel?" broke in Anstice. "Perhaps I can persuade the poor thing to come down after all you men have failed."

"Certainly, Miss Anstice; we shall be delighted to have both your company and assistance."

They found the situation to be precisely as described, except that, by this time, quite a crowd of soldiers, all laughing and shouting at the Indian girl, were collected about the tree. These were silenced by the coming of their officers, and drew aside to make way for them.

"This is a decidedly novel experience," began the colonel, as he caught sight of a slender figure perched up in the tree, and staring down with great, frightened eyes.

At that moment, Anstice Boyd, who had just caught a glimpse of the girl's face, sprang forward with a little scream of recognition.

"It is Nita! my own darling Nita!" she cried. "Colonel, order these horrid men to go away at once, and you and the others please go away, too. She is my friend, and will come to me as soon as you are all out of sight. I will be responsible for her, and shall take her directly to the house, where you can see her after awhile, if you choose."

Two minutes later the men had disappeared, and the poor, brave girl, who had determined to die rather than leave the land in which her lover still fought for liberty, was sobbing as though her heart would break in Anstice Boyd's arms. The latter soothed and petted her as though she had been a little lost child, and finally led her away to her own temporary home. Here she clad her in one of the two extra gowns she had managed to bring from the plantation, and so transformed her in appearance, that when, an hour later, the colonel called to inquire after his captive, he was more amazed than ever in his eventful career, to find her a very beautiful, shy, and stylishly dressed young lady, to whom it was necessary that he be formally presented.

He had, in the meantime, learned her history from Boyd; and, when made aware of the tender ties existing between her and the redoubtable young war-chief of the Seminoles, had exclaimed:

"Ralph Boyd, your coming here with your sister was a special leading of Divine Providence, as was the act of that brave girl in refusing to embark for New Orleans this morning. Now, with her aid, we will end this bloody war."

Proceeding to headquarters, he briefly explained

the situation to General Armistead, who had just succeeded General Taylor in command of the army in Florida, and obtained his permission for the transports to depart, leaving Nita Pacheco behind.

Upon meeting Nita in Anstice Boyd's tiny sitting-room, the colonel chided her gently for not making herself known to him at the time of her capture with the others of Halec Tustenugge's village.

To this she replied that she and her people had suffered so much at the hands of white men, and been so often deceived, that they no longer dared trust them.

"That is so sadly true, my dear girl, that it seems incredible that a Seminole should ever trust one of us again. Still, I am going to ask you to do that very thing. I am going to ask you to trust me, and believe in the truth of every word I say to you as you would in that of Coacoochee himself. If I deceive you in one word or in any particular, may that God who is ruler of us all repay me a thousand fold for my infamy."

Here followed a long conversation, in which the colonel outlined his plan for obtaining an interview with Coacoochee, through the influence of Nita, who he proposed should accompany his forthcoming expedition to the southern interior. At its conclusion, Nita gave him a searching look that seemed to read his very soul. Then, placing a small hand in his, she said:

"I will go with you, I will do what I can, and I will trust you."

"Spoken like a brave girl, and one well worthy the bravest lover in all Florida!" cried the colonel. "Now can I see the end of this war. Boyd, I of course count on you to go with us?"

"And me?" interposed Anstice. "Don't you count on me too, colonel? Because if you don't, neither of these people shall stir a single step with your old expedition."

"My dear young lady," rejoined the colonel, gallantly, "the entire fate of the proposed expedition rests with you, and I made so certain that you would accompany us, that I have selected as my adjutant Lieutenant Irwin — "

"That will do, sir. Not another word," interrupted the blushing girl. "If you get into the habit of talking such nonsense I, for one, will never believe a word you say. I don't care, though, so long as it is settled that I am to go. Now I want you both to listen while I tell you what Nita has just told me of all that has happened to her since she disappeared so mysteriously from the plantation. Nita dear, I am sure you don't want to hear it, so run up to my room, and have a good rest. I will come just as soon as I have got rid of these men."

x

CHAPTER XXXVI

PEACE IS AGAIN PROPOSED

AFTER Nita had left the room, Anstice began her story as follows :

"On the afternoon before that cold 'Norther' we had about a month ago, Nita was sitting, as she often did, by the magnolia spring. You must remember the place, colonel. There she received a most unexpected visit from her brother Louis, whom she had not seen for years. He had been sent by Coacoochee to carry the news of the battle of Okeechobee to the northern bands, and also to bring a message to Nita. After they had talked for awhile, he had to go on his way, but promised to be back in two days' time and take any message or token she might wish to send to her lover."

"That's who it was then!" broke in Ralph Boyd. "Well, I am glad to have that part of the mystery cleared up."

"Yes," continued Anstice; "and of course, Nita was awfully excited. When the second day came, she spent nearly the whole of it at the spring. Finally, late in the afternoon, as before, she heard a voice calling to her by name, very softly. Thinking, of course, that it was Louis, who feared, for some reason, to advance into the open, she followed the direction of the voice unhesitatingly. Then the first thing she knew, a cloth was flung over her head, she was seized in a pair of strong arms, and borne struggling away.

"When, to save her from suffocating, the cloth was removed, she found herself in a boat, with two white men and her brother Louis. The poor fellow's head was cut and bleeding, as though from a cruel blow, and he lay bound in the bottom of the boat. One of the white men was rowing, and the other sat watching them, with a pistol in his hand."

"Did she recognize the white men?" inquired Ralph Boyd.

"Yes, she says they were the very two who stole her mother, and afterwards stole the wife of Osceola."

"The scoundrels!" cried Colonel Worth. "In that case they were the prime instigators of this war, and ought to have been hanged long ago."

"Yes," answered Boyd, "and one of them stole my sister, colonel, and turned her adrift in the forest, where but for Coacoochee she must have perished. The same gentleman also shot me in the back at the battle of Withlacoochee, and supposed he had killed me."

"Hanging would be altogether too good for the brute," declared the colonel, excitedly. "He deserves to be burned at the stake."

" That is what the Indians thought," replied Boyd, significantly. " But go on, sister. Did Nita find out the name of the other man ? "

" Yes, she learned while with them that it was Ruffin, — Ross Ruffin."

" I have heard of him, too, as being as great a scoundrel as Jeffers himself, only more of a coward," muttered Boyd.

" They made both Nita and Louis put on boots before leaving the boat," continued the narrator, " and that accounts for our finding what we supposed were the footprints of four white men. When they reached the place where the horses were waiting, both the captives had their wrists bound together, and a rope was passed from each to the saddle of one of the white men. So they rode for two days, and Nita says it was simply awful."

" I should imagine it might have been," said the colonel.

" Just at dusk of the second day, a lot of ambushed Indians surprised and captured them all without firing a shot. Nita says, in spite of her fright, she thinks that was one of the happiest moments of her life. The Indians knew Louis, and, of course, released him and her at once, tying up the white men instead. That night they camped some miles from the road, and when Louis told who the prisoners were, and of the many outrages they had committed, especially the stealing of poor Chen-o-wah, the Indians declared they should live no longer, and began at once to make preparations for killing them. Nita says she isn't certain how they were killed, as she made Louis take her a long way off, where she could neither see nor hear what was going on; but she thinks they were *burned* to death."

"And I know it," said Ralph Boyd, grimly. "Douglass and I saw their charred remains the next day, and not knowing who they were, I expended a certain amount of sympathy on them, that I now feel to have been wholly wasted."

"Oh brother! and you never told me! I'm glad you didn't, though, for it is too horrible to even think of. Well, when Nita got to the Indian village, they treated her just as nicely as they knew how, and promised to join Coacoochee, of course taking her with them, as soon as their crops were planted. Then you came along, colonel, and captured poor Nita with the others, and brought her in here, and the rest you know. Oh, I forgot! Nita is feeling very badly about her brother Louis, who was captured with her and brought here. She says he was taken off in one of the first boats this morning, and she is afraid she will never see him again."

"He must have given an assumed name," remarked the colonel, thoughtfully. Under the circumstances, though, I am very glad that he did, and that he is well out of the country. I am afraid if it had been known a few hours sooner that Major Dade's guide was in the prisoners' camp, he would never have left it alive. In that case my course with Coacoochee, which now appears so plain, would have been beset with serious, if not insurmountable, difficulties. As it is, I congratulate you, Miss Anstice, on having Nita Pacheco for a friend, and look forward to the happiest result arising from that friendship. Within a week we shall be ready to start for the country of Coacoochee, and I can assure you that I have never anticipated any expedition with greater pleasure than I do this one."

The first of March, that loveliest month of the entire Floridian year, found Colonel Worth's command camped in Fort Gardiner hammock, on the western bank of the Kissimmee River. Here, they were more than one hundred miles beyond the nearest white settlers, and in a country so abounding with game of all kinds, including deer and turkey, besides fish and turtles in wonderful abundance, that the troops were fed on these, until they begged for a return to bacon and hardtack as a pleasing change of diet. The heavily timbered bottom lands were in their fullest glory of spring green, fragrant with a wealth of yellow jasmine, and the glowing swamp azalea, as well as vocal with the notes of innumerable song birds. It was one of the most charming bits of the beautiful land that the Seminole loved so well and fought so fiercely to retain. It was a typical home of the Indian, and one from which the soldiers of the United States had thus far been unable to drive him.

In the camp a large double tent, pitched next that of the commander, was set apart for the use of the Boyds and Nita. Here Anstice held regal court; for she was not only the first white woman to penetrate that wild region, but the first who had ever accompanied a command of the Florida army on one of its " swamp campaigns." In her efforts at entertaining the officers who flocked about her, Anstice was ably seconded by Nita, who, though demure and shy, was not lacking in quick wit and a cheery mirth that had been wonderfully developed during this expedition into the haunts of her lover.

From its outset she had refused to wear the garb of civilization, and appeared always dressed in the simple costume of an Indian maiden such as the young Seminole war-chief might recognize at a glance, and now he might be expected at any moment.

The day on which he had promised to come in had arrived, and already was Ralph Boyd gone forth to meet him. Oh, how slowly the time passed, and yet again, how swiftly! Finally, unable to conceal her agitation, Nita returned to the innermost recess of the tent, while Anstice entertained several officers with gay talk and laughter outside.

Friendly Indians, sent out long before with a white flag, on which were painted two clasped hands, in token of friendship, and with numerous presents, had found Coacoochee, and informed him of Colonel Worth's desire for a talk ; upon which the fierce young chief had laughed them to scorn.

" Tell the white chief," he said, " to come alone to the camp of Coacoochee if he wishes to talk."

" Thy friend Ralph Boyd is in the camp of the soldiers, and sends word that the white chief is to be trusted."

" Tell my friend that I am through with trusting white chiefs. I have had a sadder experience with them than he."

" Nita Pacheco is in the camp of the soldiers, and, being restrained from coming to thee, bids thee come to her. She also sends word that the white chief is to be trusted even as she is to be trusted."

For a long time Coacoochee sat silent, while the little smoke clouds from his calumet floated in blue spirals above his head; then he spoke again, saying :

" Tell the white chief that in five days Coacoochee will come to him. Tell Ralph Boyd that on the fifth day from now, two hours before the sleeping of the sun, if he comes alone, I will meet him at the palmetto hammock, one mile this side of the soldiers' camp. If he comes not, then shall I return to my own people, and the white chief shall never meet me save in battle. Tell Nita Pacheco that at her bidding only, of all the world, do I trust myself

again within the power of the Iste-hatke.   Now go,
and bear to her this token from Coacoochee."

With this the young chief detached from his turban a superb cluster of egret plumes fastened with
a golden clasp, and handed it to the messenger.   This
token had been promptly delivered to Nita, together
with her lover's message, and now she awaited his
coming.

Ralph Boyd, riding out alone to meet his Indian
friend, felt almost depressed at the utter loneliness
of his surroundings, in which no signs of human
presence or animal life were to be discovered.   He
wondered curiously, as he rode, whether that fair
country would ever be filled with the homes and
tilled acres of civilization.   As he approached the
cluster of cabbage palms named as the place of meeting, he scanned it closely, but without detecting
aught save an unbroken solitude.

Even as he pondered on how long he should wait
for Coacoochee to fulfil his engagement, he was
startled by a low laugh, and the young chief, with
outstretched hand, stood by his side.

Springing from his saddle, the Englishman grasped
the hand of his friend, and after a warm greeting
confessed his amazement that any human being could
have approached him so closely without warning.

"I remembered the magic by which your warriors
were made to appear and disappear on that former
occasion long ago," he said, "and have watched so

keenly this time that I did not believe even you could come within many yards of me without detection. Even now I know not from where you came."

For answer Coacoochee uttered his own signal, the cry of a hawk. Instantly, to Boyd's infinite amazement, the two were surrounded by a cordon of warriors, all armed with rifles, and the furthest not more than three rods away.

Coacoochee smiled at the blank expression on his friend's face, and said: "From the camp of the soldiers to this place have my braves kept pace with thee; for, while I trust Ralph Boyd, I was not yet prepared to fully trust the war-chief of the Istehatke nor place myself entirely in his power. Now am I satisfied, and will go with you."

Thus saying, Coacoochee waved his hand, and the Indians, who had stood motionless about them, disappeared within the shadows of the hammock. At the same moment there came from it seven mounted warriors, one of whom led a superb horse fully equipped for the road. The young chief vaulted lightly into the saddle of this steed, and Boyd mounting at the same time, the two friends, followed by their picturesque escort, dashed away toward the camp by the Kissimmee.

A few minutes later a blare of trumpets and a roll of drums heralded their arrival, and Colonel Worth, escorted by a group of officers in full uniform, stepped forward to greet the distinguished guest, from whose coming so much was hoped. As the two war-chiefs of different races, and yet both natives of one country, held each other's hand, and gazed into each other's face, each was impressed with the belief that he had met an honest man, a worthy foe, and one who might become a stanch friend.

After the formalities of the occasion had been exchanged, and just as Coacoochee's eyes were beginning to rove restlessly down the camp, Anstice Boyd stepped to his side, gave him the greeting of an old friend, and leading him to her own tent, bade him enter alone.

Thus there was no witness to the meeting of the forest lovers; but when, a few minutes later, they came from the tent together, there was a happiness in their faces that had not been there since that long-ago evening of betrothal in the village of Philip Emathla.

CHAPTER XXXVII

COACOOCHEE IS AGAIN MADE PRISONER

ALTHOUGH the Seminoles had generally been victorious in their battles with the whites, they were struggling against a power so infinitely greater than theirs that the four years of war already elapsed had made very serious inroads upon both their strength and their resources. Their entire force was in the field, and they had no reserves from which to draw fresh warriors. They must raise their own food supplies even while they fought. They could not manufacture powder nor arms, and could only gain infrequent supplies of these by successful battles or forays. The fresh, well-armed, and well-fed troops, operating against them, outnumbered them ten to one. Their entire country was dotted with stockaded posts, called by courtesy "forts," garrisoned by troops who were continually driving the Indians from hammock to hammock, destroying their fields, and burning their villages.

One line of these posts extended across the Territory, from Fort Brooke on Tampa Bay to St. Augustine, cutting off the northern bands from those who had sought refuge amid the vast swamps of the

south.   Another line extended down the west coast,
and up the Caloosahatchie to Lake Okeechobee ;
while a third line commanded the Atlantic coast
from St. Augustine to the mouth of the Miami River,
where it empties into far-distant Biscayne Bay.   Of
this last chain the principal posts were Fort Pierce,
on the Indian River opposite the inlet, Fort Jupiter
at the mouth of the Locohatchie, Fort Lauderdale on
New River, and Fort Dallas on Biscayne Bay.   The
last named was most important of all, because of its
size, its strength, nearly all of its buildings being so
solidly constructed of stone that some of them are
in a good state of preservation to this day, and
on account of its situation, which commanded the
Everglades and the system of waterways connecting
them with the coast.

Under these circumstances, it is no wonder that
the Indians were weary of the hopeless struggle
against such overwhelming odds, and that Colonel
Worth found Coacoochee willing to talk peace.

The two war-chiefs seemed drawn to each other,
and to understand each other from the first.   During the four days that Coacoochee remained in the
camp of the soldiers, they held many informal talks
concerning the subject of greatest importance to
them both.   For a long time, Coacoochee argued
stoutly against the removal of his people to a distant country, and pleaded hard for a reservation in
their own land.

To this Colonel Worth replied that more than half the tribe were already removed, and could never be brought back. Also that, with the great tide of white immigration setting steadily southward, no reservation in Florida, worth the having, could be secured to the Indians for more than a few years; at the end of which time the existing troubles would rise again with exaggerated violence.

These arguments finally prevailed, and with a heavy heart the young chief admitted the necessity of leaving the land of his birth. He, however, made one stipulation.

"There are among us," he said, "those of a darker skin than ours, but who are yet our brothers. Many of them were born to freedom in the land of the Iste-chatte. They have fought with us for our liberty, and have died by our side. They are with us as one people, and where we go they must also go. If Coacoochee surrenders, and exerts his influence for the removal of his people, it is only on condition that those of the Iste-lustee now dwelling with the Seminoles shall go with them, and that no one of them shall ever be claimed by a white man as his slave. Are the words of Coacoochee good in the ears of the white war-chief?"

"They are good," replied Colonel Worth, "and, were I in full command, your condition should be granted unhesitatingly. But there is another war-chief more powerful than I, who must be consulted.

I believe he will gladly accept your terms. He is now at Fort Brooke. Will you go with me and see him? If you will, no matter whether you come to an agreement or not, I pledge my sacred word, as a man and a soldier, that you shall return to your own people, free and without harm."

For some minutes Coacoochee meditated this proposition in silence. Then he said slowly:

"Micco-hatke [white chief], in the hope of ending this war, and saving the lives of my people, I will do what I have said I never would do. I will trust myself again within the walls of a white man's fort. I will go with you to talk with this great white chief. First, I must return to my warriors, and tell them where I am going, that there may be no fighting while I am gone. I give you these ten sticks. With the rising of each sun throw one away. When all are gone, Coacoochee will come again, and go with his white brother to the place of the great white chief."

So the Wildcat left the camp of the soldiers as free as he had entered it, journeyed far among the scattered bands of his people, and in ten days returned, prepared to accompany his white friends to the place from which they had set forth in search of him.

At Tampa, General Armistead expressed himself as greatly impressed with the manliness and evident sincerity of the young chief. He readily consented to the condition imposed, and bade him bring in his people at once, that they might be embarked for emigration.

To this Coacoochee replied that, while he had become convinced of the necessity for removal to the west, it would take time to convince his followers, especially as the soldiers had so driven them that they were scattered in small bands all over the country. They would not be gathered together until at their great annual festival or green corn dance, which would be held in June. Before that time he doubted if he should be able to accomplish very much.

Understanding this state of affairs perfectly, General Armistead still desired Coacoochee to go and collect his people as speedily as possible, designating Fort Pierce on the Indian River as the place at which they should assemble.

So the young war-chief having renewed his confidence in the words of the white man, departed cheerfully, and filled with a new hope for the future. He had received every mark of friendship and distinction from officers and soldiers, and had been given no cause to doubt for a moment the sincerity of these expressions.

As Colonel Worth was about to leave for Palatka, and the Boyds were taking advantage of his escort to return to their own home, Coacoochee decided to accompany them as far as the plantation on the St.

John's, where Nita was still to be left until his return from the great enterprise he had now undertaken.

About this return much was said; for it would mean the beginning of the young chief's long journey to the west, and of course on that journey, from which there was to be no return, Nita Pacheco was to accompany him. Anstice had set her heart on having what she termed the "royal wedding" take place at the plantation, and had so nearly gained Coacoochee's consent to being married according to the way of the Iste-hatke, that she already considered her pet scheme as good as adopted.

The only officer accompanying the colonel to Palatka was Lieutenant Douglass; and, on the evening of their arrival at the plantation, as he and Anstice sat together on the verandah, while Coacoochee was strolling with Nita beneath the oaks, and Ralph Boyd was entertaining Colonel Worth inside the house, he startled the English girl by asking:

"Wouldn't it be just as easy, Miss Boyd, to have two weddings as one when Coacoochee returns?"

"Why, yes. I suppose so. If there was any one else who wanted to get married just at that time."

"Well, there is. I do, for one."

"And who is the other, pray?"

"Can't you guess, Anstice? Don't you know? Won't you — ?"

Here the young officer caught one of the girl's hands in both of his, and though he was obliged to

Y

release it a moment later, as the other men appeared on the verandah, the mere fact that she had not snatched it away filled him with unspeakable joy. It was a sufficient answer to his question, and he knew as well as though told in words, that he had won something better and sweeter far than rank, or honors, or position, or whatever else besides love the world holds most dear.

During the weeks that followed this happy evening at the plantation, while Colonel Worth, with Irwin Douglass as his hard-worked adjutant was always in the field, giving the Indians to understand that the vigilance of the troops was in no way to be relaxed, by the prospects of peace, Coacoochee, in the far south, was using every effort to redeem his pledged word, and persuade his people to come in for removal. He often visited Fort Pierce, the appointed rendezvous, which was commanded by Major Chase, the same who as a captain had destroyed the swamp stronghold of Osceola. This officer had long been conducting similar operations in the south, despatching small bodies of troops in all directions from his post, on the soldierly tasks of destroying fields, capturing women and children, and burning the rude roofs that had sheltered them. Upon receipt of orders to stay his hand, and hold his troops in check, that Coacoochee might be given an opportunity to collect his scattered warriors, Major Chase became impatient at the loss of his favorite occupation. So he sent word to the general commanding, that Coacoochee was so dilatory in fulfilling his promises, that it was believed he meditated treachery.

At this, General Armistead, who was on the point of being relieved of his command, and ordered to Washington, consummated his official career in Florida by an act calculated to bring a blush of shame to the cheek of every American soldier. It was nothing more nor less than an issue of instructions to Major Chase to seize Coacoochee, together with any who might accompany him, the very next time the young chief visited Fort Pierce, and hold them as prisoners of war.

Upon the retirement of this general, the man appointed to succeed him to the command in Florida, was Colonel Worth, then at Palatka, on the St. John's, which was headquarters of his regiment. The distance between that point and the Boyds' plantation was so short, that the colonel, together with his adjutant, was in the habit of frequently visiting it and sharing its bountiful hospitality. Here were often held discussions of the war, and of the efforts then being made by Coacoochee toward securing peace. During these conversations, the colonel was apt to sigh for an extension of his powers, that he might be enabled to put some of his pet theories into practice. In these aspirations the plantation household heartily sympathized.

It was only natural, then, that, on receiving his unexpected appointment as commander-in-chief, the honest soldier should hasten to impart the glad intelligence to his friends and bid them share his satisfaction.

Thus it came about that, a few evenings later, Ralph Boyd gave a dinner in celebration of the event, at which, among other guests present, were "General" Worth, as he must now be called, and Lieutenant Douglass.

The occasion was one of unrestrained happiness, for all believed that the tedious war must now come to a speedy close. Frequent blushes were brought to the cheeks of both Anstice and Nita, by sly allusions to the rapid approach of a certain double wedding that now appeared among the probabilities of the immediate future.

When the festivities were at their height, and all were in the gayest of spirits, there came a clatter of horses' hoofs, and a rattle of arms, from outside. The next moment a travel-stained courier entered, saluted, and handed the general a despatch marked "urgent."

The commander tore it open, glanced with paling cheeks at its contents, and sprang to his feet, exclaiming:

"My God, gentlemen! all is lost, and the war is about to break forth with greater fury than ever! In violation of our plighted word, Coacoochee and

"ALL IS LOST AND THE WAR IS ABOUT TO BREAK FORTH WITH
GREATER FURY THAN EVER."

fifteen of his followers have been treacherously seized at Fort Pierce, sent in irons to Tampa, and despatched in cruel haste to the west. A transport even now bears them toward New Orleans. In this emergency there is, to my mind, but one thing to be done. Coacoochee must be brought back. Without his aid to end it, this wretched war will continue indefinitely. Lieutenant Douglass, within fifteen minutes I shall want you to start on an overland ride to New Orleans. Intercept Coacoochee and bring him back to Tampa. For so doing you shall have my written authority. Boyd, pen and paper, if you please, and quickly."

Less than a quarter of an hour later, Douglass, splendidly mounted, armed with all requisite authority, and followed by but two troopers, dashed away down the long avenue, fairly started on his momentous mission.

As Anstice bade him farewell, she whispered in his ear: "Remember, Irwin, a double wedding, or none."

CHAPTER XXXVIII

In spite of the undisguised treachery by which Coacoochee had been made a prisoner and hurried from the country, the act was hailed with joy by unthinking people all over the Territory. These cared not how their enemy was got rid of, so long as they were at liberty to seize his lands and enslave the negroes among his followers. There were many others who were making too good a thing out of the war to care to have it end. From these classes, therefore, arose a mighty clamor, when it became known that General Worth was determined to bring back the young war-chief; and for a time there was no man in the country so bitterly abused and reviled as he.

To the fearless soldier, strong in the rectitude of his convictions, and planning far ahead of the present, this storm of words, prompted by ignorance, malice, and selfish interests, was but as the idle whispering of a passing breeze. He cared not for it; and if he had, his attention was too immediately and fully occupied by matters of pressing importance to permit him to notice it.

As the general had foreseen, the outrage perpetrated upon their most beloved chieftain caused the Seminole warriors to spring to their arms with redoubled fury. Even as a smouldering brush-heap is fanned into leaping flames by a sudden fitful gust, so the spirit of revenge, burning deep in Indian hearts, was now allowed to blaze forth without restraint. Small war-parties sallied forth from every swamp and hammock, burning and killing in all directions. Nimbly eluding pursuit, these could neither be destroyed nor captured; and through their fierce acts of vengeance, the citizens of Florida were given bitter cause to regret the taking away of Coacoochee. Such chiefs as remained, bound themselves by a solemn covenant to hold no further intercourse with the treacherous white man, but to fight him to the bitter end, and to put to death any messenger, red, black, or white, whom he might send to them under pretence of desiring peace.

It was now summer, the season of heat, rain, fevers, and sickness. Heretofore, during the summer months, the Indians had rested quietly in their villages, and cultivated the crops that should furnish food for the campaign of the succeeding winter. Heretofore, at this season, the soldiers had been withdrawn from the deadly interior, and allowed to recuperate in the health-giving sea-breezes of the coast.

Now all this was changed. While sympathizing

with the wronged and outraged Indians, General
Worth's loyalty to his government was too strong
to permit his feelings to interfere in the slightest
with the full performance of his duty. The time
for an active summer campaign had arrived, and the
new commander was the very man to conduct such
a one with the utmost vigor. The Indians who had
taken to the war-path quickly found, to their sorrow,
that the whites had done the same thing.

From every post in Florida detachments of troops
scoured the neighboring territory, carrying desola-
tion and dismay into every part of the country
known, or supposed, to be occupied by the enemy.
No hammock was so dense, and no swamp so trackless, that the white soldier did not penetrate it.
During the month of June thirty-two cornfields of
from five to twenty acres each were despoiled of
their growing crops, and as many Indian villages
were destroyed. Even the watery fastnesses of the
widespread Everglades were invaded by a boat expedition from Fort Dallas, which destroyed crops
and orchards on many a fertile island that the
Indians had fondly believed no white man would
ever discover. During this same month of June,
more than three thousand men, stricken by fevers
and kindred disease encountered in the swamps,
were enrolled on the sick list of General Worth's
little army.

By the end of the month nearly every Indian in

Florida had been driven into the impenetrable recesses of the Big Cypress, a vast swamp bordering
on the southwest coast, and most of the troops were
recalled to their respective posts.

Now, if Douglass had been successful in his mission, it was time for Coacoochee to be expected at
Tampa, and the commander moved his headquarters
from Palatka to Fort Brooke, that he might be on
hand to receive the exiled chief. With him went
the Boyds; for they had become too deeply interested in this game of war to remain at a distance from its most important moves. Of course,
Nita accompanied them, alternately hopeful and
despairing, longing for news from her lover, and
yet fearing to receive it. Their old cottage being
again placed at their disposal, the Boyds were at
once as comfortably established as though they had
never left it.

On the third of July, a strange sail was reported
beating slowly up the bay, and that same evening
Lieutenant Irwin Douglass, in speckless uniform,
walked into the Boyds' cottage, as quietly as though
he had left it but an hour before. As he entered,
Anstice was the first to discover him, and sprang to
his side.

"Irwin Douglass!" she cried. "Have you brought
Coacoochee back with you? Tell me quick!"

Close behind her stood Nita, silent and motionless,
but with shining eyes that gained the coveted in-

formation from the young officer's face long before
he could give it in words.

"Didn't you say it must be a double wedding or
none?" he asked, laughingly.

"Yes. Tell us quick!"

"Well, I didn't know of any one besides yourself
who wished to get married, except Nita."

"You horrid man! Why don't you tell us?"

"And as I didn't suppose she would accept any
other Indian —"

"You brought Coacoochee back with you?"

"I didn't say so."

"But you have! You know you have; for you
would never have dared come here if you hadn't."

"Well then, I have, and he is aboard the transport
out there in the bay, alive, hearty, and filled with
happiness at once more breathing his native air."

"Irwin Douglass, you are a dear fellow, and I love
you! which is more than I ever admitted before,
except to Coacoochee," cried Anstice, throwing her
arms about Nita and hugging her in her excitement. "But why didn't you bring him ashore?
Didn't you suppose we wanted to see him? And
didn't you know that poor Nita was wearing her
heart out with suspense?"

"I feared so, but I couldn't help it. You see,
when a man in the military business runs up against
orders, he finds them mighty stubborn facts, and
not lightly to be turned aside. So as I had orders

to leave our friend under guard aboard ship, until he had been visited by the commanding general, I thought it better to obey them."

"Never mind, dear," said Anstice, turning consolingly to Nita. "We will have him ashore to-morrow, and his coming will be a fitting celebration of the Fourth of July that the Americans make so much fuss over."

On the morrow, the general, accompanied by his staff, together with Douglass and Boyd, visited Coacoochee on board the transport. As these gained the deck, they beheld the distinguished prisoner thin and haggard, with manacles on both wrists and ankles, but still standing straight and undaunted, with eyes gazing beyond them and fixed on the dear land that he had thought never to see again.

Stepping directly to him, General Worth grasped his hand, saying :

"Coacoochee, I take you by the hand as a warrior and a brave man, who has fought long and with a strong heart for his country. You were not captured and sent away by my orders, but by the orders of the great chief who was then in command. Now I am in command, and by my order have you been brought back to your own land that you may give it the peace you promised me. For nearly five years has there been war between the white man and the red man. Now that war must end, and you are the man who must end it. You will not be allowed to go free until your whole band has come in, ready for removal to the west. You may send a talk to them by three, or even five, of your young men. You shall state the number of days required for your people to come in. If they are all here within the limit of time fixed, you shall be set at liberty, and allowed to go on shore to them. If they are not here by the last day appointed, then shall its setting sun see you, and those with you, hanging from the yards of this vessel with the irons still on your hands and feet. I do not tell you this to frighten you. You are too brave a man for that. I say it because I mean it, and shall do as I say. This war must end, and you must end it."

For some minutes there was a dead silence, as the company reflected on the terrible words they had just heard, and Coacoochee's breast heaved with emotion he struggled to control. At length he said :

"Micco-hatke, you are a great chief, and I believe you are an honest man. Other white men have lied to me and cheated me. They could not overcome Coacoochee in battle, so they captured him by their lying words. With you it is not so. I will trust you. Let my young men go. If in thirty days the warriors of Coacoochee have not obeyed his voice and come to him, then let him die. He will not care longer to live."

After a conversation with his companions, to whom

all this had been interpreted, Coacoochee selected five of them, and with the earnest words of one placing his life and honor in their hands, charged them with a message to his people.

Then the irons were stricken from the limbs of those five, and they were allowed to pass over the side of the ship into a waiting boat. Coacoochee shook hands with each one, and to the last he said : " If thou meet with her whom I love, tell her — No, tell her naught. Already does she know the words that the heart of Coacoochee would utter. Give her this, and bid her wear it until I once more stand beside her or have gone from her life forever."

With this he handed the messenger a silken kerchief of creamy white, that, in honor of the occasion, had been knotted about his head.

Among those who thronged the shore to witness the return of the boats, none watched them with such straining eyes and eager impatience as Nita Pacheco. She stood with Anstice, a little apart from the rest, clad in the forest costume that she knew would be most pleasing to her lover.

General Worth had told no one of his plans, and so the girl did not doubt for a moment that Coacoochee would be allowed to come ashore that day. She was the first to make certain that one of the boats contained a number of Indians ; and from that moment her eyes did not leave it.

As it drew near to the shore, the happy light gradu-

ally faded from her face, and in its place there came
a look of puzzled anxiety. "He is not there," she
finally said to Anstice, in a tone that betrayed the
keenness of her disappointment. "Let us go ; there
is nothing now to stay for."

"No," objected Anstice, "there must be a message
from him. Let us wait and learn what has happened."

Boyd and Douglass came directly to where the
girls awaited them ; but ere either of them could enter
into explanations, Nita darted away toward the warriors, who had just landed. With these she engaged
in rapid conversation for the next five minutes,
during which she learned of all that had passed
aboard the ship, and of her lover's imminent peril.

When the girl rejoined her friends, her jetty hair
was bound with the kerchief of creamy silk. She
walked with a resolute step, and her eyes flashed
with determination. Speaking to Anstice alone,
without regard to those who stood near her, she
said :

"The Micco-hatke will kill him if every member
of his band is not here, ready to emigrate, within
thirty days. The Seminole chiefs have sworn to
receive no proposals for peace. They will even
shoot the messengers of Coacoochee before they can
be heard ; but they will not kill a woman. It is
for me, therefore, to go with those who bear the
talk of Coacoochee. If, at the end of the allotted

time, every member of the band is not here, then
I, too, shall be far away; but, as the sun sinks
into the sea on that day, the spirit of Nita Pacheco
will be forever joined with that of him to whom
she plighted her troth. Come, let us go and make
ready."

No persuasions nor suggestions of danger or hard-
ship could alter the girl's determination, or cause
her to waver from her fixed purpose. So she was
allowed to have her way, and at daylight of the
following morning she set forth, in company with
the five warriors, on her perilous and fateful mission. They were amply provided with horses, provisions, and everything that could add to the success
of their undertaking, and, as they rode away from
the fort, every soul in it, from the general down,
wished them a heart-felt "God speed."

CHAPTER XXXIX

THE BRAVEST GIRL IN FLORIDA

DURING the month that followed Nita's departure there was in Fort Brooke but one all-absorbing topic of conversation and speculation. Would the brave girl succeed in saving the life of her lover? or must he die like a dog, without ever again treading the soil of his native land? Except for being kept a prisoner, the young war-chief was treated with distinguished consideration, and every want that he made known was gratified, so far as was consistent with safety. At the same time, he was still manacled, and his irons, together with those of his comrades, were carefully examined by a blacksmith, under supervision of an officer, every morning and evening. The guard on the transport was doubled, and at night a chain of sentinels was posted along such portions of the shore as lay adjacent to the ship. No boats were allowed to approach or leave the floating prison between sunset and sunrise, and no other precaution that human ingenuity could devise for the safe-keeping of the captives was neglected.

Ralph Boyd, often accompanied by some officer

from the post, made daily visits to cheer Coacoochee
with his belief that all was going well, and to carry
him the very latest news. On the occasion of his
first visit he took Anstice, who claimed the privilege
of telling the young chief what his sweetheart had
undertaken in his behalf. As the stern warrior listened to the simple recital, his face became very tender, and a tear, hastily brushed away, glistened for
an instant on his cheek. Then he said : " Now do
I know that all will go well," and from that moment
he was cheerfully confident of the final result.

No word was received from the messengers for a
week, at the end of which time one of them returned,
bringing with him ten warriors and a number of
women and children. The messenger reported that,
but for Nita, their mission, so far at least as this
particular band was concerned, would have been
fruitless. Upon their approach, the warriors had
sternly ordered them away, covering them with their
rifles, and threatening to shoot if they dared speak
of peace. Upon that, Nita, who had until then remained in the background, boldly advanced to the
very muzzles of the brown rifles, resolutely pushed
them aside, and then pleaded so effectively with the
warriors who held them that, ere she finished, their
hearts were softened, and they announced themselves
as not only ready to surrender, but willing to follow
their young chief wherever he might lead them.

Coacoochee had given General Worth a bundle of

z

small sticks which, by their number, represented the entire strength of his band. Upon the arrival at the fort of these forerunners, the general counted them, and returned to Coacoochee an equal number of his sticks. From day to day after this, other small parties of Coacoochee's followers straggled in, and for every new arrival a stick was sent to the young chief, who gloated over his increasing pile as a miser over his hoard, or a politician over the incoming votes that promise to save him from defeat.

In the meantime Nita, with an incredible exhibition of endurance, was scouring the distant country lying about the headwaters of the St. John's and Kissimmee. Here in little groups, the widely scattered members of Coacoochee's once numerous and formidable band had sought refuge amid the vast swamps and overflowed lands, which constitute that portion of Florida. Here, from swamp to swamp, from one tiny wooded island to another, or from hammock to hammock, the dauntless girl followed them. Sometimes she was accompanied by a small escort; but more often she was alone. There were days on which she had food, but many others on which she went hungry. The howl of the wolf became her familiar lullaby, while the scaly alligator and venomous water-moccasin regarded her invasion of their haunts with angry eyes. She travelled on horseback, by canoe, and on foot, scorched by noontide suns, and drenched by heavy night-dews that fell like rain, but always the image of Coacoochee was in her heart, as she bore his *talk* from band to band of his scattered followers.

As fast as they could be persuaded to go, she sent them to the far-away fort by the salt waters of the west, and bade them hasten or they would be too late. She, too, knew the number of Coacoochee's warriors, and kept a close count of those who had gone, as well as of those who still remained to be persuaded. With jealous care she noted the passage of each day, and murmured that they should fly the more swiftly as the fatal date drew near.

At length the last hiding-place was found, and the last sullen group of eight warriors, with their women and children, was persuaded to go in with her who was beloved of their young chief. By hard riding they could reach the fort on the twenty-ninth day, leaving but one to spare for safety. The brave girl, who had borne up so wonderfully during this month of suspense, was filled with joy at the success of her mission. At the same time, she was so utterly wearied that she often slept, even as she rode, and but for the quick support of willing hands, would have fallen from her saddle. But she would not pause. There would be plenty of time for resting afterwards. Now, they must push on.

On the evening of the last day but one of the month, the fort was only a score of miles away. They would keep on and reach it that night. So said Nita Pacheco. But there were enemies on whom she had not counted. Halec Tustenugge, with the fourteen Miccosouky warriors who had escaped with him from their ravaged village, roamed that part of the country and infested that particular road like ravening beasts. They had sworn never to surrender themselves, nor allow others to do so if they could prevent them. Now they confronted the little party from the eastern swamps, and bade them turn back or suffer the consequences.

There was a moment of hesitation and consultation. Then Nita Pacheco sprang to the front.

" Are the warriors trained by Coacoochee to be told what they shall do, and what they shall not do, by a pack of Miccosouky dogs?" she cried. "No! It cannot be! Let them get out of our way, or we will trample them in the dust! Yo-ho-ee yo-ho-ee-chee!"

As this war-cry of the Wildcat rang out on the evening air, and Nita's horse sprang from under the stinging lash, in the direction of those who blocked the road, the warriors of Coacoochee, echoing madly the cry of their leader, plied whip and spur in an effort to charge by her side. The Miccosoukies, though numbering nearly two to one, were on foot, while Nita's followers were mounted. The former fired one point blank volley, and then fled precipitately from before the on-rushing horses.

The battle had been fought and won, and the

enemy dispersed in less than a single minute; but
it was the victors who suffered the heaviest loss.
One warrior killed outright, two more wounded, one
horse so severely wounded that he had to be killed;
and, what no one noticed at first, not even Nita herself, a stream of blood spurting from an arm of the
girl who had led the charge.

So delayed was the little party by this fierce interruption, that the sun had climbed high above the
eastern horizon, on the last day of the thirty allotted
to Coacoochee, ere the last of his followers, travel
worn, staggering from wounds and weariness, but
filled with pride at the feat they had just accomplished, and fully conscious of their own importance,
filed slowly into Fort Brooke.

For days their coming had been eagerly awaited.
For hours they had been watched for with feverish
anxiety. Now the tale of sticks in General Worth's
possession was complete, for Nita had insisted upon
the living warriors bringing in him who was dead,
that he might be counted with them.

The soldiers of the garrison uttered cheer upon
cheer at sight of these last comers. The friends
who had preceded them thronged about them with
eager questions and congratulations; and the news
that Coacoochee was saved, repeated from lip to lip,
spread like wildfire throughout the post.

Ralph and Anstice Boyd, seated at a late breakfast, heard the glad shouting, and ran to the porch

of their cottage to discover its cause. They were just in time to greet Nita as she rode up, and to catch her as she slipped wearily from her saddle.

Her clothing was torn and stained, and her unbound hair streamed wildly about her head. Her eyes were bright and shining, but her cheeks were hollow, and glowed with spots of dull red. Coacoochee's silken kerchief that had confined her hair, was now bound tightly about her arm, and its whiteness was changed to the crimson of blood.

"He still lives? I am in time?" she whispered huskily as Anstice met her with a mingled cry of joy and terror.

"Yes, you dear, splendid, brave girl. He still lives, and you are in plenty of time. But, oh Nita! if you have killed yourself, what will it all amount to? Ralph, you must carry her in. She isn't able to walk."

Very tenderly they bore her into the house, and laid her on the tiny bed in her own room. Then Boyd hastened to find the surgeon, while Anstice bathed the girl's face with cool water, and talked lovingly to her. Ere an hour was past, the deadly fever of the swamps, that she had defied so long and so bravely, held her in its fierce clutches, and the girl, who by her own exertions had brought the war to a close, lay with staring eyes, but unconscious of her surroundings.

To Irwin Douglass was assigned the congenial

task of notifying Coacoochee that he was free, and bringing him ashore. He hastened to execute it, and, on reaching the ship, at once ordered the hated irons to be struck from the limbs of the captive leader. As they fell clanging to the deck, the whole appearance of the young chief changed. He again lifted his head proudly, his form expanded, and he paced the deck with the stride of a free man.

His first query was for Nita, and when told of her triumphant return, leading the last remnant of his band, he smiled proudly, and said that she was indeed fitted to be the wife of a warrior. At that time Douglass did not know of the girl's wound, nor of the illness that was even then developing its true character. Consequently, Coacoochee was allowed to go ashore filled with happy anticipations of meeting her whom he loved and to whom he owed so much.

He arrayed himself in a striking costume for the occasion, and one that well became his rank. From his turban drooped three black ostrich plumes. His frock was of scarlet and yellow, exquisitely made. Across his breast glittered many medals. In his silken sash was thrust the silver-hilted hunting-knife, by aid of which he had escaped from the fortress prison of St. Augustine. His leggings were of scarlet cloth, elaborately fringed, and on his feet he wore beaded moccasins.

A great throng of people, including every Indian at the post, was assembled to greet him; and as the boat neared land, these raised a mighty shout of welcome. As he leaped ashore and trod again his native sands, the throng drew back. Then with outstretched arms, and his form extended to its fullest height, Coacoochee gave utterance to the ringing war-cry that had so often carried dismay to his foes, and thrilled his warriors to desperate deeds.

" Yo-ho-ee yo-ho-ee-chee yo-ho-ee ! "

It was answered by a sound of hearty cheers from the assembled troops. Then the throng parted to make way for him, and up the living lane the young war-chief walked proudly to headquarters, where he exchanged greetings with General Worth as one with whom he was in every respect an equal. This formality concluded, he turned to the crowd of Indians who had followed him, and addressed them briefly, but in ringing tones :

" Warriors : Coacoochee stands before you a free man. He sent for you, and you have come. By that coming you have saved his life, and for it, he thanks you. The Great Spirit has spoken in our councils, and said: ' Let there be no more war between my children.' The hatchet is buried so that there may be friendship between the Iste-chatte and his white brother. I have given my word for you that you will not try to escape. For that I am free. See to it that the word of Coacoochee is kept strong and true. I have spoken: By our council fire I will say more. Now, away to your camp."

As the throng melted away in obedience to this command, Coacoochee turned to Lieutenant Douglass, and asked to be taken to Nita.

At the cottage in which she lay, he was met by the Boyds, from whom he learned what she had undergone on his behalf; of her wound incurred in fighting his battle, and of her present dangerous illness. He insisted on seeing her; and, on being led to where she lay tossing and moaning in the delirium of fever, the proud warrior knelt by her side, and, hiding his face, wept like a little child.

CHAPTER XL

For days Nita Pacheco hovered between life and death. During this time, almost hourly bulletins of her condition were demanded, not only from the Indian encampment, but from the garrison, every man of which had been won to admiration of the gentle girl by her recent heroism. As for Coacoochee, he was as one who is bereft of reason. He would sit for hours on the porch of the Boyd cottage, heedless of any who might speak to him, motionless and unconscious of his surroundings. Then he would spring on his waiting horse and dash away to scour madly through miles of forest, before his return, which was generally made late at night or with the dawning of a new day. When food was offered him, he took it and ate mechanically; when it was withheld, he seemed unconscious of hunger.

The mental condition of the young chief so alarmed his friends that, one morning when he returned from a night spent in the forest, in a cheerful frame of mind, gentle and perfectly rational, they were greatly relieved, and welcomed him as one who had come back from a long journey.

"Take me to her," he said. "She is watching for me. From this moment she will get well. I have seen Allala, and she has said it."

They had not noted any sign of a change for the better in the sick girl, and so it was with misgivings as to the result that they complied with his request.

Nita lay as they had left her; but, upon the entrance of her lover into the room, her eyes unclosed. She smiled at him, and feebly held his hand for a single moment. From that hour her improvement was steady and rapid, and from that time forth Coacoochee was again the leader of his people, the firm ally of the whites, and unwearying in his efforts to persuade those of the Seminoles who still remained out, to come in and submit to removal.

During the two following months he spent his time as Nita had done, in visiting distant bands of Indians and explaining to them the folly of a further resistance. He possessed two great advantages over all others who had labored in the same direction. He had fought by their side, no one more bravely, and they trusted him. He had also crossed the salt waters and returned again in safety, so that, of his own experience, he could refute the assertion made by their prophet, that every Indian taken to sea by the whites was thrown overboard and drowned.

In this service the young chief often found himself in desperate situations, and he made frequent hair-breadth escapes from death at the hands of those Indians who were either jealous of his power or distrustful for his honesty of purpose. In spite of discouragements and dangers, he persisted, and as the result of his convincing talks beside the red council fires of many a wild swamp retreat, band after band under well-known leaders and renowned fighters came into Fort Brooke, until only a scanty remnant still defied pursuit amid the impenetrable labyrinths of the Big Cypress.

The Indian encampment at Tampa occupied a space two miles square, and the task of guarding this large area was so great that, early in October, General Worth concluded to embark those already collected before they should become dissatisfied or rebellious and without waiting for more to come in. Accordingly the transports were made ready and the day for departure was fixed.

Now ensued most active preparations. For three days and nights the monotonous sound of the great wooden pestles cracking corn for the journey was heard from all parts of the camp. Vast quantities of fat pine knots were collected by the women, for they had heard that the country in which they were to live was destitute of wood. The entire area of the camp was illuminated at night by huge fires, so that there might be no cessation of the work.

The crowning event of all, or, as the general termed it, "the peace contract that ended the Seminole

War," was the double wedding that took place in the
open air, under the great live-oaks in front of headquarters, on the evening before the day of sailing.
The scene was as remarkable as it was picturesque.
On one side were gathered the hundreds of forest
dwellers who acknowledged one of the bridegrooms
as their leader. Among these were proud chiefs,
conspicuous in feathers and gaudy finery, stern warriors who had never known defeat in battle, plump
matrons wearing many rows of beads and silver or-
naments, slender maidens, and chubby children.

On the other side were ranks of troops as motionless as though on parade, and groups of officers in
glittering uniforms. A superb military band rendered its choicest selections of music, and the simple
ceremony was performed by the post chaplain.

Nita, fully recovered from her illness, and having
emerged from it more lovely than ever, like gold
that is purified by fire, was clad in the fawnskin
dress of a forest maid, though about her neck lay a
chain of great pearls, presented by the commander
and his officers in token of their devoted admiration
of her who had ended the war.

Beside her stood the young war-chief who had
fought so bravely, and accepted defeat so man-
fully, and with whose fate hers had been so closely
entwined during all the long years of fighting.

These two were married first, and after them came
the beautiful English girl, whose heart had passed

into keeping of the dashing American trooper, standing so proudly beside her.

Ralph Boyd, after giving away both brides, declared that he could now appreciate the feelings of a parent bereft of his children.

The moment the double ceremony was concluded, the band played its most brilliant march, the troops raised a mighty cheer, there came a salvo of artillery from a light battery stationed on the parade-ground, and the assembled Indians gazed on the whole affair with curious interest. All that evening there was music and feasting and dancing ; but on the morrow came the sorrowful partings, and, for hundreds of those about to become exiles forever, the heart-breaking departure from their native land.

As Coacoochee and Nita stood together on the after-deck of the steamer that was bearing them down the bay, straining their eyes for a last glimpse of the stately pines that they loved so dearly, she murmured in his ear :

"Without your brave presence, my warrior, I could not bear it." And he answered : "Without you, Ista-chee, I would never have come."

Across the blue Mexican Gulf they steamed, and for one hundred miles up the tawny flood of the great river to New Orleans. There the followers of Coacoochee were so impressed by the numbers and evident strength of the white man, that they were filled with pride at having successfully resisted his soldiers so long as they had.

At New Orleans the exiles were transferred to one of the great river packets, that, with its glowing furnaces, and the hoarse coughing of its high-pressure exhaust, seemed to them by far the most wonderful creation of the all-powerful Iste-hatke.

Being embarked in this mighty Pith-lo-loot-ka (boat of fire), no stop was made until they came within a few miles of Baton Rouge, where, by special request of Coacoochee, the packet was swung in toward the eastern bank. Guided by one familiar with that country, the entire body of Indians followed Coacoochee to the land. He bore a great basket, very heavy, and covered with palmetto leaves. None save himself knew what it contained.

A few rods from the shore the guide halted, and pointed to a lowly mound that was evidently a grave. Standing silently beside this, and waiting until all his people were gathered about him, the young chief said, with a voice that trembled, but so clearly that all might hear :

" Under this grass lies a great chief of the Seminole nation ; one whom you knew and loved. He was an old man when the soldiers tore him from his home. His heart broke with its weight of sorrow, and he died on his way to that new land to which we are now going. He lies cold in this strange earth ; but I have brought that which will warm him. With this soil from the land of his fathers, I now cover the grave of Philip Emathla." Thus saying, Coacoochee emptied the contents of his basket over the mound at his feet.

At mention of Philip Emathla's name, a great cry of grief and loving reverence went up from the dusky throng, and they pressed tumultuously forward. They struggled to see, to feel, and even to taste the earth that now covered his grave. It was only coarse gray sand; but it was sand from Florida, from the dear land they would never more see. Through the magic of its shining particles they could hear again the whispering pines, the rustling palms, and the singing birds of Florida. They could see its shadowy woodlands and white beaches. Its myriad lakes and tortuous waterways lay outspread before them. The fragrance of its jasmine and palmetto was wafted to them. Its glinting clouds of white-winged ibis circled before their eyes. The countless details mirrored indelibly on their hearts rose before them in all their alluring beauty. The warriors stood stern and silent; but the women tore their hair, with piteous cries.

After a while Coacoochee succeeded in restoring quiet, and, with many a backward, lingering glance at the lonely grave of Philip Emathla, the company was re-embarked, and the steamer continued on its way up the mighty river. Turning from it into the Arkansas, they continued up the muddy volume of that great tributary, across the whole State to which it gives a name, and on into that territory that the United States Government had recently set apart for the occupation of its Indian wards. Here, at Fort Gibson, the journey by water ended, though they had still to traverse the country of their old-time neighbors and enemies, the Creeks, ere they could reach the narrow tract reserved for them, in which they were to make their new homes.

At Fort Gibson a joyful surprise awaited Nita and Coacoochee; for Louis Pacheco, long since established in the west, and previously notified of their coming, had travelled that far to meet them. For them he had brought saddle-horses, while for the others a long train of wagons had been provided.

It was late on the day after their arrival before all was in readiness for the last stage of their journey; but they were now so anxious to press forward that Coacoochee gave the order for a start. Then, vaulting into his own saddle, and with Nita and Louis riding beside him, the young war-chief dashed away in the direction of the setting sun. As they gained a crest of the rolling prairie, he waved his rifle toward the infinite glories of the western sky, and, turning his face to those who followed him, thrilled their hearts with the ringing war-cry that had so often led the Seminole to victory:

"Yo-ho-ee yo-ho-ee yo-ho-ee-chee!"

2 A

www.ingramcontent.com/pod-product-compliance
Lightning Source LLC
Chambersburg PA
CBHW021710110726
47902CB00005B/1136